HIS PERFECT CRIME

Emily Slate Mystery Thriller Book 1

ALEX SIGMORE

Dark Woods Press

HIS PERFECT CRIME: EMILY SLATE MYSTERY THRILLER BOOK 1

1st Edition

ebook ISBN 978-1-957536-02-6

Print ISBN 978-1-957536-03-3

Chapter One

DON'T SCREW THIS UP.

As I approach the yellow caution tape, a familiar pit forms in my stomach, the one that always comes when I'm near a corpse. I can't seem to help it, despite seeing many bodies over the years. But this time is different. This time I feel like an imposter, like I shouldn't even be here.

I shouldn't be nervous; this is my job. A job I've done a hundred times before. I'm a trained FBI agent, this is what I do. But this is the first one back after...the *incident,* and I can't help but feel the weight of the situation bearing down on me. It's a test; we all know it. And if I can't keep it together then I'll be out of a career, no matter what they say. More than that, I'll have lost the last thing in my life worth hanging on to.

Frost crunches beneath my boots and I pull my overcoat tighter as I near the scene. If it weren't for the murmurs of the beat cops who were on patrol all night guarding the site, this place would be as quiet as a grave. For being in the middle of the woods, there's not a sound out there. No birds, no small mammals scuttering around, nothing. It's like they know something bad has happened here, and they want no part of it.

I pull the collar of my coat up around my face, bracing myself against the cold. It's the type of cold that isn't from a blowing breeze, instead it's biting, from another temperature drop overnight. Once the sun comes up it'll warm, but right now it's a shock. I wish I hadn't left my coffee in the car.

"Morning," I say, nodding to the cop standing beside the yellow tape. He's bundled up too, a wool hat with the word POLICE embroidered on the front pulled down over his brow, but I still see his eyebrow arch. He's wondering what a five-six, hundred-and-thirty-pound brunette woman who looks like she's a couple of years out of high school is doing on a crime scene. I've always had a young face, so I get that a lot. It comes in useful sometimes. Other times, like this one, it makes my job harder.

I show him my badge. "Special Agent Slate," I say. "I was called in."

The change in demeanor on his face is almost comical. It goes from skepticism to downright loathing in half a second. I wish I could say that my reputation precedes me, but I know this is just normal local cop bullshit. Anytime the FBI steps within a half mile of one of their crime scenes they can't help but make a fuss about it.

He pinches his face like he might try and argue with me, and I catch sight of his name badge: Rutherford. He must see me eyeing it because he lifts the tape up and ushers me through.

God, I hate politics.

They've cordoned off an area that looks to be about three hundred feet in all directions. And from my approach, this means I have to make my way down a shallow hill to reach the place she was found. Thankfully, these are reliable boots, and I have no trouble navigating the hill, even with the frost.

Another officer stands at the bottom of the hill, his arms wrapped around him as vapor escapes his mouth. He's tall like a basketball player; I'd be surprised if he didn't play when he was younger. He eyes me, doing nothing but rubbing his hands on his arms as he tries to stay warm.

"You're early," he calls out when I'm close enough. "The detective won't be here for another thirty minutes, at least."

That was the point. "Where is she?" I ask.

He motions to a dark area about fifty feet behind him. There's a small clearing, surrounded by bare trees. A portable light and generator have been brought in, but both are off. The sky beyond is beginning to show signs of life, but it's barely a dark blue now and all I can make out are the tops of the trees against it. The sun won't be up until seven-thirty. Maybe it was foolish coming out here before daylight, but I wanted to get a jump on things. It's an axiom in my life: if I'm not early, I'm late, no matter the appointment. I also wanted to make sure I was here before anyone else, so I'd have the site to myself for a few minutes. It's another one of those things that helps other members of our profession take me more seriously, despite my looks.

Still, it's always an uphill battle.

"Need any help?" the cop asks.

I don't reply, instead I pull on some gloves, switch on my flashlight and make my way to the scene, careful not to disturb anything. Until the crime scene techs get here, I don't want to make a dent; I just want to have an understanding of what I'm looking at.

"Whatever," I hear him mutter as I press forward, having not responded to his inquiry. He's obviously new, otherwise he wouldn't have scored such a cushy assignment such as standing out in the cold all night. In fact, he's probably younger than I am, despite the fact that he looks like he could pass for someone in their late thirties.

I sweep my light beam across the path in front of me. Even though it's light enough to see, I'm looking for anything that might stand out. Though, from what I understand about how she was found, I'm unlikely to find it.

According to the initial report that was filed with the FBI, the body was only found because this area has had some heavier-than-normal rains over the past few months, causing a lot of erosion, which probably explains the slippery hill back there. The site itself is on a partial hill as well, and as I reach it, I can see where water has cut drainage valleys into the soft dirt. Near the edge of the clearing is a shallow pit, and a small pile of dirt off to the side. The report said she was found by a trapper, out with his dogs. In reality it was probably the dogs who smelled her first, drawing the trapper here, who, judging by how much dirt he moved, had probably figured he'd found buried treasure instead of a body.

Imagine his surprise.

Any residual evidence of the burial site is no doubt long gone by now, either from the weather or from the trapper himself, but I look around anyway. No one is perfect, and no matter who left her out here, they left a trail. All that remains to be seen is if anything has survived the weather. There's no telling how long she's actually been here, at least not until the coroner gets a good look at her.

I'm intentionally avoiding the site itself because I know it's not going to be pretty. And despite always having a strong stomach, I can't help but feel some connection with my victims. Seeing them in death…especially lately…let's just say it hasn't been good. But I *need* to do this.

I perform another sweep of the surrounding area, finding nothing. When the sun comes up and provides me more light to work with, I'll take another look, but for now, all that remains is the big show.

I take a deep breath, forcing myself to calm down. *It's not him. It's not him.*

Bending down, careful that I don't get too close to the edge, I shine my light in the shallow grave. The trapper dug down deep enough to uncover the top of what looks like a small shipping crate, or maybe even a footlocker, though I haven't seen one of these in a long time. The lid is down, but he'd already broken the seal on the side and inspected the contents, otherwise we wouldn't even be here. I reach down and slowly pull back the lid on its hinge.

I turn away at the smell, which is more concentrated than I'd expected, the body reeking of spoiled milk. Once I have my reflexes under control, I look back to see what I'm working with.

She's in an advanced state of decay. Parts of her skeleton are clearly visible, though bits of skin still hang on in places. She's still dressed, though the clothes have been ravaged by all the organisms slowly eating the body from the inside out. If it weren't for her clothes and long, red hair, we wouldn't even know the sex of the victim.

But what stands out most is her eyes. Sewn shut with a thick thread, they now hang from pieces of skin barely connected to the sockets.

Equally as strange is how she's folded up into this box. A human child can easily fit in a footlocker. An adult, not so much. She's been contorted and shoved inside, like someone was packing a too-full suitcase. I don't see how they got her in there without at least breaking a few of her bones, especially around her pelvis, to get her legs to fit. Not only would that take an immense amount of strength, but it would have been cumbersome. And messy. We might be looking at more than one killer here. But first, we need to figure out who this woman is, and if she matches any of the missing persons reports from the area. But I can already tell this isn't recent. Which makes my job even more difficult. Pinpointing her time of death will be crucial to finding out who did this, and based on what I'm seeing, she's been here months instead of weeks.

No wonder they called us in. Stillwater is a tiny town two hours outside of D.C. They're not equipped to deal with this kind of thing.

Light begins to peek through the woods as the sun finally

breaks the horizon, illuminating the skeletal face of the victim. I purse my lips and slowly close the lid of the locker again. This person, whoever she was, deserved better than this. And she deserves a respectful resting place, not being left out here, forgotten, in the middle of nowhere.

Part of me curses Janice for sending me here. And yet, another part knows it was completely warranted. It wasn't like she was going to throw me a softball after what I pulled. I stand, watching the sun illuminate the skeletal trees, finally reaching me.

Last chance, Emily. Better make it a good one.

Chapter Two

"HEY!" A VOICE CALLS OUT FROM THE DIRECTION I approached the site. At first I think it's the same cop, until I see two other figures making their way down the hill, carefully. Behind them is a small team of two more, both carrying cases with them. The cavalry has finally arrived. I check my watch. They're earlier than I'd expected.

"What do you think you're doing?" the man leading the group asks. He's big, heavyset with a graying beard and accusatory eyes, doing his best to intimidate me, even from a hundred feet away. "You're not authorized to be here; this is a crime scene."

I see the courteous gentlemen who granted me access to the site didn't think to mention to them I was already here. I swear, if we could just drop all this pretense and actually work together, things would go so much smoother. People would trust their local police more, the FBI could actually do its work rather than be hamstrung by a bunch of self-important idiots, and I wouldn't have to explain myself over and over again. That was the one nice thing about taking some time off—I didn't have to put up with men like the one now approaching me, his face red and full of indignation.

I take a step back, pulling out my badge. "I'm Special Agent Slate. Here at your request."

The man deflates a little; but retains his superiority. I notice he's not being careful with the site itself; instead, it seems like he's more interested in getting to me. I take a few more steps away from the body, hoping to alter his trajectory because I know a head-on confrontation is just what he wants.

"William Burke, Chief of Stillwater," he says brusquely. "And let's get something straight. *I* didn't want you here. The mayor did, against my express concerns. We can handle this."

"I have no doubt of that, Chief," I say. "I'm just here because my boss told me to be."

He narrows his eyes. I think he was hoping I'd put up more of a fight. "What are you, twenty-five?"

"I don't see why that matters," I say.

"It matters because I need to know if I'm working with some wet-behind-the-ears rookie who doesn't know her head from her ass. I swear, if they sent me a—"

"I've been with the Bureau four years," I reply, gritting my teeth at already being put on the defensive. "So, don't worry, I'm crate trained."

He turns to the side with a sardonic smile, and I get a good look at the other man who was following him. He's on the younger side, but not as young as the cops I came across when I arrived. He's trim, with a soft complexion covered by stubble that's probably seven days old at least. His blonde hair is trimmed short, but I don't get the same kind of ambivalence from him that I get from Burke. "This is Detective Liam Coll," Burke says. "He'll be taking the lead here."

Coll holds out a hand and I give it a quick shake. "Plea-sure," he says. Funny, from his name I figured he wasn't from around here, but he has a typical northern Virginia accent. I also have trouble tearing myself away from his hazel eyes. They're soft in a way I'm not used to seeing in law enforce-ment. I have to remind myself that Stillwater, Virginia is nestled in the mountains and the people here aren't used to these kinds of horrors. The worst these officers have probably had to deal with is a missing cat.

Still...those eyes.

To distract myself, I turn back to Burke. "I'm surprised to see you on site. Didn't know the chief was involved in all of Stillwater's cases."

"I'm not," he replies. "But we don't see many dead bodies up here and you can bet when we find one, it's all hands on deck."

"Good to know. I've already done an initial inspection, but I want to—"

"Listen," Burke says. "You're here to assist only. And as soon as this case is wrapped up, I want you back out of my town, got it, little lady?"

I give him the most pleasant smile I can muster, but it takes a lot of effort. "Chief, you may not realize this, but when you call in the FBI, this automatically becomes a federal case. Technically, it belongs to me and your job here is to make sure I have everything *I* need to do my job effectively. I will be happy to leave once I am satisfied with the outcome."

He grits his teeth. "Which will be?"

"Finding whoever killed this woman and bringing them to justice."

Burke stares at me a few moments, towering over me. He's got to be at least six-two. But I've faced bigger men than him and never backed down before, I'm not about to start now.

"Coll," he says.

"Yes, sir."

"Make sure *Agent Slate* has whatever she needs to wrap this case up as quickly as possible."

"Right," Coll replies.

"And report back to me before you leave." Burke turns and pushes past the techs, who are still standing off to the side, waiting for the go-ahead from either Coll or myself.

I watch him leave, apparently so wrapped up in his own ego that he didn't even consider there's a dead person not more than thirty feet from him. Someone whose life was cut short and was unceremoniously disposed like a piece of trash.

"Great guy," I mutter. It's both an honest opinion and a gauge for Coll. I'm having a hard time reading him, and I can't tell if he's one of those yes-men who do exactly everything their superior officer says, or if he sees just how ridiculous Burke is being.

"Yeah he's...well, the chief is his own brand of special," Coll finally says, and I catch the two techs exchange a knowing look, smiles on their faces. Coll turns back to me. "Anyway, now I guess we can get some real work done."

I smile. At least they're all not idiots up here. But I'm not about to open up to Coll or anyone else. I'm not here to make friends. I'm here to catch a killer.

"If it makes you feel any better, I agree with the mayor," he adds. "We don't get murders in Stillwater, at least, not like this. Occasionally, two people will get mixed up in a drug swap gone wrong but we always know who it is, and if we don't, we know the community well enough to find out quickly. We may only have twenty-five thousand residents, but we still deal with crime, like any other city. But this..." He puts his hands on his hips. "We just don't see it."

"Were you here last night?" I ask.

He shakes his head. "I didn't get the call until just after midnight. Our guys down at the station said it would be better to wait until daylight, since they didn't get up here until close to two a.m." One of the techs switches on the generator, sending a flock of birds nesting in a nearby tree out into the sky, which has brightened considerably. I'm not even sure we'll need the portable light, though they switch it on anyway, focusing right on the center of the site.

I bend down beside the locker again. "It's not like anything would have changed if you'd spent all night out here in the cold." I slip on another glove and lift open the lid again. "She's been here a while."

I'm looking to see how he handles it, and Coll manages to impress me. It's not that he doesn't react at all, but his face falls when he sees her, and I can see some real empathy in those hazel eyes. That's exactly what I needed. Because otherwise we wouldn't be able to work together. If he'd been one of those cops whose become so hardened to the realities of this job and had just checked out, I'd be much more likely to handle this case on my own. I can't do a job with someone who thinks of her as just another vic. I need to know they'll fight for her, that they'll do anything they can to find her killer. Just like I would.

"Jesus," he says, bending down. "You weren't kidding."

I wave the two techs over. "Start here and spread out to two-hundred feet in all directions. Tag anything that isn't a leaf, stick or rock." They nod and begin going to work.

Coll stares at me. "She's been here for months, at least. With all the recent rainfall—"

"Yeah, I agree. But you never know. We might get lucky." I survey the area as I'm squatting, staring back up at the hill we've all come down. It looks like the most obvious path someone would have taken to bring her here. "I want to know if she was already in the box before she got here, or if the killer staged the area with the box waiting for her, and carried or dragged her here."

"You sound like you've seen this kind of thing before," Coll says.

"Not exactly," I reply. "This is my first person that's been folded in half with her eyes sewn shut."

"You said you've been with the Bureau for four years. Any murder cases before?" he asks.

"I could ask you the same thing."

He grins, and it lights up his face. I attribute my noticing to the fact I'm a good detective; I see what others don't. It's why I'm in this job. I hate that I'm feeling a slight pull in my gut; a subconscious part of me just wants to trust him. But that's how I get in trouble. It just means I'll have to be extra vigilant. Plus, I'm not an idiot. Coll is Burke's man on the inside, here to keep an eye on me. I can't forget where his loyalties lie, even if he doesn't have the best opinion of his boss.

"Okay," I say, standing back up. "Let's get to work."

Chapter Three

THREE HOURS LATER I MAKE MY WAY BACK TO MY RENTAL CAR. Coll and I went over the scene with the techs inch by inch, but there really was nothing out there. Either our killer was supremely talented at covering his tracks, or she's just been out there too long and any evidence of who put her there has washed away. No prints on the box itself, inside or out. And nothing they could pull from her clothes, but once the coroner has her all laid out they'll take a second look.

Coll seems like a competent detective. With the two of us working together, we were able to establish she was brought in the same way we'd come, which is a small trail that comes off a county road out here. The techs were also able to confirm she'd originally been buried deeper, but the erosion and the rising water table had pushed the box to the surface over time. All of that is good news, because it means her killer wasn't expecting us to find her, at least not so soon. It's not much, but it's better than nothing.

I reach the top of the hill and huff. The coroner is down there now, helping to remove the body from the locker and get it into a watertight bag for transport back to the morgue. Coll stops just behind me, looking back. "Something we missed?" he asks.

"No," I reply. "Just looking at the scene as the killer saw it. He's buried her, leaving her in the middle of nowhere. Do you think he takes a moment to admire his cleverness? Or is he someone on a timetable? Someone who needs to be somewhere?"

"Hard to say," Coll replies. "Have you had breakfast yet?"

"What?" I ask, blinking away my thoughts.

"Breakfast. Did you eat yet?"

"I don't eat breakfast," I reply, making my way back down the trail and ducking under the yellow tape.

"It's the most important meal—" he begins.

"Coffee," I reply. "Nothing is more important than coffee. Plus, it's easy, and portable."

"Right. Where they got you set up?"

"The Nite Owl, off Route twenty-two," I say.

"I'd have thought the FBI would provide for better accommodations," he says. "There's a nice Holiday Inn only a few miles down that road."

I don't reply, not wanting to reveal the reason the FBI didn't exactly roll out the red carpet for me on my first assignment back after…the *incident*. I took one step inside that motel and immediately felt like I needed a shower. But it's just another test from Janice, trying to put the screws to me to see if I can still take it. I know exactly what she's doing, and I know the second I complain, it's all over. An accommodations complaint wouldn't be enough to file any kind of official report or anything, but in her mind I'd be done, and I'd get nothing but desk jobs from then on. I can't do that; I have to be in the field. Six weeks at a desk was long enough to make me feel like I was going stir crazy as it was.

"You get in last night?" he asks.

I look over my shoulder as we walk. "What's with the third-degree, Coll?" Even though my tone is light, there's a seriousness under my words. If this is Burke's idea of subtlety, he picked the wrong guy.

He's taken aback. "Nothing, I just…was curious."

"I got in at three a.m. if it's that important to you."

"You're an early riser," he says.

I turn back down the path, and we pass another officer headed toward the site. "I don't like being late."

"So how do we play this?" he asks.

"I want to talk to the trapper who found her, see if he can remember anything about the site before he disturbed it. I want to make sure there wasn't any kind of sigil marking the…" I almost say grave but think better of it. "…location. Make sure we're not dealing with some kind of ritual." Given what I've seen, I don't think that's the case. There weren't the normal identifiers that usually come with a ritual killing. No symbols, identifiers, or any evidence of a ceremony of some kind. I just need to cross that possibility off before moving along. This job is all about looking at a given situation from every angle, then whittling down the things that don't fit until you're left with the truth. That's been my experience, anyway.

"After that we'll have to wait on the M.E.'s report. Probably have to ID her using dental records."

"She still had some jewelry on," Coll says.

"We'll take a look at those too. If we can find the original seller it will help. How many jewelry stores in town?"

"Just one," he replies. "Unless you count the Wal-Mart out past the interstate."

It's a possibility, but we'll check the jewelry store first.

"Where's the trapper?"

"I had Rollins drive him down to the station early this morning."

I stop. "Why not just take him home?"

Coll shrugs. "He insisted, said those dogs of his don't like visitors, and he said he didn't mind. I think he's the kind who likes the company."

We reach the small area off the road where everyone has parked. There's one black and white with its lights flashing, just to slow any traffic through here. People probably aren't expecting to come up on four cop cars, an ambulance and three regular vehicles this far out, and all bunched up together off the side of the road. If I know anything about back roads like this, is people take the rules of driving a little more loosely out here. Someone could come screaming around one of those corners at sixty-five, clip one of the vehicles, and end up in a tree.

I look around, but don't see Burke anywhere. He must have gotten bored or decided he'd harangued me enough. I feel like the only reason he came out here at all was to make sure I knew who was in charge of this investigation. For every-one's sake, I think I'll just stay out of his way as best I can. The less contact we have, the better.

I head over to my rental, a white Ford Fiesta. I would have preferred something in gray or black, but it was this, or an SUV, and I wasn't about to drive that thing two hours here.

Coll heads for one of the other unmarked cars, a gray hatchback. "You want to follow me to the station?"

"Lead the way," I say, slipping into the car. I doubt I'll spend much time there, but I might as well get a lay of the land while the day is still new. As much as I would prefer to work in an office, the level of distrust between me and the locals goes both ways. And I don't need them screwing up my last chance at keeping my career. I sacrificed a lot for this job and to get where I am; it's all I have left.

As I follow Coll to the station, I attach my phone through the car and call back to headquarters.

"Simmons," Janice says when she picks up.

"It's me." I wait a beat to see if she's going to ask or if I'm going to have to lead. I guess I'm not surprised when she doesn't say anything. "Just finished up at the site. It's going to be a tough one; she's been out there a while."

"You need additional resources?" my boss asks.

"Not yet. We're just getting started. But I wanted to let you know local PD isn't happy about me being here. It might cause some friction."

"Make sure that it doesn't," she replies. Her voice is completely emotionless, which is just how Janice operates. I've been working under her for a few years now and she's tough, but one of the best agents I know. I respect the hell out of her. I know the only reason I'm here is because of my own actions.

"Yes, ma'am."

"If there's nothing else?"

I hesitate. "I just wanted you to know that I appreciate you trusting me with this one. I won't let it slip through my fingers."

Her voice softens, but only a hair. "That's why I chose you. Good luck, Agent Slate."

When we arrive at the Stillwater station it's coming up on eleven a.m. and the place is as quiet as a church on a Monday morning. The stations I usually see are always bustling with activity, but not this one. It's a standard granite building that looks like it was built sometime around the start of the 1900's. Two floors, with thin windows on all sides. It sits right on the street in downtown Stillwater, though there's a parking lot off to the side. Behind the building is a small jail, attached by a modern-looking glass hallway. It looks to me like the jail was something else at one point and it was acquired by the police and integrated into the station.

When we pull in there are only three other cars in the entire lot.

"It's not much—" Coll begins, as I step out of my car, surveying the area.

"Don't you say it," I snap, slamming my door, my warm breath visible in the cool air of the midmorning.

"What?" he asks, an easy smile on his face. Spending the morning working with him has endeared me to the man a little more. He's one of those people it's easy to joke with, and you can tell won't get offended at every little thing you say. So far, everything I've prodded him with has rolled off his back.

"You're about to say, 'but it's home'."

"Maybe," he replies. "Then again, maybe I was about to say, 'but it's small and dirty too.'"

That produces a smile which I have to work to hide. "Sounds lovely."

"Nah, you were right. I was going to say it's home. And the dirt isn't too bad, once you get used to it." He motions for me to follow him in. Automatically I'm on the defensive again. I've been in this exact same situation a dozen times before. It never goes well. And if Chief Burke is any indication of the rest of his force, I don't expect them to be much better.

Inside the main entrance are rows of chairs on either side, with a partition in the middle of the room, bisecting it into a front section and a back section. A woman sits behind the desk in the middle of the partition, reading a worn paperback.

"Mornin', Trish," Coll calls as we walk past.

"Mornin'," she replies, not looking up. "Visitors gotta sign in." I turn to her and see her gaze follow me over the top of the paperback. Not so oblivious after all.

"This is Agent Emily Slate, with the FBI," Coll tells her. "She's here to assist with the case of that woman they found last night."

"Hmm," Trish replies, then goes back to her book. Coll motions for me to follow him and we pass through a security door into the back section of the station.

The whole area is partitioned off. To the right look like the interview rooms, as well as some desks for cops on rotation.

But Coll leads me to the left which seem like they're all offices. He enters the third one down, flipping on the lights.

Inside there are three desks, though only one is occupied with anything other than a computer, the other two remain empty. "Behold," Coll says, "The Stillwater Detective wing."

I look around. "This can't be it. You have to have more than one detective on staff," I say.

He shrugs. "We did. But Morrison just retired and Laufey took his vacation last week. Won't be back until the end of the month. That just leaves me for the moment." He points to the two empty desks. "Take your pick. I'll get you set up in the system so you have access to everything you should need." He takes a seat at his own desk and begins working.

I have to admit I'm a bit surprised by his behavior. Most of the time when I get assigned to work with a local precinct or sheriff's office, I get stuck in a broom closet with a bad internet signal. But Coll is going out of his way to make me feel welcome. Maybe relations between the police and FBI aren't as hopeless as I'd thought. "Thanks," I say, taking a seat at one of the desks.

"Yeah, no problem."

I wonder how much contact Coll has had with the FBI in the past. If I had to guess I'd say little to none. Because as bad as the local cops treat us, we give as good as we get. At least, a lot of my colleagues do. They seem to get off on the power trip and I just don't get it. There are people in my own department who can't seem to quit dick-swinging long enough to actually get any work done.

And yet, they're rarely reprimanded.

"Okay," Coll says. "I've got your basics set up. Private VPN, secure systems. You'll have access to our case files if you need them, but you should also feel secure logging into the FBI systems from here."

I turn to him, consternation on my face. "Why are you being so accommodating?"

He furrows his brow, his lips turned down. "Sorry?"

"You're just being overly generous. I don't normally get this much cooperation from local PD."

"Yeah, well," he says, his easy demeanor on full display. "Most people are morons." He gives me another one of those smiles, then motions to the door. "He's over in interview one. Let me know whenever you're ready."

I stand, feeling pretty good about this place. Maybe this won't be a total failure after all. "Let's go see what he has to say."

Chapter Four

"GOOD MORNING, MR. BERMAN. WE JUST HAVE A FEW questions for you," Coll says as he strolls into the room. I stick to the back, my arms crossed while I watch Augustus Berman, the trapper who found the body.

"A'yuh," he says, his mouth full of chewing tobacco. It has left a lingering smell in the air that turns my stomach. He nods to me. "She supposed to be here? I don' mean to be insensitive, but this is some heavy subject material. I wouldn't want a young'un to be scarred."

"I'm Agent Slate, with the FBI, Mr. Berman," I say, keeping my voice even.

Coll gives me a sheepish look, like he knows he should have introduced me when we came in. Honestly, at this point, I don't care. I've had to do this so many times it's like a reflex.

"Sorry, ma'am, I didn' mean to insult ya." Berman says, working the juice in his jaw. I know he's looking for a place to spit it, but because this is one of the nicer interview rooms I've been in—not the kind that are all concrete walls and metal tables—he has no choice but to keep it in his mouth...or swallow it.

"This won't take long," Coll says. "We just need to go over a few details." Coll opens the thin file folder in front of him which contains little more than the initial report of finding the body. "Can you tell us what happened last night?"

"A'yuh," he says again. "I was out with my dogs—they're huntin' dogs, but I got 'em trained to sniff out when we got an injured animal. See, not all injured animals cry out. And I got traps all over them woods. Surprised you folk didn't step on one."

"Is that your property, Mr. Berman?" Coll asks.

"Well, no," he says. "But I got an agreement with the landowners out there, they own somethin' like a hundred acres or more, I dunno. They don't care if I'm out there." Coll turns to me. We're going to have to follow up with the landowners. I'll do a search when we get back to the office.

"Anyway, I was out with my dogs, checkin' all the traps when Ricochet gets a sniff of somethin'. 'Course I think it's one of the traps, so I let 'em off the leash and hightail it after him. By God, that dog can be fast. My knees start actin' up in this cold so it takes me a little longer than I'd like—"

"Mr. Berman," Coll says with an impatient tone.

"Right. So I followed 'em over to this small clearin'. I knew there wasn't no trap there, but he'd gotten into somethin' like it had possessed 'em. For second I thought it was a deer carcass or maybe even a bear. One time, Trigger, that's my other dog, he came back so bloody from findin' this racoon family that somethin' had left. I swear I jus' about had a heart attack when I seen 'em, I figured that was *his* blood after all. But as soon as he walked up to me, waggin' that tail of his, I knew he was alright. He led me back to the scene of the crime, like you folk say. Turns out a bobcat had—"

"Mr. Berman," I say. "Please try to stay on subject here. We don't want to take up your entire day."

He waves his hand in the air, dropping his head. "Right, right. Sorry. I'm just a little nervous. Never found a body like that before. I get Ricochet back on the leash and figure out he's done uncovered somethin' while he was diggin'. The ground's pretty hard this time of year so I couldn't do much else myself without a shovel, so I marked the spot, took my dogs back to my truck and returned just as it was gettin' dark. But I got pretty good GPS up here if you know what I mean, so I weren't worried about not findin' my way back." He taps his head for good measure.

"So I'm out there diggin' by flashlight, thinkin' I've hit somebody's secret stash, ya' know? Who else would leave a big box like that, buried, out in the middle of nowhere? I manage to uncover the top and enough of the sides to get it open, and when I do…" he trails off, holding both hands up.

"That's when you found her," Coll says.

"A'yuh. Scared the ever lovin' hell out of me. I know I prolly screamed out, but nobody out there for miles. I doubt anyone heard me."

"What happened next?"

"Well, I closed her back up, headed back to my truck and took a long swig of the Evan Williams I keep in the—" He stops, his eyes wide. "I mean, uh…"

"It's fine," Coll says, motioning with his hand. "Continue."

"And then, I uh, I called you folk. That's pretty much it." He sits back, holds his hands up for a brief moment, then drops them again.

"Mr. Berman," I say, stepping forward. "When you first found the clearing with your dog, did you notice anything strange about it? Any kind of markings or anything else to signify what was there?"

He shakes his head. "Nope. Just a little area with no trees. 'Course by the time I got up on Ricochet, he'd already pawed the ground apart. If there was somethin' there, I didn't see it."

The rest of the interview is standard measure, and we're done in half an hour. Coll was right, Berman is one who likes to talk. The man is probably just lonely; it's sad in a way. I'll make sure he gets an escort back to his house. At least he'll have someone to talk to during the trip.

We return to the office, and I immediately do a search on who owns that land out there. I'm so used to dealing with state-owned property it didn't even occur to me that it was private land. Being so far away from any dwellings, you tend to forget people out here own large swaths of undeveloped property.

"Mr. and Mrs. Jerimiah Willis," I say, reading off the land deeds. "Both in their eighties, childless."

Coll looks up from his desk. "I'm going out on a limb and saying they didn't drag that locker all the way out there."

"Probably not. And no other living relatives…that seems odd though, doesn't it? Elderly couple, living out by themselves on a huge piece of property? No one else around for miles?"

"Not really. Not for this area. Ask anyone local they'll tell you people here are cut from a different cloth. A stronger brand. There's a rugged individualism that runs through places like this, where people don't like to advertise they need others to rely on." He grins. "Personally, I think it's just people being stubborn."

"Still," I say, tapping my lips with the pen in my hand. "I want someone to follow up on them. Let's make sure they haven't died out there and someone is squatting in their house, collecting their social security checks."

"I'll get a patrol on it this afternoon."

I check the time. One-fifteen. I didn't tell Coll that I didn't even bother going to sleep last night, instead I popped a couple of caffeine pills and stayed up watching TV. I have a hard time sleeping before a big case, especially one that could make or break my career. I always end up tossing and turning, my mind going through the thousands of possibilities of what might happen, or what I might find. But now I'm good and exhausted, considering I've been up for close to thirty hours.

I grab my coat. "You said it'll take the M.E. at least a day to do the autopsy?" He nods. "Call me when it's ready."

"Where are you headed?" he asks.

"Just need to go work a few things out."

Chapter Five

"GOOD MORNING, SLEEPYHEAD," A SING-SONG VOICE SAYS ON the other end of the line. I knew I should have looked at the phone before picking it up.

"Morning, Zara," I say, yawning.

"Did you do it again?" she asks.

"Do what?"

"Stay up all night after you got there?"

I crease my brow and pull my phone away from me, checking the time on the too-bright screen. I grit my teeth and put it back to my ear. "Are you seriously waking me up at four in the morning?"

Her laugh bubbles in my ear. "You deserve it! Plus, you've probably been asleep since what, five o'clock yesterday? You need to get up already."

As much as I want to reach through the phone and strangle her, she's right. Zara Foley is probably the only other person at HQ I actually talk to on a regular basis. If anyone were to ask her, she'd say we're best friends, but I don't know if I'd go that far. Not that there's anything wrong with her, or I don't appreciate her attempts, but I'm just not the kind of person who gets close to people. Every time I've done that in the past it's backfired, especially this most recent time. But since I have few other friends and don't talk to my family much, she's the one constant that's always there for me. She likes to joke that as an extrovert she "adopted" me and is the only reason I go anywhere other than work or my house. "Thanks for the wake-up call," I say, resigning myself to actually getting up. "How's Timber?"

"The perfect houseguest, as always. I let him sleep under the covers with me again last night."

I groan. "Don't do that, he'll expect me to do it when I get home."

"But he's such a good baby," she says in an overly sweet voice, and I can just imagine her rubbing him behind the ears.

"How's the case going?"

"It's going to be a tough one," I say. "Weather washed any possible evidence away. We're supposed to get the autopsy report today. Hopefully then we can actually ID her."

"Are you...doing okay with it?" she asks delicately. I know what she's doing, and while I appreciate the effort, it's not necessary. I can hold my own out here. Maybe that wasn't true three months ago. If it hadn't been for her, I'm not sure where I'd be right now.

"Yeah, of course. I just want to find the bastard that did it."

"Okay," she says, and I can tell she was hoping for more. Despite my best attempts, Zara keeps trying with me. I know I should open up to her more, but right now I just can't. Maybe one day. "If you need any help, just let me know. Your stuff always goes to the top of the pile."

"You don't have to do that," I say. "There's a procedure for a reason."

"Well, I'm just that good," she says with the confidence of someone who can back it up. "I can add yours in and no one ever knows the difference because I get them done so fast." Zara is strictly an in-office analyst. On rare occasions she'll leave headquarters for an op, but I think it's only happened twice. She's the person who's always behind the screen, helping the agents in the field, like me, be more effective. She's also something of a book nerd, but that's part of why I like her so much. She doesn't have all the grand ambitions every other agent who comes into the FBI starts out with. And she's great at her job.

"Thanks again for the wake-up," I say, sitting up. "Now all I have to do is make sure the shower works before finding some decent coffee in this town."

I hear the tapping of keys on the other side of the phone. "You'll want to check out the Early Derby, off Chestnut. They open at five-thirty."

"You're too good to me," I say.

"Have a great day!" she hangs up, leaving me staring at the blue light of my phone, longing for a connection I have no idea of how to make.

———

After a quick stop at the Early Derby and a steaming coffee in my hand, I'm at Stillwater PD by five 'till six. Trish is nowhere to be seen, instead another officer sits behind the partition, glaring at me as I walk in. I show him my badge and he opens the door to the back where I sit down and get started, searching all of the missing persons' reports for the last six months a hundred miles around Stillwater. Without a presumed name, there's no way we'll be able to find dental records on this person, so it's time to get to work. I could wait on the autopsy, but I'm impatient, and I can narrow down the search parameters with just what I observed on site yesterday. Fortunately for us, there aren't that many natural redheads in the general population. Which should narrow things down quickly.

However, by the time Coll makes his way in around seven forty-five, I've come up with nothing.

"I'm going to have to start getting up earlier if I want to beat you in," he says, leaving a coffee on my desk as he passes.

"What's this for?" I ask.

"You said you didn't eat breakfast, so I figured you might need one since you've been here for..." he waits for me to finish.

"Two hours," I reply sheepishly, not even sure why I'm embarrassed.

He nods at the other cup on my desk. "I see you've already found the best in town."

"I had some help," I reply, turning back to the missing person's database. "Thanks for the coffee."

He points to my screen. "I went through them all yesterday too, after you left. I don't guess you're having any luck?"

I shake my head. "As much as I hate to admit it, I think we're going to have to look nationally. There's a good possibility she was brought in from somewhere outside the general area."

"Yep," he says and lays a file folder on my desk. In it are seven reports, all featuring red-haired women of varying ages.

"How late were you here?" I ask.

"I left around nine," he replies.

"This can't be all of them," I say.

He chuckles. "No, just Virginia and Maryland. Who do you think I am, Superman?"

This is good. I should have been here to help him, and I can feel that pressure building up inside me. The pressure to be the best at this job. If I'd just gotten sleep that first night... but I stop. I can't do that to myself right now. It's already in the past, and he's started on the legwork. And staying up before a big case is part of my process, which I need to accept. We can probably cover a few more states before the coroner finishes with the autopsy, assuming she's the first thing on the schedule this morning.

"I'll take south and west if you want north and east," I say, grinning. We won't get them all, but the more we have when the report is ready, the better prepared we'll be. If she's not from the general area, more than likely she'll be from an adjacent state. I just hope this isn't one of those where the killer transported her all the way from Oregon.

"Sounds good," he says. I find despite my best efforts, I'm liking Detective Coll more and more. Working with him is easy, unlike most of the people I have to interact with on a daily basis. Part of me wants to lean into that, but then the other, more practical part of myself tells me what I already know: it's only going to turn out bad in the end, so I need to keep my distance. I give him a curt nod and turn back to my screen, starting with North Carolina.

"Well, you had one thing right," the medical examiner says, snapping off a pair of gloves as she addresses us in the county examiner's office, which is only three buildings down from the police department. "She's a woman."

"Good to know," I reply. I suppose we could have been dealing with a cross-dresser, but somewhere in my gut I knew that wasn't the case.

"Here's all her effects," the M.E. says, handing us a small tray with all the jewelry she had on. I give it a quick visual inspection. We'll be following up with these later.

"So?" I ask. "Any idea of what killed her?"

She eyes me carefully. I don't get the same kind of ambivalence from her that I got from the other cops, save Coll. But she's careful, guarded. She isn't sure if she can trust me or not. I don't blame her. When we first came in she waited a beat before introducing herself as Sybil Crowley, chief coroner for

Stillwater. She's in her mid-fifties, and I get the sense from this woman she doesn't take shit from anyone, including Burke. As I speak to her, I hear Janice in the back of my head not to make things harder here for the locals.

"Given the advanced state of decay, it's hard to tell," Sybil says. "But we can rule out gun shot or blade wounds. The clothing was mostly intact and I'm not seeing any scratches on the bones or bullet holes." She takes us over to where the woman's remains are lying on the table in the middle of the room. "There was also no blunt-force trauma to the head or spine. Eyes were sewn shut post-mortem. And as you probably already saw, there was a tremendous amount of damage to the pelvic area, given the way she was crammed into that box."

She indicates what is left of the woman's pelvis and femurs, which have been realigned. "Someone wedged her in there with a lot of force," she says, "But based on the pooling, she was probably already dead by the time they did."

"Why would someone do that?" I ask. "What benefit does it have?"

"Well, first off, you don't have to dig as large of a hole," Sybil says. "But as far as I can tell, there is no advantage. Other than rage. If she'd been alive we'd be seeing more damage around what's left of her nail beds or other residual bruising or breaks."

"Couldn't she have been drugged?" Coll asks.

Crowley shakes her head. "Even if she were, there would have been evidence inside the box showing some kind of struggle. I am reasonably sure she was already dead when they stuffed her in there."

"How long was she out in that clearing?" I ask.

"Best guess? At least two and a half months. She's reached a state of butyric fermentation, where the flesh begins to break down. Normally this begins about twenty days after death, but in this case, confined in that little box, I believe it's slowed the rate of decay that we'd normally see. Based on that and the condition of the body, I'd say she was probably killed some-time in mid-January."

"At least that's something," Coll says. "I was afraid it was going to be longer."

I agree. Two and a half months means this isn't a complete cold case. Still, it's not going to be easy. And some-thing about this tugs at the back of my memory, though I can't recall exactly what. "Fingerprints?" I ask.

"That's where we might be in luck. Because of the cold, the skin has been preserved. There's a process called thanato-practical processing, which might be able to restore the fingers enough to get a print, but we'll have to send the body off to do that; we don't have the equipment here. Do you have any idea who the vic is?"

Coll shakes his head. "Nothing. But we're hoping we might get a break on the jewelry."

"Honestly," Sybil says. "You've got better luck getting a dental match than with the fingerprints. If you can get a lead on her identity, I can confirm with her dentist. It will be a lot quicker than trying to get the prints reconstructed."

I walk over and bag the jewelry. "Anything else? Other identifying details?"

Sybil shakes her head. "Just that she was relatively young; in her mid-to-late-thirties. Too young for knee or hip replace-ments, no metal plates, not even a broken bone as far as I can tell, unless, of course, you count the body stuffing."

My mind is trying to take in all these details. Based on her jewelry alone I can tell this wasn't a poor woman, none of this stuff is costume jewelry. And it seems she was in generally good health, given what Sybil has told us.

"What about the eyes?" I ask. "Any particular reason?"

"None that I could find," she says. "Seems ritualistic."

"Religious maybe," I tell Coll. "Something else to consider."

"Thanks, doc," Coll says as I return with the bagged evidence.

"Of course. I'll keep her in the freezer until you decide what you want me to do. Just keep me in the loop." She wheels the table over to the wall of compartments. They remind me of a mausoleum, and I have to shake away the thoughts.

Coll takes notice and gives me a look for a second, but I wave him off. "Pleasure meeting you, Sybil," I say. "Thanks for your help."

She gives me a dispassionate nod. "Just doing my job."

Chapter Six

AFTER LEAVING THE COUNTY EXAMINER'S OFFICE, WE DECIDED to head directly to the jewelry store. Coll offered to drive, and I didn't feel like objecting. Any hope I had of breaking this case is quickly fading. With little to identify her and similar women not showing up in any of the local missing person's reports, I'm starting to think this is a long shot.

"So I'm thinking," Coll says. "We know she's only been missing a few months, and that she's reasonably well off—"

"And that she's married," I say, flipping a gold wedding ring over inside the bag. Unfortunately there is no engraving on the band itself. There's also an engagement ring, a bracelet, and a pendant with what looks like a ruby inside.

"—And that she's married," Coll repeats. "Do you think she knew her killer?"

"More than likely," I say. "The lack of violent contact to cause her death would suggest as much. She was probably either strangled, or injected with something…and like Sybil said, she didn't put up much of a fight. Which means our unsub could get close without fear of being exposed."

"Unsub?" he asks.

"Unknown subject," I reply. "It's what we call our perpetrators when we don't have an ID."

"We just call them unidentified assailants."

I turn to him. "Don't you know? The FBI is all about efficiency. There's not an acronym out there we haven't co-opted for our own use."

It takes him a second before he busts out laughing, and I can't help but grin myself. Sometimes the FBI really can be full of itself, and that's something I have to remember when working with local cops.

We pull into the jeweler's parking lot. It's a small building, crammed in between two larger buildings that both show VACANT signs. At one point in time they were probably department stores or local shop fronts; part of a bustling downtown in a growing city. But now they just sit there, the small jewelry store having outlasted them both.

Coll leads the way as we enter to the sound of a bell overhead. I look up, and realize it wasn't an actual bell, but an electronic monitoring system that was designed to sound like a real bell. A quick glance at this place tells me the owners are serious about their security. This might be a small operation in a tiny town, but they're not leaving anything to chance here.

"Morning," the clerk at the counter says. He's in his mid-forties with glasses on his face, and a second set of glasses perched on his balding head. He greets us with a smile. "Let me guess, shopping for wedding rings?"

Coll and I exchange an uncomfortable glance before I pull out my badge and show it to the clerk. "I'm Agent Slate, with the FBI. This is Detective Coll. We're here to see if you can identify some jewelry for us off a crime scene."

"Oh," the clerk says, taken aback. "I'm sorry. Not often we get the FBI in here. What do you have?"

I lay out the bag for him.

"May I remove these?" I nod. They've already been

sampled for prints, DNA and anything else. He takes a minute, pulling the second set of glasses down over his first, and I realize they're magnifying glasses. After an inspection of all four items he looks up. "Well, the good news is they're all authentic."

I let out a satisfied breath. "What can you tell us about them?"

He places each item on a small scale in turn. Then he uses a small caliper on the stones.

"Wedding ring, gold, twenty-four karats. Diamond engagement ring, three karats set within an eighteen-karat band. Diamond and ruby tennis bracelet, of varying degrees of quality, and a five-karat ruby set within a diamond-studded necklace. All told, you're probably looking at twenty to twenty-five grand worth of gems and metals here."

Coll lets out a low whistle. I can't blame him. "Can you tell us if your shop sold any of these items?"

"It's possible," he says. "We do have a lot of high-paying clients, especially those that commute into the city. Let me check our inventory to see if any of these match items sold recently."

"It wouldn't be recent," I say. "At least, not within the past two months."

He nods, pulling his second pair of glasses back up before heading over to his computer.

"Is your entire inventory digitized?" Coll asks.

"Everything back to the late nineties," the clerk says. "Makes it easier for record-keeping. People come in missing a stone or need a repair, it's much easier to see what they originally bought than to try and guess. Then we can reconstruct it much closer to the original item." He searches for a few moments. "Hmm. The wedding ring I won't be able to tell, we've sold literally hundreds of those over the years. The engagement ring though…no. Doesn't look like that was us."

I let out a frustrated breath. I'm not feeling optimistic about this. Our killer probably drove in from Canada or—

"Wait, looks like we did sell the necklace."

My heart jumps. "Are you sure?"

"Pretty sure. That's an R4 ruby inside a setting decorated with four half karat, C6 diamonds. The odds of another one like that being sold anywhere are low. It was a unique item; we've never had another like it in the shop."

"Who was the buyer?" I ask.

He purses his lips. "This is odd. I don't have a buyer listed. It says they paid cash."

"*Cash?*" Coll asks. "How much total?"

"A little under nine grand," the clerk says. "Same day pickup."

I put my hand on the jewelry case between us, leaning forward to see if I can get a look at his screen. "Are you telling me someone walked in off the street with nine grand in their pocket and purchased that?"

"It seems that way," he replies.

"When?"

"Invoice is dated…November third, twenty-fifteen."

I look up at the cameras that have all angles of the shop covered. "I don't guess you have footage that goes back that far."

"No, and we've replaced the system since then. Even if we'd had it, the records are long gone."

Damn. I turn and head for the door.

"Thanks for your help," Coll says, and I hear him gathering up the jewelry. I'm standing outside by the car by the time he reaches me. "Not what you wanted to hear?"

I shrug. "I knew this wouldn't be easy. But at least it tells us one thing: she might be local after all."

"I don't get it," Coll says. We've been back at the office ever since the jewelry store and the day has dragged on with little

progress. The first thing I did when I returned to my tempo-
rary desk was read over the coroner's report. But there
wasn't anything in there I didn't already know. Now we're
back to searching the missing persons' reports, with little
luck.

"Don't get what?" I ask.

"Wouldn't someone have reported her missing? I mean,
we get reports on homeless people going missing all the time.
You would think, with someone walking around that has
twenty-six grand of jewelry on her person, *someone* would
notice her missing."

He's right. People with that much money don't drop off
the face of the earth without somebody taking notice. And
unless she bought those items for herself, someone else at least
knows of her existence. I still can't get over her eyes. It's such a
strange thing to do to someone, and something about it is
bugging me. I pull out my cell and dial.

"Howdy!" Zara says.

I grin. "Howdy? That's new."

"I just figured I'd give you a good ol' country welcome,
considerin' you're workin' in the sticks." Her voice too upbeat
and cheerful. And a little bit mocking too, even though I know
she'd give anything to be here as well.

I laugh. "You're not far off. Can you do something for me?
I've got a hunch."

"Ohhh, those are the best," she replies, back in her
normal voice. "Lay it on me."

"Can you work your magic and check the CDE for me on
any other victims that match similar circumstances upon being
found? I'm updating her file now with everything we know." I
notice Coll perk up.

"You're thinking she's not the first?"

"I don't know, there's just something…familiar about this
case and I can't put my finger on it. Just check for me, okay?"

"Sure thing. Gimmie a couple hours. I'll have to run a

couple of different syntax searches since we don't have a name. I'll be back in touch soon."

"Thanks, I owe you a drink when I get back." I hang up and turn to Coll.

"What's going on?" he asks.

"Just checking on a hunch. I want to make sure our unsub hasn't done this before."

He sits back, his eyes wide. "Shit. You really think it's possible?"

"Anything's possible," I reply. "We just have to figure out how probable it is."

"Well," he says, standing and grabbing his coat. "I'm about useless for the rest of the day, how about you?"

I stare at the search screen some more. We've managed to pull nineteen more names for the file, but they're all out of state. If the jewelry was purchased here, then more than likely the victim lived here and we're just wasting our time. I feel like I've completely gone off the rails and we've just barely begun.

I run my hands down my face. "Yeah. I'll come back to this tomorrow. I need to catch up on my sleep."

"That's a myth, you know," he says, slipping his coat on. "You can't really catch up. Sleep isn't something you can bank, like money. Once it's gone, it's gone."

"Are you *trying* to depress me?" I ask, putting my own coat on. "I covet my naps."

"Now naps are a different thing," he says, leading me down the hallway. "They act like a recharge. Naps are great, I take naps all the time. But once you've lost that night-time sleep, you are S.O.L., sister."

"Why do you know so much about sleep?" I ask.

"Suffered a bit of insomnia when I was younger. Endured tons of tests. Not something I'd recommend if you can avoid it."

"What helped you get over it?" We exit through the back of the station, which is closer to the parking lot.

"Liberal amounts of alcohol."

I chuckle until I see his face. "You're serious."

"Don't get me wrong, I'm not a drunk or anything, but I find having one or two after work helps calm me down. So I'm not drowning in these dark thoughts every day. Seeing that woman...that was rough."

"Is that where you're headed now?"

He nods. "I was hoping you'd join me. I mean, I'll be plying you for FBI secrets the entire time, just so you're aware."

Normally I'd say no and just go back to my hotel room. But given that it isn't the most comfortable place, and Coll has been more accommodating than most anyone else, I figure I owe him at least one drink. "Fine. But you start hitting on me and your ass will be on the floor."

"Promises, promises," he says, grinning.

Chapter Seven

"DID YOU ALWAYS WANT TO BE WITH THE FBI?" COLL ASKS, taking a seat across from me. He's brought me to a place called *The Road Stop*, which is barely more than a one-story cinder-block building with a few windows carved out. A row of pool tables and over-used dartboards are in the back and the place has the distinctive smell of beer. I'm glad I followed him in my own car; I don't plan on staying very long.

"Slate?"

"What?" I ask, snapping back to attention.

"I said, did you always want to be with the FBI?" There's a lot of people in here tonight. I wouldn't exactly call the place "jumping", but there's enough ambient noise that Coll has to raise his voice.

"This where you bring all your dates?" I ask with a smirk, dodging his question.

"Oh no, this isn't a date," he says. "I think we need to be clear on that. This is just a friendly after-work drink. I save the nice places for special occasions."

I grin and have half an urge to throw my drink at him, but I take a sip from my glass instead. He flashes a smile, tipping his own bottle back. "Actually, this is where most of the off-duty cops come to blow off some steam."

"Awesome," I say. "Cop bar."

He makes a little gesture with his hand. "Atmosphere isn't the best, but you can't beat the price. But you keep avoiding my question."

I take a deep breath. I guess I have to participate after all. "I didn't have a childhood dream or anything like that. I just wanted to be the best, at whatever I was doing."

"Lemme guess, valedictorian?" I'm about to contradict him, but he's right. I don't say anything, just take another sip. "Early acceptance into Quantico? Field-training at what… twenty-three?"

"Twenty-four," I correct him.

"Black belt?" he asks.

"Two. Aikido and Karate."

His eyes widen just a hair, but his smile doesn't go anywhere. "So that crack about me being on my ass was—"

"Dead serious," I reply, but there's a smile on my lips. I immediately wipe it away. I'm not going to do this. I'm not about to be sucked into something, not when things are so…raw.

"What about your family?" he asks. "Any brothers or sisters?"

"Just me," I reply. "Only child and the one they pinned all their hopes and dreams on."

He raises his bottle to me. "Looks like you're doing all right from this side of the table."

"You don't know the whole story," I reply.

"Care to tell me?"

"Not really."

"Fair enough." He squints. "Let's see…I'm gonna say… private school. K through twelve."

I have to stifle a full-belly laugh at that. "Not even close. I'm from a town smaller than Stillwater. My graduating class had less than forty people in it. We didn't even have a private school."

He leans forward. "All of a sudden, that valedictorian isn't looking so impressive after all."

"Now you know the worst secret of all." I take another sip then nod to him. "What about you? Career cop always in your sights?"

"Runs in the family, just not the immediate family," he says. "My granddad was a cop, back in Ireland in the eighties."

"Whoa," I say.

"Yeah. Made the ultimate sacrifice fighting off a bunch of thugs who were just out causing trouble. One of them pulled a knife on 'em and..." He takes a swig.

"Liam, I'm sorry," I say.

"Yeah, it's sucks. I wish I could have known him. Anyway, my da moved here shortly after and met my mom. They got married and that's all she wrote."

"I was wondering why you didn't have an accent," I say. "With a name and complexion like yours?"

"What, not Lucky-Charms enough for ya?" he says in a bad impression of an Irish accent.

I almost spit out my whiskey.

"Have you ever been? Trace back your family heritage?"

"I'd like to," he says. "But I doubt I'll do a lot of traveling on a cop's salary. At least a cop in Stillwater. Maybe the pay's better where you are."

"The pay might be better, but the hours are murder," I reply. "I've got a dog that I barely see because they've got me working so much."

"Then why get the dog?" he asks.

I wince. "I...he...he was a friend's. I don't want to give him up." *Dammit.* I did not want to be talking about this. I should just finish my drink and go.

I knock back the rest of the whiskey, draining the glass.

"I'm gonna hit the hay, try to get some of that sleep I can't catch up on." I produce a ten from inside my coat and place it on the table. "Thanks for inviting me."

"Emily, hang on," he says, leaning to the edge of the booth as I get out. It's the first time he's used my first name and I hate myself for liking how it sounds coming out of his mouth. "You don't have to go. We can talk about anything else. Anything at all."

"Thanks," I say. "But I'm really tired. I'm gonna get back."

"Okay." Funny, I don't detect the normal anger or frustration I'm used to hearing when I blow guys off. "See you tomorrow?"

"Yeah, of course," I say, then head out to the parking lot.

What the hell am I doing? I'm supposed to be here for a job, not to go out and have drinks with the local cop shadowing me for the police chief who I *know* has it in for me. No matter how nice Coll is, I have to remember he's on the other side of this. If he were FBI, it might be different, but I have to keep my wits about me, and going out for drinks with him isn't doing me any favors.

I slam both of my hands on the steering wheel as I'm driving back. How could I be so stupid? What would Matt say? How would this make him feel?

My phone rings as I'm halfway back to the motel. At first I'm afraid it might be Coll, trying to coax me back. But when I see it's Zara I let out a sigh of relief.

"Hey, Zara. What's up?"

"Got some good news and bad news for you," she says. "What first?"

"Hit me with the bad news. Might as well get all the crappy parts over with first."

"Wait," she says, her interest piqued. "What does that mean? What else is crappy?"

"Nothing, I just...I went out for a drink with the detective I'm working with. It was stupid, I shouldn't have done it."

"Because of Matt?" she asks, and I'm struck by her bluntness. She's never said his name before, at least not ever since... that day. At first, I'm too stunned to even answer.

"I mean...yeah," I finally say. It isn't like I can get mad at her; she's not wrong.

"Was it a date?" she asks.

"No, not technically. But some parts felt...date-ish."

She chuckles. "Date-ish? What does that even mean?"

"I don't know," I say. I'm not making sense to her because she's not in my position. No one is. No one has been through what I've been through, not at my age.

All I know is sitting there with Liam Coll felt...familiar. And I've only ever felt that once before.

"Try not to beat yourself up," she says. "What you went through...it's going to be raw for a while. But you're still human. You're allowed to have feelings."

"I guess," I say. Though I've always prided myself on not getting bogged down with the stuff that trips up normal people. I guess I'm not immune after all. "Thank you."

"Anytime," she adds, her voice full of cheer. "So I can't really tell you the bad news without the good news first."

That brings a smile to my face. "Then why did you ask me which I wanted first?"

"Cause you're supposed to say the good news! Everyone says the good news!"

I relent. "Okay, what's the good news?"

"I found another victim in a similar condition." I pull the car off the road, my tires screeching. "Em? Are you okay?"

"You're shitting me," I say.

"Nope. I had to dig deep, though. Six years ago."

"Tell me that's the bad news."

"I wish." She pauses and I can hear the trepidation in her

voice. "The killer was never identified. Even after an extensive search."

"How was she found?" I ask.

"Almost exactly the same. Eyes sewn shut, body folded up into a box half her size. Report says she was in there for probably at least three years. Advanced state of decay."

"Holy shit," I practically scream. This information has turned this from a one-off into a possible serial, with a matching M.O. Who knows how many other victims could be out there? "Where? Are there any others?" I ask, taking a moment to breathe.

"A town called Soft Bend, a few hours from you. I haven't found any others yet. I'm going back further to see if anyone else matches. We might have an offender who only works once every couple of years or so."

"Which means catching them is going to be next to impossible. Did you inform Janice yet?"

"Nope, that's your job. I'm just the desk-jockey."

"Zara, thank you for this, really. You might have just blown this case wide open."

"Wasn't me." I can practically see her blushing through the phone. "It was your hunch. How did you know?"

"I didn't," I reply. "But something about it felt...off. Like it was too perfect. No trace evidence, no residual prints or anything to give us an ID. It's like the unsub planned the perfect murder. You don't get that lucky on your first try."

"Well, you were right," she says. "When are you going to tell Janice?"

Suddenly, I'm no longer tired or worn down. It's like the conversation with Coll happened a year ago. I feel the invigoration of a fresh case moving through my veins. The victim was from here, *and* her killer has struck before. That doubles the chances of them screwing up, of leaving some clue behind. Something that will allow me to find them. "Tomorrow," I say. "I need time to process this. To work the case a little more. Is my laptop encrypted?"

"Should be, why?"

"Can you send over everything you have on this second victim? I need to do some work tonight."

Chapter Eight

"GOOD MORNING," COLL SAYS, STROLLING IN. HE STOPS IN front of my desk, making sure he has my attention. Already I know this is going to be about last night, but I'm past that already. I've made a huge breakthrough, but I have to wait on Sybil before I can be sure. "Listen, about last night, I didn't mean to make you run off. I was just—"

"It's fine," I say. "I'm not great with people, so don't take it personally."

"If I said anything to offend you, I didn't mean to," he says.

"I know, and it really doesn't matter right now." I grab the file I pulled from records this morning after I arrived. "What do you know about this?"

The consternation on his face is easily visible, and he seems frustrated at my dismissal of his "apology". But honestly, I really don't care. Not after what I found last night.

Coll takes the file and opens it, flipping through the pages. "Victoria Wright?" he asks. "What does she have to do with anything?"

"You know the case?" I ask.

"Sure, the chief handled this one a few months back.

Family friend or something, I'm not sure. But he took point on it. It's a closed case. She wasn't missing; she flew off to Italy with her new boyfriend or something and just happened to never tell anyone."

I take the file back. That's what I'd read too. After I got back to my motel room last night, I started doing some digging into the second victim Zara found. She turned out to be a young woman named Laura Allan who had been missing for almost three years. They only found her because she'd been buried in an abandoned building. When the building was demolished for a new urban housing project, her remains were uncovered in a box almost exactly the same as the first victim. By some kind of miraculous luck, they were able to identify her due to a series of broken bones from an accident she'd suffered as a child.

But the most interesting part about the case was Laura Allen had been reported missing originally, then "found" a few days later when she was discovered to have taken off to California in her Geo Tracker. The Police had even spoken to someone over the phone who insisted she was Laura Allen and her car was spotted on I-40 around Amarillo and again in Flagstaff.

When her body was found and identified, it was assumed the note she'd left had been faked, and the woman they'd spoken to must have been paid by someone to impersonate her. But no other evidence was found of who might have killed her. Her vehicle hasn't been spotted since.

As much as my heart hurt for Laura Allen, her case gave me the push I needed to get a break. So I went back through all the closed missing person's cases and found this one: Victoria Wright. Originally reported missing by her husband over three and a half months ago, Victoria was well-known in the community, though she kept to herself. She also had naturally red hair, which, from the pictures I've seen, made her hard to miss. After the missing person's report was filed, an investigation was opened, and eventually closed, from circumstantial evidence, that she'd emptied her bank accounts and left the country with someone she'd been seeing without her husband's knowledge.

And yet, when I look at the similarities between Victoria Wright and our victim, I can't help but see everything match up. They're the same height and build, same age, same hair color and she went missing close to the time the body was most likely dumped. The only thing we'd missed was that she had been a *closed* missing case and not an open one.

"You think this is our victim?" Coll asks.

"I'm almost sure of it," I reply. "I've got Sybil checking her dental records right now. When those come back, we'll know one way or the other."

Coll screws up his face before taking a seat at his desk. "But…she's supposed to be on the other side of the Atlantic."

"Did anyone ever follow up?" I ask.

He shakes his head. "I don't know. Like I said, it wasn't my case. The chief handled that one." I'd seen that on the file. Burke's name had been all over it from day one, and it was his signature that closed it up. I look back over to Coll. His eyes have gone glassy as he's trying to wrap his mind around the possibilities. I know the feeling; I was doing the same thing half the night.

"Do you think she came back?" he asks.

"Clearly she did," I reply. "And someone was here waiting for her."

"We need to let the chief know," Coll says.

I shake my head. "Not until we're sure. I'm already on my boss's shit list and I don't need to get up in Burke's craw if I can help it. Let's wait until we get the dentals back before we do anything."

"Right," Coll says, collecting himself. He picks up the stack of other missing persons we've already printed out. "I guess these are useless now."

"There's something else," I say. I debated with myself all night about whether I should tell him we're looking at a possible serial here, but I have to believe we can work better together than apart. Plus, Coll has shown me he's not like the normal cops I deal with. I don't think sharing this with him will blow up in my face; at least I hope it won't. And if he's going to be of any use to me, he needs to have all of the information too. "I received intel last night that she may not be the first victim."

He almost spits out the coffee he'd brought in with him but manages to keep it in his mouth and swallow. "What?" he sputters.

"I had a friend at the Bureau run a search for me. Similar death circumstances. She found one other from six years ago, in a town on the other side of the Maryland border, Soft Bend."

"Another body like this one?"

I nod. "Found in an advanced state of decay, shoved and crammed into a small footlocker. Remnants of thread around the eyes indicating they were sewn shut. The killer was never found, and a motive couldn't be determined."

"Holy shit," he says. "Are there any others?"

"She's still looking, but I'm willing to bet the body out in Soft Bend wasn't our unsub's first. But she might have been the first of a new M.O. Victoria here suffered a similar fate."

Coll sits back, running his hand across the side of his face and through his hair. "How...how did you do all of this in one evening? Yesterday we had little more than nothing."

I give him a knowing smile. "I don't often get this frustrated this quickly. Usually we find something at the scene, or something on the body to indicate who did this. The fact that we didn't says something in itself. It says this person is careful; they know what they're doing, and they are obviously skilled at covering their tracks. Only someone with practice would be able to do that. From there it was as simple as figuring out our victim was part of a pattern. And once I had the information from Soft Bend, I *knew* she had to be in the missing person's database somewhere, even if it had just been a phone call to report she hadn't picked up her newspapers off her front porch."

He laughs. "Who uses newspapers anymore?"

I narrow my eyes, but there's a smile on my face. "You know what I mean. Someone like this makes waves in a community. Their absence is noticed, if by no one else but the gossip crowd."

Coll lets out a low whistle. "That's pretty impressive. So as soon as the ID comes back, we can let Burke know?"

He seems awfully anxious to loop his boss in on this. Then again, I guess that's how they operate out here. Even though I'm coming off a suspension, I still have all the power of the FBI at my disposal, as well as the autonomy. I don't have to notify Janice of anything until it looks like we're closing in on a suspect. But it looks like Coll wants to get Burke in on this right away, something I don't look forward to. The man is a pompous bully, and it's obvious he screwed up the original investigation, otherwise we'd already know who our vic was, given her case should still be open.

"We'll inform Burke when the time is right. If this really is Victoria Wright, we'll need to reopen her investigation." Coll averts his eyes. "What?"

"I can just tell you now he won't like that. Burke has a pride about his record; he's not going to want to see a closed case dredged back up."

I scoff. "That's just too damn bad. We're dealing with a potential serial killer and a victim who has been buried in a box for two months. I don't care what part of his ego gets bruised; I'm not backing down off this."

"No, I know," Coll says. "Just…be prepared for the backlash."

Great. But it can't be helped; not given what we know

already. If that really is Victoria Wright down there, Burke is just going to have to deal with the fact that he screwed up. He strikes me as the kind of man who isn't used to being held accountable. But he's in for a big surprise if he thinks I'm not going to throw this failure right back in his face.

I can already feel Janice's silent judgment. This isn't about embarrassing Burke; it's about finding justice for this woman. And I'm going to have a much harder time doing that if I have to fight the Stillwater Police Department the entire way.

"Let's just wait and see what Sybil comes back with," I reply. "In the meantime, I want to start going over all this 'evidence' in Victoria's file."

"Sure," Coll says, tapping on his computer. "I've got all the digitals right here."

I position myself over his shoulder. "Show me everything."

Chapter Nine

FOUR HOURS LATER AND MY EYES FEEL LIKE THEY'RE ABOUT TO pop out of their sockets. I've been staring at the screen so long I'm going to be seeing windows in my dreams. But Coll and I went over every piece of evidence in Victoria Wright's file, in addition to what little physical evidence was present, which wasn't much.

According to Burke it was an open and shut case. After the husband reported her missing, they took her computer, found a bunch of messages and emails to and from a man named Patrick Wood over the course of almost a year. The messages had started out innocuous enough, but eventually they had built a relationship, and she'd decided to leave her husband for Patrick. After that they found ATM footage of Victoria emptying her bank accounts and then purchasing two tickets to Italy out of Dulles on January 17th. After confirming with the airport they were on the plane, Burke summarily closed the case, chalking it up to a wife who no longer wanted to deal with her husband and wanted out of a bad marriage.

There were a few witness statements and some other background information, but none of it is what I'd call in-depth. I can see why Burke thought this was an easy win: it seems so clear-cut on the surface. Maybe that's why he decided to take the case himself, add another closed case to his record with little legwork. But there's nothing in the file about how the husband took the news about his wife having an affair. And now that we've got a body, I find myself very anxious to interview him in person.

After going over all the case notes, I had to take a break. Fortunately, today is a bit warmer than the past week has been, even for these parts, and I recalled seeing a little deli only a few stores down from the police station. Turns out they have a pretty good pastrami sandwich. At first I thought Coll would want to join in, but he never said a word, probably still trying to figure out how to approach me after last night. I can't help that, though. I didn't mean to be rude, but any time anyone brings up anything even closely related to Matt, I... just can't. It's too much, even now. Timber was ours together, I rescued him from a dog-fighting ring and we both trained him. He had been used as a "bait" dog, for the larger, more powerful animals to dominate. I could tell when I first saw him he'd been broken by humanity, and I wasn't going to let that stand. Even though animal control said it was dangerous, I didn't care. We took him in, showed him loving care and tenderness for the first time in his life, and he's never once snapped at anyone.

But every time I think of Timber I can't but help think about Matt too. And being away from my dog in a way feels like I'm even farther from my husband.

Detective Coll doesn't need to know about my private life. It's like the more people I tell, the worse it gets, because it just cements in my head the fact that he's gone. Part of me wants to pretend that Matt is still back in D.C., waiting with Timber for me when I get home. And right now, that belief, misguided as it is, and this job are the only things that are keeping me going. The fact that I can focus on someone else's pain and redirect my own is what keeps me getting out of bed in the mornings. It's the reason I can't fail on this case. I can't let it get away from me. Because if they force me to sit behind a desk for the rest of my career, I don't think I can handle it.

I take a deep breath as I leave the deli, soaking in the warmth from the sun and the mild air. I barely even need a jacket today, it's so fair and breezy. It isn't often I get to visit small towns like this one. Usually, I'm stuck in D.C. or Baltimore, working cases there. It's always noisy and busy and sometimes it's hard to think. But here, where there's barely a car on the road and all I can hear is the distant sound of a train somewhere off in the distance, I'm reminded of how peaceful life can be.

I walk back into the station, smiling at Trish as I pass her. She barely looks up from the book she's reading and doesn't return the sentiment. I don't really expect her to. She buzzes me through and I head back to my makeshift office, hoping to find a report from Sybil on my desk.

Instead, however, I find Chief Burke, with his huge ass right on the side of the desk I've been using, looking at Coll as I walk in. I can tell by their body language they were discussing something regarding the case, because as soon as I enter, they both turn to me. While Coll immediately looks away, Burke locks eyes with me, a grimace on his face.

"Chief," I say, standing close to the door. I don't want to try and get around him to my workstation. It would be pointless anyway, considering he's taking up half my desk. My laptop is off to the side, still closed, but I can't help but wonder if he's opened it up, trying to take a peek.

"Agent Slate," he says. "I understand you're looking to reopen a closed missing person's case."

I shoot a pointed glance at Coll, but he avoids me like the coward he is. *Damn.* I knew I shouldn't have trusted him. I ask him not to inform Burke about Victoria Wright yet and what does he do? Goes behind my back. I'd hoped to have taken care of this diplomatically, once I had the proof back from the coroner. Now that's all down the drain. Looks like he's just a stooge for Burke after all.

I square my shoulders, addressing Burke. "That's right. The missing person from that file may be our victim."

"We didn't call you here to open cases that have already been solved, Agent," he says. He's trying to restrain himself, but I can tell there's a lot of vitriol behind those words. His burning eyes say it all.

"And I didn't come here to half-ass my job," I reply. "If a case wasn't thoroughly investigated the first time, you can bet your badge I'm reopening it."

Burke shoots to his feet. "This isn't the big city, little lady," he says and I can feel my palms burning. He's baiting me, trying to get me to go off. And if he pushes me much farther, he might just get his wish. "We have a code around these parts. You don't have any direct evidence the body down in that locker is Victoria Wright, do you?"

"What's wrong, Chief? Afraid I'll expose some shoddy police work from the lead detective? Oh wait, that was you, wasn't it? I don't think you're entirely impartial on this matter."

"That's it," he says, pushing past me. I actually feel his shoulder connect and for a split second I have the urge to grab it, shove my leg out and drop him like a bag of potatoes onto the floor. Thankfully my self-control kicks in and I manage to step out of his way before I can react further. "Let's just see what your supervisor has to say about this."

"Be my guest," I reply, though I can feel the heat rising up my back. Getting Janice involved won't be good for me, especially if I don't have anything to show for it. I need that report.

Burke storms out of the office and I head for the door.

Coll stands. He never said a word to help me. "Emily——"

"Don't," I say, the sharpness in my voice clear. "I don't want to hear it." I spin on him and head back out of the station and to my car. I need to get over to the county examiner's office, right now.

"Hello?" I ask as I traverse the halls of the building. I don't remember it being this big when I came here with Coll, though I was more focused on getting information back from the body than I was on the layout of the building. "Dr. Crowley?"

"Back here." Her voice rings through the halls but it's immediately clear where she is. I follow it to the back where a series of small office rooms are adjacent to the primary examining room. There aren't any windows in here, which makes it feel just a tad claustrophobic for me. Not enough to be uncomfortable, just enough to be noticeable.

"Oh, Agent Slate, good," Sybil says, looking up as I approach. "I was just about to email you. I heard back from Victoria Wright's former dentist, they still had everything on record."

"And?" I ask.

"Perfect match. There's no doubt it's her. I've got all the details right here," she says, pointing to her computer.

I feel like a huge weight has been lifted from my chest. This happens sometimes in big cases like this when we get breakthroughs. Sometimes agents don't realize just how much pressure they're under until they're proven right or wrong. The fact that this hunch has panned out means I haven't completely lost my touch. Not yet. "Can you email all that over to me now?" I ask.

"Of course," she replies. "To be honest, I thought this was a long shot. Usually the longer they're in the ground, the less likely we are to get a positive ID."

"That was my thought too," I reply. "But sometimes we get lucky."

She stares at me a moment, probably trying to decide if I'm being humble or cocky. I can't tell which way she goes with it. "There you go."

My phone buzzes, indicating an incoming email. "Great. Thanks for your help."

"Anytime," she says. "I'm always happy to do my job when I know the results will be put to good use."

I stop, interested to see where this thread goes. "Does that not happen often?"

She gives me a small shrug. "Let's just say the chain of command gets in the way out here. I thought working in a small town would make things easier."

"You from D.C.?" I ask.

She frowns. "Is it that obvious?"

"I know a professional when I see one."

Sybil leans up against one of the tables. "I moved out here a few years ago to get away from all that. I just got so tired of the constant interference from politicians always trying to twist the truth. Turns out I didn't go far enough. A lot of people that live over in the richer neighborhoods still commute in. I don't know how they stand it."

"When you say your results don't get put to good use…" I say, allowing my words to hang. I've put my investigator hat back on, wondering if she can tell me anything that might be helpful.

"I wish I could help," she says, "But I don't get into all that. I just do my job. It's up to you to make something happen."

"Well," I hold up my phone. "I appreciate it all the same. I've already experienced the kowtowing personally."

"Just so you know," she calls after me as I leave. "It's not all of them. There are a few good ones left. Ones that aren't so…career-obsessed."

"Thanks," I say, heading back through the door into the hallways. It's obvious from both Coll and Sybil that Burke has a stranglehold on this town. Normally I wouldn't care, but this could affect my investigation. He's an obstacle that might need to be removed. As much as I wish I could tell him that just to see the stupid look on his face when—

My phone buzzes and I check the screen. An urgent text from Coll, just one sentence.

You better get back here.

Chapter Ten

WHO THE HELL DOES HE THINK HE IS, THREATENING ME? FIRST Burke and now Coll? They really are cut from the same cloth. I'm not sure who Sybil was talking about, but it wasn't him.

I grit my teeth as I drive back to the station, all thoughts of what a nice day it is outside forgotten. Part of me is mad that I didn't see Coll for the snake he was in the beginning. I had some suspicions, but he seemed different. Now I can see it was all an act, just so he could get close and report back to his boss.

He'll be lucky if I don't deck him.

I'm so mad I want to hit something, but I can't do that. I represent *the Bureau* and have a *standard* to live up to. Not to mention I'm a woman and God forbid any woman show any emotion one way or another and not be branded a lunatic who can't control herself.

It doesn't matter. I have the evidence, and we now have a positive ID. If I have to do all of this by myself I will. I've got no problem with that at all.

I pull into the parking lot, my tires screeching as the little car fishtails at the entrance. I manage to get it into the spot and I'm out, storming up the stairs while rational thought still lives somewhere in my brain. Blowing through the doors, I see Trish actually look up for once, her book lowering to the desk.

"Chief wants to see you," she says.

"The feeling is mutual," I growl, and she buzzes me through. In the back I stroll right past my "station" and down into Chief Burke's office, not bothering to knock. He's alone in the room, sitting behind his wide desk with a grin plastered on his face.

"Ah, here she is now," he says. I look down and notice one of his phone lines is active, the little red light indicating it's live and on speaker. Burke stands. "I've got someone here who'd like to speak with you."

"Slate?"

It takes all my strength not to wince. "Yes, Special Agent Simmons," I reply. "I'm here." When Burke said he was going to call Janice, I half thought he was just blowing hot air. But it seems he really thinks he's in the right here.

"The chief has expressed his concerns about the job you're doing there." Burke's smile is a mile wide. And all I want to do is roundhouse kick it right off him.

"I'm aware," I reply. "The chief doesn't want me looking into a missing person's case that he closed two months ago. But I've just learned that this particular case matches our murder victim." I look up at Burke. "Dental records just came back." Burke's smile disappears.

"So you have a positive ID?" Janice asks.

"Yes, ma'am. I'm officially reopening the case. It was classified as solved being as the person in question, Victoria Wright, was thought to have fled the country with a lover. It seems she ended up buried in a box just outside of town instead."

"Chief?" Janice asks.

"I haven't seen the evidence connecting the two yet," he says, but I don't miss the sweat on his brow.

"Here, allow me to forward it to you," I say, holding up

my phone dramatically, and going through the motions to forward the email from Sybil.

"This seems…looks like Agent Slate is correct," he admits, looking at his own computer.

"Good job, Slate," Janice says. "Sounds like you're making some good progress there. Let me know when you have a suspect."

"I'm about to go put together a list right now," I reply, beaming.

"Thank you for taking my call, Special Agent," Burke says.

"Chief Burke," Janice says, and I can already hear it in her voice. A tone that I'm more than familiar with. "Next time you want to question the FBI's motives, make sure you pull your head out of your ass first. I don't have stupid people working for me. Let Agent Slate do her job, or I'll file a formal injunction with the State of Virginia. Are we clear?"

"Yes, ma'am," he replies, his entire face flushed crimson. I can't tell if it's from embarrassment or anger. Probably both.

"Don't waste my time again." She cuts off the line which goes to a dial tone. He reaches over and ends the call.

I stand there, daring him to say something. But he just glares right back at me, the fire burning in his eyes. "Anything else, Chief?" I ask.

"No," he growls through his teeth.

"Good. Because I have a case to work. Maybe next time don't be so defensive. Someone might think you have something to hide."

This really gets him worked up and I can see his fists opening and closing, like he can't hold himself together. For a brief second I think he might take a swing, but even he's not that stupid. He just glowers at me until I turn, making sure my hair flits back over my shoulder as I leave him standing there.

My good mood is almost immediately soured when I realize I have to go get my stuff from the joint office I was sharing with Coll. His betrayal has told me one thing: I can't trust him not to blow this case to Burke. Which means I'm officially on my own. That's fine, it's what I expect anyway. I'll just set up shop in my motel room, like usual. I just hope there's a place with decent coffee close by.

When I enter the office, I'm surprised to see Coll's desk is dark. Apparently he's done for the day. Shrugging, I head over and gather up all my items, including all the relevant case files on Victoria Wright. Now that I know who our victim is, I can put together a better profile for her killer. It's time to start digging up some dirt.

By the time I get everything set up in my room it looks like a very organized bomb has gone off. I'm a visual person, so it helps me to spread everything out. That way I can see it all at once to help me see the bigger picture.

Before I left the office, I made sure to print out everything from the digital case file. It's always a ton of paper, but I'm sure Chief Burke won't mind. It's not like it's his money, after all. But I didn't want to need to go back to their systems, so taking things all the way back down to paper it is. I actually ended up leaving with a supply box full. If there's one constant in the universe, it's the never-ending paperwork of law enforcement.

As I stare at the small piles before me, I realize this is going to be difficult to do on my own. Without Coll, it means I have to dig through all of this myself. And given that we're dealing with someone who has already struck twice, I feel the pressure of the case on the back of my neck. If I let things stall, someone else could be killed. In fact, the killer might already have another victim lined up. Given how they've been able to cover their tracks so successfully thus far, it's not a stretch to say that they're probably confident in their abilities by now. They may have already struck again.

I'm deliberately trying not to assign the unsub pronouns yet, not until we have a better idea of who it could be. But all my training and experience tells me the killer is a man. And obviously my prime suspect is going to be Victoria's husband: Gerald.

Despite the fact he called in the missing person's report, it doesn't mean he couldn't have committed the crime. Not to mention Burke never followed up with him after Gerald Wright was told his wife was having an affair. It's very possible that information could have sent him over the edge. Maybe he even went to Italy to convince her to return home, and when she did, he killed her. I won't know until I actually talk to him, which is the first thing on my agenda tomorrow.

But the case file has a couple of other nuggets of information. Briefly, Victoria's boss, Rex Fuller was considered a suspect, before the ATM footage was found. I'm not about to leave any stone unturned, so I'll be going to see him as well.

Additionally, there's this mystery man she ran off with. All I have is a name, no picture. Patrick Wood. There's not much data on him in the file; I might call Zara and get her to do a background on this guy for me. Obviously Burke didn't see much need in investigating him, given they ran off together. But it's possible when they arrived in Italy, Victoria began to regret going and wanted to go home to her family. Patrick might not have taken very well to that. Maybe he came back with her, killed her when they arrived.

Finally, I can't help but think something else is going on with Burke himself. He's too protective of this case, too invested. No one is that much of an asshole for no reason. I'm not saying he actually did anything to Victoria, but something is going on. I just need to figure out what.

I shake my head. There's too many possibilities and not enough information. I'll have to get deeper into the investigation before someone stands out. But I do know this: the killer is smart, they are ruthless, and they are a total narcissist—

operating outside the law without impunity. And I'm not about to let them get away with this.

By the time I look up, it's past seven and my stomach is grumbling. I feel like I'm on a roll, so I order a pizza from a local joint down the street. By the time it arrives I've got my game plan together, and I'll be starting bright and early, ready to suss out a killer. But I'll need to be smart. If they get wind of me poking around, they might get nervous. And a person like this, one who doesn't make stupid mistakes, might end up disappearing forever.

I only end up eating a few bites before hitting the bed. This day has worn me down and I still haven't caught back up on my sleep. But then I hear Coll's words in my head about not being able to catch up. It makes me hate him even more because now I see those hazel eyes as I'm trying to go to sleep. Instead, I try to focus on something else. Something pleasant.

My last thought before falling asleep is of the frown on Burke's face, when everything blew up in it.

Chapter Eleven

I SNAP AWAKE AT FOUR-FIFTEEN; MY ROOM COMPLETELY DARK. At first I think the power must have gone out, because I always leave the bathroom light on when I stay at hotels, but then I remember the bulb burned out last night while I was brushing my teeth. Unsurprisingly, the room doesn't even have a digital clock, just one of those old kinds that flips down the numbers as the minutes count down. I check my phone and find I've missed three emails overnight, though none of them are important.

I could try and go back to sleep, but I can already feel the excitement of moving forward on this case. Instead, I get up and grab a quick shower, though the water takes forever to get warm. You'd think in a motel with only two other guests, it wouldn't be that hard to get warm water in the middle of March.

After dressing in my standard attire and pulling my coat on, I gather all my files and set them back inside the box. I'm not entirely convinced about the security of this place, so all my case files are staying with me. My first stop this morning will be Gerald Wright's office, which according to my information is located near the middle of downtown. Which means I can grab some coffee from the Early Derby and stake out a spot. I want to see how this man acts when he doesn't know he's being watched before I announce my presence to him.

I grab my laptop bag and my service weapon, making sure it's safe to handle before putting it in my holster and closing up my jacket. I push down the handle of the door and prop open the door with my foot, grabbing the box to head out to my car.

Just then, out of the corner of my eye, I see a dark figure rushing me. I drop the box and my laptop bag, pulling my weapon and leveling it at the figure. "Freeze!"

"Jesus!" he yells, stumbling back and tossing something up in the air as he falls on his ass. Since there's no light outside my door and the sun hasn't come up yet, I have to pull my phone out of my pocket and use the flashlight on it to shine it on his face.

I see Liam Coll, his butt in what looks like a brown puddle. An overturned coffee cup on its side beside him.

I lower my weapon, replacing it in my holster. "What the hell are you doing?" I ask.

"Sorry, I was...you looked like you were having trouble with the door, so I was coming to help."

I let out a long breath. It's not often my adrenaline spikes before six in the morning. "Here," I say, holding out a hand to help him up. "C'mon."

He takes it. Once he's up he starts trying to inspect his backside. From what I can tell given the light from my phone, his pants are soaked. "What are you doing here?" I ask.

He gives me a sheepish grin. "Trying to make amends?" He indicates the overturned coffee cup on the ground.

"Oh, you mean for going behind my back when I explicitly asked you not to?"

He looks at the ground. "Yeah. It was a shitty thing to do."

"Yeah, it was," I say, turning off the light and heading

back to the door to grab my things. I pull the laptop bag over my shoulder again and grab the box, hoisting it up.

"Need some help?"

"You know what would be really helpful? Go back to yesterday, *don't* tell Burke about the case, and let me do my job. What if those records hadn't come back as a match? What if I'd been wrong about Victoria Wright?"

"But you weren't," Coll says, going for my door. I get there before he can.

"But I could have been. And even though my boss doesn't answer to yours, if she'd heard I was just down here spinning my wheels...I'm not sure what would have happened. I'm on thin ice, got it?"

"I'm sorry, Emily, I didn't know," he says. I can't decide if I like him using my first name or not. Part of me wants to reject him and push him away, while another part, the betrayal part, is glad he's here. "I wasn't trying to circumvent you. But Burke came in during lunch, wanting an update on the case. He saw where we'd been pulling the missing person's files and he saw Victoria's there on my desk."

I shove my box and laptop bag in the back seat. "You could have told him we didn't have anything yet."

"You're right. I should have," he says. "I should have just stuck to my guns. But I've never had a reason to question Burke's motives before. After what happened yesterday, I couldn't stop thinking about it. It's like he has some personal stake in this case; he just won't let it go. I think there's something going on."

"Uh-huh," I say. "Let me guess, you're recording this so he can accuse me of undermining him or raging some kind of disinformation campaign against him. No chance, buddy. I'm done talking to you."

"No, Emily, I swear," he says. "Look. We don't deal with this kind of stuff here. We have drug raids, missing kids, domestic abuse cases. But not murders. And certainly not potential serial killers. I'm used to always trusting Burke's judgment. I have been ever since he hired me. But there's something different about this case. He's acting different, cagy, like he's trying to hide something. And if he'd done his job properly the first time, we might not have a dead woman down in the county morgue. I'm not so blind I can't see it. Yesterday was a lapse in judgment. It won't happen again. Especially now that I see him for what he really is."

I like to consider myself a pretty good judge of character. Yet, at the same time I don't really get very close to people, because I've learned more often than not, they end up disappointing you when everything is said and done. I'm not what you'd call a trusting person. The easy thing to do would be to dismiss him out of hand, accuse him of working for the other side and just work this all this by myself. But part of me knows I could use his connections to the community to get closer to people than I could on my own. People are intimidated by the FBI. Not so much when it's the local cop they see every day at the diner.

"What do I have to do to prove it to you?" He pulls out his phone. "Look, see? Not recording."

I cross my arms. "That's very convincing."

"Do I need to show you I'm not wearing a wire? I'll do it," he says, reaching for his jacket and unbuttoning it. Suddenly some deep part of me ignites and I realize if he opens that shirt things are going to get very complicated, very quickly. Which is the absolute worst thing that could happen right now. Especially considering who he might be working for. I let him get as far as the first button of his collared shirt before I reach out and stop him.

"No, but you need to understand you violated my trust. And I'm not someone who gives that out very often."

He holds my hand that's on his button a moment before he realizes what he's doing and lets it go. In that moment I feel a spark and do everything in my power to tamp it down. *Not.*

Now. Never again. "I am really sorry," he says. "I didn't mean... no. I was being selfish. Cowardly, even. Only thinking about myself."

"Yes, you were." *Button that damn jacket back up, right now.*

"I understand if you can't trust me anymore. I'll be happy to send you all the files from the case and that way you don't have to interact with me or anyone else at the station."

I motion toward my car. "Already got them."

He seems to see the box for the first time. "Ah." I smile because I'm enjoying this. He's basically prostrating himself before me and he has nowhere else to go. Nothing else to offer. "Okay then. Well, if you need anything else, just give Trish a call. We can have it sent here or over to your official email." He begins backing away. The entire time I'm appraising him, looking for any further signs of deception. But as far as I can tell, he's genuinely sorry.

"I didn't mean to jeopardize your job, especially not for Burke's benefit. Good luck with the case. I'll head home to change," he says, continuing to back away, waiting for me to save him from this humiliation. But I need to enjoy it just a second longer. "This getting up at five thing isn't for everyone."

I let out a long breath. Why do I feel this magnetism to him? And why is it so hard to resist? I know the smart thing would be to just let him walk away; to work this case all by myself. But I've been by myself for three months, and his presence the past few days I've been in Stillwater has been a quiet comfort. It's nothing overt, instead it's like the comfort you get after a long day, when you can just sit on your porch and relax, watching the sun set. That's the feeling I get from him. Part of me hates myself for it, and another part wants more. But I realize now it's been something I've been craving that I couldn't put into words. Despite the fact he betrayed me, part of me doesn't even care. I'm too emotional to make a decision like this. And yet...

"Come on back," I say, waving him back over. This might be the stupidest thing I've done in a while. Actually, no. I can't even say that. The *second* stupidest thing.

He stops. "What?"

"Come on. I get it. You're a sad puppy. If you were any more pitiful, I'd have to put an adoption tag on you."

He sputters. "I'm not...that's not what..." He runs a hand through his hair. "I wasn't trying to..."

"You got a change of clothes in your car?" I ask.

"Yeah."

I motion back to the motel. "You can change in my bathroom. We need to go over some stuff."

Chapter Twelve

"THIS SUCKS," LIAM SAYS, GLARING OUT THE WINDSHIELD UP at the building.

I take a sip of my coffee. "Yup." After he got changed, I looped him in on what I was doing. I truly believe he knows he screwed up. But he's going to have to prove to me that I can trust him again. I'm not giving him anything he doesn't already know from the original case file; all I've done is outline my strategy for approaching this...for finding Victoria's killer.

Despite the fact that he's our prime suspect, Gerald Wright is the only next-of-kin listed in any official documentation anywhere. Her parents are no longer living, and I can't find any evidence of siblings. And given that she was still married when she ran off with Patrick, legally, we have to inform Gerald of her death. Thankfully we don't need him for an ID, though I'll be interested to see how he reacts. There may be an element of performance to his reaction, which is what we need to be on the lookout for. We need to determine if this really is news to him or not. It can be cruel, and I hate that it has to be this way. There's also the possibility he's as much of a victim in this as Victoria is. And if that's the case, I don't look forward to what we're about to do.

Correction, what Detective Coll is about to do.

"I still don't think I should have to be the one—" He stops when he looks over at me.

"You want to be on this case, you get the honors. Think of it as your penance," I say. "You're Catholic, right?" I *hate* informing families that their loved ones are dead. I can't imagine a worse part of the job. No agent I know looks forward to it, which is probably a good thing. If any of them did, there might be some cause for concern.

Liam lets out a low sigh. "I guess I deserve this. But I've never had to do it before. At least, not like this. We've had people killed in accidents, sure. But never by a—"

"That part you keep to yourself," I say. "Unless *he* brings it up." It's a long shot, but I'm not about to make this any easier for the killer than necessary. Everything I know about our unsub is that they're smart, and capable. If Gerald really did this, he's smart enough not to slip up in front of us, but I'm not about to reveal that we know there's more than one victim. That's a good way to lose someone in the wind and never find them again. If he thinks we're doing nothing more than delivering bad news, he'll keep his guard lower.

Liam takes a deep breath. "Okay," he says.

"I'm not just using you as a sacrifice," I say. "While you're talking, I'll be able to keep a close eye on him, look for any tells. By not telling him myself, it allows me the capacity to watch his movements more closely."

"That makes sense," he says, then nodding. "Is that him?"

I look out across the parking lot to where a nice, blue Mercedes has pulled into one of the spots. According to the file we have on him, that should be Gerald Wright's car. A semi-heavyset man gets out. His suit is immaculate and dark glasses cover his eyes. I can see a hint of gray at his temples, but otherwise his thick, dark hair is perfectly coiffed. He pulls a briefcase out of his backseat before heading into the building with his name on the side.

"So this guy is a real estate developer?"

"Real-estate *buyer*," I correct him. "From what I can tell, his company purchases parcels of land all over the country then divides them up and sells them to commercial home builders."

"So, subdivisions basically."

"Yep. And it looks like he's doing pretty well for himself," I say, watching him stroll through the lobby. It's an impressive building in Stillwater's small commercial part of town, on the other side from the police station. One of the few that isn't a reclaimed older building. No, he built this one himself, his name is on the front of it.

"How long has this building been here?" I ask.

"I think it was built sometime in the late 2000s," Liam replies. "At least that's what I seem to remember. When I went off for college it wasn't here. But when I got back, it was."

I turn to him. "I didn't know you went to college."

He gives me a smirk. "We might be rednecks, but we're well-educated rednecks, Ms. Slate."

I smack him on the shoulder. "I never said you were rednecks. Plus, you're half Irish. You've already got more red in you than you can handle."

He laughs. "I guess that's true." We both wait a beat before he turns back to the building. "Shall we get this over with?"

"Sure," I reply. "Best to do it first thing when he's fresh. Let's see what kind of reaction we get."

Liam and I stroll into the office building. Being Stillwater, they don't have keycard or punch lock doors. Anyone can get into the lobby. It isn't what I'd call opulent, but it is of a higher quality than most other buildings I've seen in town. Part of me is already screaming that this is our guy. He's got the money and he's got the power. We just need to establish his motive, which, more than likely is either revenge or jealousy.

We check the small board by the elevators, that tells us we're headed for the fifth floor: the building's top level. Again, I'm surprised at the lack of security here. No guards in the lobby, no access keys. If someone wanted to, they could just waltz right in and go to any level.

I have to remind myself, living in D.C.—the most paranoid city in the world in my opinion—not everywhere else is like that. This is Stillwater; they probably don't have a large homeless population that is always looking for a warm place to sleep. Nor do they have massive crime organizations that are looking to take advantage of any lapse in security. The most they probably worry about is some strung-out junkie, wandering into the wrong place.

Once off the elevator, we go through another set of glass doors into the offices of Wright Properties, Limited. A young receptionist sits behind a wide oak desk and greets us with a smile. "Good morning. How may I help you?"

I hang back while Liam shows the woman his badge. I'm trying to get a good look beyond the reception area, but it's mostly hidden by walls. I can see some glass back there, looking out on to the town, along with a few individual rooms or offices.

"We'd like a moment with Mr. Wright, please," Liam says.

The girl's features crease. "I'm sorry, but he's booked for the morning on calls. I could squeeze you into his schedule either late this afternoon or tomorrow."

I step up to the counter holding out my badge as well. "Ma'am. This can't wait. We need to see him, right now."

Either the sight of an FBI badge or the fact I'm using what I call my "intimidation voice" seems to get the ball rolling as she nods, then taps on the phone in front of her. "Mr. Wright. The police and FBI are here to see you," she says into the earpiece. She nods, then hangs up. "Please come with me."

When she stands, I realize she's taller than she looks, almost Liam's height. She leads us back past the main partition to the offices I saw when we first came in. The very last one is a corner unit, with windows on two sides. Inside sits Gerald Wright at a wide desk with a computer that has two monitors. His suit jacket is on the small couch in the room right under one of the windows, along with the briefcase we saw him with.

"Thank you, Ashley," he says and she retreats out, closing the door behind her.

Liam sticks his hand out. "I'm Detective Coll with the Stillwater Police," he says. "And this is Agent Slate with the FBI."

"FBI?" Wright says with genuine surprise. "I would have figured it was the other way around."

Well, we can add *arrogant snot* to his dossier.

"What's this all about?" he asks.

"May we take a seat?" Liam asks.

"Of course," he says, returning to his chair as he indicates the two sitting in front of his desk. So far, I haven't seen anything that tells me he's nervous about us being here, or that he even knows the reason. As best I can tell, it's genuine confusion.

Liam glances at me and I give him a subtle nod. Best to start with the hard stuff. "Sir, I'm very sorry to inform you, but your wife's body was found a few days ago, just outside of town."

Wright doesn't react. It's almost as if he didn't hear him. He blinks, then finally shakes his head. "I'm sorry. What?" He's incredulous.

"She had apparently been out there for some time. A few months, it looks like."

Wright shakes his head again. "No, my *wife*, is in Italy." He puts special emphasis on the word wife, as if it's nothing more than a title. I still haven't seen much emotion from him. He doesn't believe it yet, or he's an incredible actor.

"No, sir. I'm sorry. We have a positive ID. We were able to match her dental records," I say.

He gives us another subtle shake of his head, but I begin to see the reality of the situation dawning in his eyes. He puts his hand to his face, covering up his mouth, but I can already tell its downturned. And his eyes are wild, trying to process what we've just told him. Still, he shakes his head, like he doesn't want to let himself believe it.

"That can't...I mean...you're sure you've got the right person? How could she...she's supposed to be in *Italy!*" The last sentence comes out with a lot of force, and I watch as the storm of emotions tears through him. This is not a man who was expecting this information.

"H-how?" he asks.

"We're not sure yet," Liam says. "But we suspect either strangulation or suffocation."

Suddenly his brow creases and his entire face darkens. "It was *him*. That bastard who stole her away from me."

"Mr. Wood," Liam says.

"Have you arrested him yet?" Wright asks. His face softens again like he's alternating between angry and sad. His hand that remains on the desk is trembling.

"We don't have a prime suspect at the moment," I say. "Right now, we're just notifying next-of-kin."

"What do you mean? You have to arrest him," Wright says, more forcefully this time. "It was obviously him. He was the last one she was with."

"You know this?" Liam asks, withdrawing his notepad.

"Everyone knows," Wright says.

"Everyone?"

"Her friends. My friends. Family members. Work colleagues." He motions to the door we came through. "Everyone." I can see the fact she left him is a source of great embarrassment for him, which puts him firmly into the motive category. But when he speaks, his words are colored more with shame than anger.

"Can you tell us the last time you spoke to Mrs. Wright?" Liam asks.

"It was the day she left," Wright says. "Just a normal Friday morning, like any other."

"And you were the one who reported her missing," I ask.

He nods. "When she didn't come home that night I tried calling and didn't get anything but her voicemail. I waited until about nine p.m. before calling the police to let them know. I was sick the entire weekend with worry."

"She never responded to your call?" Liam asks.

"Didn't call, didn't text. Didn't ask about the kids…Oh my God. What am I supposed to tell our kids?" This brings tears to his eyes that he has to wipe away.

"She hasn't spoken to them since that day either?" I ask.

He gives me the most pitiful look. "I couldn't bear to tell them she was missing. I told them she went on a work vacation. That she'd be back home soon."

"But that never happened," Liam says.

He shakes his head. "By Monday the police had figured out she'd left. I think it was Saturday or Sunday when I realized one of her suitcases was missing, along with some of her stuff. They showed me the footage of her at the bank. I called over there to confirm and they told me she'd emptied her accounts. After that the police showed me where she'd booked a ticket out of Dulles that night. Here I was, with our two kids, worried sick at home and she'd flown off to *fucking Italy!*" He yells this last part, the tears coming in earnest now.

We wait a moment for him to regain some semblance of control. "And you haven't heard from her since?" I ask, gently.

He shakes his head. "I just figured she was done with us. That she'd either had enough of me or the kids or this life… who knows? I've tried calling and texting, I've even tried emailing all her accounts but all I get is silence." He stares at us under a hooded brow. "I guess now I know why."

"What did you tell your children?" I ask. According to his file, the kids are five and seven. They wouldn't have bought that vacation lie for very long.

"I had to tell them the truth, or what I knew of it," he says. "That their mother had decided to take some time to herself, and that I didn't know when she'd be coming back. That was a hard night." He takes a few deep breaths, steadying himself. "And now, I have to do it all over again."

"Can you tell us, what was your relationship with Mrs. Wright like before she left?" I ask.

"Fine," he says, all the energy seeming to drain out of him. "Normal. Two working parents, you know how it is. Not enough time together, but…I thought we were happy. I thought things were okay. But ever since then I don't know what to believe."

I shoot a look at Liam. He's thinking what I'm thinking: this isn't our guy. This is a distraught husband and father, who just learned the woman who spurned him for another man ended up dead. I can see he's not doing a very good job of keeping it together.

Wright's phone rings, startling him. He grabs the receiver. "What? No. And Ashley, cancel my calls for the rest of the day. I'm taking a personal day." He hangs up then looks back at us. "So how does this work? Do I have to come down to… see her, or anything?"

I shake my head. "We already have a confirmed identification. You don't need to do anything."

"Except have the hardest conversation with my kids that I'll ever have to have," he replies. "And here I thought I'd already done that when she left." He seems beside herself. "Her friends…I guess I'll have to be the one to plan the funeral. How do…I mean…" He's trying to ask the difficult questions that always follow a murder. For people who aren't used to it, they don't know how to act. They're looking for a procedure, some sort of structure that will make sense for them during a time when they're facing so much senselessness.

"Don't worry, we'll have someone from the precinct contact you regarding all the details. Right now, we're not ready to release her body yet."

"If you need it to nail that bastard, then be my guest," he says, choking back another sob.

I nod to Liam and we both stand up. "We're very sorry for your loss, Mr. Wright. As I said earlier, this is an open investigation. When we have a suspect, we'll be sure to let you know." We both hand him our business cards.

"I'd appreciate that," he says.

We head for the door, but right as we reach it, I turn. "Oh, one other thing," I say. Wright looks up. "If you knew your wife left with another man, why not file for a divorce?"

He gives us a noncommittal shrug. "I guess…I hoped we could work something out," he says. "Victoria and I were together for eight years. That has to count for something. I thought maybe she just needed to get it out of her system and that she'd come back and…" he trails off.

I nod, satisfied with his answer. "If you need anything, just call," I say. He gives me a subtle nod, but his eyes, still brimming with tears, have gone glassy. He's already lost in either the memory of her or working out how he's supposed to go on without her.

It's a feeling I know all too well.

Chapter Thirteen

"So," Liam says once we're back in the car. "What was your read on him?"

I sigh. "Unlikely. He seemed genuinely surprised to hear the news. And despite their complex relationship, he got emotional pretty quick."

He leans over conspiratorially as I start the car and I take in a hint of his musk. "I have to ask, is there some kind of FBI field manual that tells you all this stuff? Because the Police procedures we received were...brief."

"No individual field manual," I say. "But it's baked into the core of being an agent. We have to be able to spot fakes a mile away. It doesn't do us much good if we can't tell who is lying and who isn't."

Liam sits back and pulls his seatbelt on. "We need a better manual. At the academy, we went through the basics, but I feel like you guys have more in-depth training."

"Don't you know?" I tease. "We're a federal agency. We always know what we're talking about and are never wrong."

He chuckles. "I'll hold you to that. So how did I do breaking the news to him?"

"Just like I would have done it," I say. I have to commend

him for stepping up to the plate. But it still doesn't mean I'm ready to trust him yet. Honestly, I'm not sure I can get back there, after what he did. But he's a competent detective and as long as I keep him at arm's length, we should be able to get through this okay.

"Next suspect?" he asks.

"Right," I say. The next obvious suspect is Patrick Wood, who is conveniently out of the country. Or at least he was at last report. There are literally hundreds of Patrick Woods in the United States, and without more information, finding the one we're looking for is going to be next to impossible, considering he's not even supposed to be here.

"According to Burke's original investigation, he was only briefly considered a person of interest," I say, reading through the file that I've pulled from the backseat. "Once they figured out he and Victoria had been messaging back and forth for months, and matched up the plane tickets, Burke closed the case." I sit back, trying to think through how the original case proceeded. It doesn't make much sense.

"Burke has to be covering something up," Liam says. "I went over the files again last night after the uh…after what happened at the precinct. He didn't even interview Patrick Wood. Not over the phone, nothing. He just found out they escaped together, then decided that was enough and shut it down."

"And because he doesn't report to anyone, he didn't have to justify himself," I say. I'm glad Liam is at least entertaining the possibility of my side of things. If nothing else, it's getting him to think critically about his boss.

I flip through the report again. "All I have in here on the man is a previous address. No prior work history, no known associates. It's like he didn't do any legwork on this guy."

Liam turns to me. "There has to be something about this case he doesn't want investigated. But I have a hard time believing he could have had something to do with her death. He's been the police chief here for seventeen years."

I give him a noncommittal look. "I'm not ruling anyone out at this point. Not until we have more information. But we need more on Patrick Wood. This isn't going to be nearly enough. And given that there might already be another victim out there, we don't have time to sit around trying to figure out who is who." I pull my cell out of my inside jacket pocket.

"Using one of your lifelines?"

I glare at him as it rings. "Hey, Em!" Zara says when she picks up on the other end.

"Hey," I say, not wanting to be too familiar with her while Liam is in the car. "Need another favor."

"How are things going with your detective? Been on your second date-ish yet?"

I pull to the side and try to cover up the receiver, but I already see the smirk on Liam's face. To his credit, he keeps his eyes straight forward and doesn't say anything. Zara can be *loud* when she doesn't mean to be.

"No, I need you to find someone for me. Possible person of interest in this case. Name is Patrick Wood, DOB on his boarding pass shows ten-eleven-eighty-two."

"Ten-eleven-eighty-two, got it. I don't guess you have a social?"

"Info is scant on this guy, we're lucky to have the birthdate. We don't even have a picture yet."

"Sounds like your detective isn't much of an axe to the grindstone kind of guy."

I practically hush her while still trying to cover up the receiver, though the way I'm jerking about, there's no way I'm hiding anything. "It wasn't his case," I say in a low voice. "And he's sitting in the car right now."

"Oh!" Zara says. "Sorry, I didn't know. Patrick Wood. I'll get right on it."

"Zara," I say, before hanging up. "It's time-sensitive. We need to get this info back fast."

"Got it," she says. "Be in touch soon."

I put the phone away, but I can already feel my face burning with embarrassment. I turn to Liam, trying to come up with a way to open the conversation that doesn't make me sound like a complete fool.

He turns to me, and I brace for it. "So, if we can't go after Patrick Wood, who else should we interview?"

I'm honestly astonished. I thought for sure he'd use this as an opportunity to embarrass me, or at least give me a few jabs, especially after I made him deliver the news to Wright. But, for some reason—maybe because he's still trying to make up for going behind my back—he doesn't.

"Um," I say, turning back to the file. I don't usually find myself in situations like this and it's throwing me off. To say I'm conflicted would be an understatement. "Rex Fuller, PLLC. He was Victoria's boss at the law firm."

"Right," Liam says, bringing up images of the files on his phone. "The original case file had him listed briefly as a person of interest before it was revealed Victoria had left with Patrick. You think he's still worth a look?"

"Absolutely," I say, closing the file. "Even if it's just to eliminate him as a potential suspect, I think we need to have a run at him, see how he responds."

"Does the file say *why* he was considered in the first place?" Liam asks.

I don't even have to open it to answer. After pouring over all of this last night, I have a good bit of it memorized. "I believe it was because someone had complained of personal misconduct at the law firm, though it isn't clear if that was Victoria or not as the complaint was made anonymously to the Virginia State Bar two years ago."

"Enough to flag it on a missing person's case," Liam says.

The State Bar had done an investigation and found no

incidence of wrongdoing, but the fact that someone reported something at all is noteworthy. It could have just been a frustrated employee who was sick of their boss, but then again, it could have been genuine, and Fuller might have found a way to sweep it under the rug. Either way, I'm not going to let him off the hook so easily.

"I say it's time to see what Mr. Fuller has to say."

Chapter Fourteen

As we head to Rex Fuller's office, I find I'm not as confident about this case as I'd been this morning. Watching Gerald Wright break down upon hearing the news has put a real kink in my optimism. I only hope Zara has some luck locating Patrick Wood, and if she does, that he's within reach. If he's still out of the country, we may have to get Interpol involved, which is not something I want to spearhead. I doubt Janice would be very happy about it either.

My other concern is Liam. He seems to have turned a corner and is doing and saying all the right things, but something in the back of my mind is niggling me, telling me not to let my guard down around him, even though he's a very easy person to be around. I like joking with him, and he has the sort of easygoing manner a lot of guys don't. Back before Matt, dating had been a nightmare to the point where I was ready to give it up. Of course, I'd been a lot younger and still in college, but still...guys were idiots back then. And from what I've observed, most still are.

It makes it that much harder that I see Liam differently.

I shake my head. I'm not here to get into a relationship, not that I would anyway, and I'm not here to make a new friend. I'm here to find a killer, get my career back on track, and get back to D.C. where I can be effective again. Everything else is just going to have to fall by the wayside.

"This is it," Liam says, pointing up ahead. It's a one-story building right off the main highway, with a modest sign out front proclaiming the building as belonging to Rex Fuller, PLLC. We're further out from the main part of town, in an area known for strip malls and homes that have been converted into commercial buildings. The parking lot is full of cars—mostly sedans and a few SUVs—and I get the distinct feel of a dentist's office from the place. One floor, all brick, long floor-to-ceiling windows spaced at even intervals. I'm willing to bet the second we walk in we'll be accosted with soft jazz.

This time I take the lead as we head through the single door to the office. There we're greeted by a reception area, but no receptionist. I give Liam a shrug and head back through the single door that leads to the rest of the building.

Inside is another small waiting area, then it opens to different wings. There's a conference area in the far-left corner, while a cafeteria makes up the far right. In the middle are large bookcases holding hundreds of books, documents, and cases, a resource library. The library is surrounded by a bevy of partitioned-off desks. Around the other edges, large rooms with glass walls make up the rest of the space. In each one, someone sits behind a desk, typing furiously. There are three people in the cafeteria, six in the conference room, and another three at the library, all searching through records. So far, no one has even noticed us yet.

I clear my throat and a young man near the stacks turns and looks up. He sets the two books in his arms down and scrambles over to us. "I'm sorry, our receptionist is out sick for the week, did you have an appointment?"

I show him my badge. "We're looking for Rex Fuller."

His eyes go wide at seeing the badge itself and he seems to have a hard time meeting my gaze. "R-regarding?"

"Just point us in his direction," Liam says.

"I'm sorry, but Mr. Fuller is in court all day," he replies. "He won't be reachable until after five."

I check my watch. It's barely past eleven a.m. Shit. So much for catching him unawares. His staff will no doubt notify him we were here. "Will he be back in the office at all today?"

"He usually heads home after being in court," the man says. "But you're welcome to leave him a message. I'll make sure he gets it."

I let out a frustrated breath. "We'll just come back later."

The man nods and heads back to the rows of books, resuming his search. I put my hands on my hips and glance around, trying to figure out our next move.

"You want to stop by his house later this evening?" Liam asks.

"Not particularly," I reply. "With our luck he'll have a gated house with guard dogs. You know how cagey lawyers get. Odds are he'll point us to one of these people as his representation anyway."

"Only if he has something to hide," Liam says.

"You'd be surprised. I swear half of them just like to screw with us because they know they can. Then they get to tell all their lawyer buddies about it in the cigar room, drinking brandy."

Liam glares at me. "I'm getting the feeling you don't like lawyers very much."

I give him a placating grin. "Look at that, those police classes weren't as much of a waste as you thought."

He chuckles, nudging me. "Jerk." The second he touches me I feel a surge of electricity through my body. It's something I haven't felt in months, maybe even longer. I tamp down the feeling, willing myself not to respond.

"I guess we'll have to come back tomorrow. Just be prepared for battle."

He nods and heads for the door. Just as I'm about to leave I catch the gaze of one of the women in the cafeteria. She's standing near the sink with a mug in her hand, looking at me pointedly. "You go ahead," I tell Liam. "I'll be there in a minute."

He looks over my shoulder. "I'll be right outside."

Once he's gone, I make my way over to the woman, only for her to avert her eyes the closer I get. She's very pretty. Tall, blond, with virtually flawless skin and expertly applied makeup. I notice she's wearing an expensive-looking bracelet, not unlike the one Victoria had. "You work here?" I keep my voice light.

"Yep, paralegal," she replies, dipping the tea bag in and out of her mug. It looked like she wanted to get my attention before, but now I'm not so sure. "Are you with the police?"

"FBI, actually." I show her my badge.

"Oh! And here I thought you might be here to serve Rex his divorce papers." She gives me a nervous laugh.

"Why would we do that?" I ask.

"No reason. I just…his wife…you know how lawyers are," she says, clearly uncomfortable.

I nod. "Have you worked here long?"

"A few years now. I started when I was still going for my law degree, but I never could pass the bar. Now I'm just trying to pay off the debt."

"Don't I know it," I say. I actually don't, but there are so many people with student loan debt in this country I've found it's best to present myself as someone who's in the same position. I'm extremely fortunate; my parents had the money to pay for my college degree. I know these days not a lot of people can say that. They either worked their way through school, or they're saddled with a debt they can't repay. Not to mention law school makes everything ten times worse.

But I was one of those rare birds. I still had a job in college, of course. But if I lost it, I was never under the threat of not being able to pay my tuition. Not having that kind of pressure is a luxury not many people get to afford, and it's not a good idea to flaunt it around.

I hold out my hand. "Agent Emily Slate."

She shifts the tea mug to her other hand, taking mine. "Sarah Ellis. So if you're not here for Rex, what's going on? The firm isn't involved in money laundering or something, is it?"

"Why do you think that?"

Her eyes go wide. "Oh, I was just joking," she says, and I catch her fingers tremble. "I just meant…it isn't every day the FBI waltzes into your building. Especially here in Stillwater."

This sometimes happens when people are around the FBI, they become extremely nervous, even when they have nothing to hide. Usually this is because they automatically think we're there to arrest them for something petty they did a decade ago, when often we're just out gathering information. It's the ones that don't get nervous that I watch out for. The ones who almost expect us to be there, like they're waiting to get caught.

Still, I feel like Sarah is hiding something. Something she might want me to know, but can't come out and say. Otherwise, why draw attention to herself like that? "Did you happen to know Victoria Wright?" I ask.

She nods, watching me intently as she takes a sip. "I did. We used to sit right beside each other."

"Would you say you knew her well?" I ask. This trip might not be the dud I'd originally thought. We haven't had a chance to dig into Victoria's life much. I wanted to get these interviews out of the way first, eliminate the biggest suspects. But if I've happened to come upon a friend of hers, I'm not about to waste the opportunity.

"Yeah, I'd say we knew each other pretty well. We'd spend

time together outside of work sometimes. Occasionally I'd go over to her house."

"Then you knew her family."

Sarah shrugs. "Sure. Once in a while. Gerald's okay, but I can see why she didn't stay. The kids though…"

A little alarm bell is going off in my head. "Things not so good with them at home?" I ask.

"It was nothing," she says. "She just thought Gerald wasn't paying her enough attention. I guess she got bored, and that's why she skipped off to Europe with that guy." She shoots a look over to the main offices. "Must be nice."

I'm struggling with my conscience. Normally I don't notify anyone other than immediate family of a deceased loved one, but in this case, Victoria had no other family. And given the fact Sarah seems to know more about her life than we do, I feel it's prudent to tell her. Not only so she can grieve, but because it might also help with the investigation.

But at the same time, I don't want to compromise interviewing Fuller. If I tell Sarah, word will no doubt get back to him before we can interview him tomorrow. So unfortunately, I have to keep it to myself for now.

"Did she ever talk about any particular problems with her husband?" I ask.

"Not in any specifics," she says, turning back to me. "What's going on? Is this about Victoria? Is that why you're here?"

I could straight up lie to her, but I won't. "It is," I say.

"Damn, I knew it. So it *is* about Rex after all."

I screw up my features. "Can you elaborate?"

"Well, obviously someone made another complaint, right? I mean, it wasn't me. And I *know* it wasn't Victoria. But I guess when it happens more than once…" She trails off.

"How do you know it wasn't Victoria?" I ask, going with this gem of a lead.

"Because we both agreed not to. I can't afford to lose my

job. Of course, that was before she took off, so maybe she changed her mind. I suspected she might report it when she left with that guy, but when nothing happened after a few weeks I figured she'd just let it go."

I get the distinct impression that Fuller is being inappropriate with Sarah, and possibly was with Victoria too. But they were both too scared of what might happen if they reported it? As far as I know, there's been no second harassment case on the record, just the first a few months back. I need to bear this out, but at the same time, I can't compromise Sarah's position here, or she'll clam up. I decide to leave her out of it completely. "Can you tell me exactly what went on between Victoria and your boss?"

She looks around. "Is any of this going to come back on me? I told you, I have *bills*."

I shake my head. "I can't promise that it won't. But I'm just asking about Victoria, who isn't even here anymore. I'll do everything I can to keep your name out of it."

Sarah eyes me with more suspicion than I'm expecting and I'm afraid I've already lost her. But then she sighs and lets her guard down. "Rex is...well...he's an asshole, to put it lightly. He thinks every woman that works for him is here for his entertainment. And he likes to flirt. A couple of months ago, before she left, Victoria came to me to tell me he'd made a move on her when she was alone with him in his office. He's pressed himself up against her, pinning her between him and his desk before she pushed him off. She told him to knock it off and that if he did it again, she'd file a formal complaint."

"Why didn't she file one then?" I ask.

Sarah shakes her head. "I don't know. Maybe she was dealing with other stuff. When she told me, it seemed like it was more of a nuisance for her than an actual attack." She takes another sip from her mug.

"Did he ever do it again, before she left?" I ask.

"I don't know. If he did, she never told me about it." She

goes in for another sip but stops. "But she must have, right? Otherwise why would you be here?"

This is good, but I think I've gotten all I can get for now. I reach into my pocket and produce my card for Sarah, who takes it with her empty hand. "If you think of anything else that might have happened between them, my personal cell is on that card. Doesn't matter what time, got it?"

"Wait, is Rex in trouble?" she asks. I can see something in her eye, something telling me if he is, that she could end up going down with him. It's a look I've seen before.

"Sarah," I say. "You have nothing to worry about. And if anything has ever...happened...between you and your boss—"

She shakes her head and drops my card. "I need to get back to work," she says, leaving me standing there in the makeshift kitchen. I bend down and retrieve my card, watching her disappear behind the stacks of books in the middle of the room.

So much for not spooking her.

Chapter Fifteen

"Wow, that's..." Liam trails off as we're on our way back to the motel. He wanted to head back to the station, but with Burke gunning for me, I'd rather just keep working out of my motel room. I've got everything I need there, and I don't have to worry about Burke eavesdropping or berating me while I try to figure out what's going on here.

As soon as I met Liam back in the parking lot, I informed him of what Sarah had told me. I'm pretty sure now she is being harassed by her boss, who may be involved in multiple inappropriate sexual relationships with his employees. Now I understand why he was originally part of the suspect pool. It seems Burke did something right for once on this one, though he never looked very deeply into Fuller either. Another casualty of a botched investigation.

"Do you think they were sleeping together?" Liam asks.

"Maybe. But it seems more likely that Victoria was getting tired of his behavior. Maybe she really was going to report him, and a second violation, even after the first one found no wrongdoing, would have shut down his firm for good, no matter what excuses he came up with."

"Certainly gives him a motive." Liam turns down the adjacent street leading to my motel.

"But when would he have had the opportunity?" I ask. "Obviously he didn't fly to Italy to kill her, then bring her body back." I think about it for a minute. We don't have any data on what happened to Victoria Wright after she went to Italy. Zero timeline. It's like when she left the United States, she ceased to exist. "We need to get flight records for around the time when her body was found. We need to figure out when she came back."

"And who knew it about it," Liam adds. He pulls into the motel parking lot.

We've spent all this time on suspects and little time on Victoria herself. If we're going to solve this, we need to focus on our victim. "I want to put together a timeline of her last few weeks here," I say, getting out of the car. "Figure out every move she made up until that plane left the ground. Hopefully Zara can come up with something for us after they landed." I turn back to see Liam still in the car, the driver's side window down. "What?"

"You still want my help?" he asks.

"You're the local detective on this case," I say. "Do you *want* to help?"

"I just don't want you to think I'm trying to do anything inappropriate," he says, nodding to the motel room.

Ah, I get it. Going into that room together carries a lot of implications. A lot of assumptions. I look into the backseat of the car with all my case files, my laptop, all of it. If he wanted, he could drive away right now, leaving me with nothing. I'd have to tuck tail back to the station and beg Burke for all my stuff back. But he's not. He's more worried about what I might think of him if we go in there together. In a way, it's sweet. But right now, I don't have time for sweet. We've got a killer out there.

"Get your ass out of the car and come help me with this

case," I say in the most authoritative voice I can muster. "And don't worry, the minute you make one wrong move, I break both your arms. Have you ever tried to use a toothbrush with two broken arms?"

He shakes his head, a smile on his face. "I don't think I want to find out."

"Then grab that box," I say, opening the back door and pulling out my laptop. He gets out, takes the box and follows me to the room. I motion for him to put the box down on the only table while I pull my coat off and toss it on the unused bed. "I'd offer you a refreshment, but we're all out."

He hooks a thumb over his shoulder. "There's a little convenience store down about half a mile. If you're looking for a nutritious, fat-injected lunch."

I press my lips together in a line. "Quit trying to get out of work. I have those organized in there, lay them out in a grid pattern, on the floor."

His forehead creases. "A grid pattern? On *this* floor? You know they probably haven't cleaned it in ten years. Not to mention this isn't the sort of place that gets the best clientele."

"Thanks for the reminder," I say, opening up my computer. "I've got a strong immune system; I'll be fine."

He shakes his head and begins removing files. "I still can't believe this is all the FBI can afford. I mean, don't we pay taxes so you super cops can get better digs?"

"This isn't a budget issue," I reply, scrolling through the files I have on Victoria herself. "This is my punishment for—" I pause, realizing I almost just let my guard down again. I keep doing that around him and not meaning to.

He looks over, his eyes questioning, but he doesn't come out and say it. It's rare to find someone who knows their boundaries and not to butt into other people's business. It's even rarer to find someone like that in law enforcement. It makes me want to tell him even more.

But if I open up to him, could he use that against me? If

Burke finds out what I did, he could claim me as an unfit agent. Janice can only defend me so much; to save face she'd have to pull me. And that would be all she wrote.

"Okay, so we know she and Gerald were having issues. How long were Victoria and Patrick in contact with each other?"

He hesitates a minute like he's going to say something, then turns back to the files, flipping through the ones he's already pulled out. "Looks like the first emails were back in January of last year."

I try not to let his reaction throw me. I'm just not there yet. After all, it was only this morning that I was thinking I'd have to work this case by myself. But something sticks in my mind about their first contact. "That means she left with him almost exactly a year after they met online."

"So?"

"Just seems like an odd coincidence, that's all," I say. "What do we have on her last few days before she left?" I set the laptop to the side and focus on the floor in front of me, not looking at anything in particular, just trying to analyze the case in my mind.

"Statement from the husband—"

"—saying everything was normal. What else?"

"ATM footage on the day she left. We see her going into the bank, then coming back out. Bank records show she withdrew close to three thousand dollars from her account."

"Did she close it?"

He shakes his head. "No. Left it with open with the minimum balance."

Why would she do that, especially if she was leaving the country? What would be the point of leaving the account open? "What else?"

"That was at two-fifteen in the afternoon. There's no trace of her again until nine-twenty-two p.m. when she boards the plane at Dulles."

I look up. "That's it?"

He flips through a few pages. "Her vehicle was found a couple of days later at the Motel Five." Liam pauses. "Oh man."

"What?" I ask.

"If this is the same Motel Five I'm thinking of then that's not good."

I get off the bed, taking the file from him. "Why? What's wrong with it?"

"It's not known for…well, let's just say I've spent more time out there than I care to. It's not the kind of motel where people sleep if you get my meaning. You want to talk about a dump—just be glad you're not holed up in that place."

"Yeah, I get it," I reply, looking over the file. "Why does this town have so many shitty motels?"

He shrugs. "Trust me, you're staying in the Hilton compared to that place."

"This says her car was returned to her husband. They never even investigated it?" I want to throw the file across the room. "This is looking less like an investigation and more like an intentional coverup." The absolute incompetence about this entire case has set me on edge. Burke is going to have to answer for this. As soon as I have some time alone, I'll be starting a new file on Stillwater's police chief himself. The fact he didn't even investigate the vehicle screams of intentional negligence in this case. What if there had been some evidence in there regarding her plans? Maybe she'd been planning on coming back but hadn't told Patrick.

"Call Dulles, see if you can get anything on her return flight," I say.

Liam nods, pulling out his cell phone. While he makes the call, I go back over the scant information we have about Victoria Wright. For all intents and purposes, she was a normal suburban wife. Husband, two kids, and a lecherous boss. And a fling on the side. It isn't surprising, nor is it particularly interesting. If people understood just how often people in marriages looked outside those relationships for comfort, I think they'd be surprised. But the truth is most people don't want to know. They ignore the truth right in front of their faces, because to confront it would require admitting to their own shortcomings.

The point is, Victoria didn't seem to have anything strange going on in her life. Based on her biographical file, it all seems to line up. Her father moved away when she was little, leaving her and her mother. Mom worked, and the father at least paid support until Victoria was seventeen when he passed away. Her mother died a few years later, a victim of an undetectable heart murmur.

I feel my eyes welling up and I shove the feelings back down, forcing myself to focus on the rest of the information in her biographical profile. She graduated from Northern Virginia Community College in 2001 and moved around for a few years, never really landing on a solid career. Eventually she found herself in D.C. where she met Gerald. They were married in 2011 and moved to Stillwater not long after, where she got a job with Rex Fuller.

I sit back. From what I can tell, Gerald is doing pretty well. Why would Victoria want to work at all, especially if it didn't seem like she had any career prospects? Because until she met Gerald, it looks like she was jumping from one thing to another, never staying in any one field for very long. And then after they get married she gets this job as a paralegal…for eight years.

Something about it doesn't add up. Like most of the details of this case. The more I uncover, the less sense it all seems to make.

"Okay, thanks," Liam says and hangs up. His face drops when he turns back to me. "No records of her coming back."

At first, I'm dumbfounded. "Did you check *all* the airlines?"

"All the ones that have international flights out of Dulles, yeah," he replies.

"She must have come back through another airport," I say. "Because she obviously came back. She's sitting in the M.E.'s office right now." I pull out my phone to start looking up the phone numbers for other local international airports and stop, glancing up at Liam. Our eyes match and go wide at the same time. "Unless she never left!" we both say at the same time. It's a strange sort of serendipity that makes me want to laugh or yell jinx. But I'm not a kid anymore.

"We need that footage from the airport that shows her getting on the plane," I say, grabbing my laptop again. It should be in the video files for the case. I hadn't reviewed any of those yet because I was too focused on my suspects. Plus, I (stupidly, I admit) assumed everything in the file was above board. I'm just not used to working after a cop who was obviously actively trying to cover up a case for whatever reason. As I scroll through the files, I don't see one from the airport. Big surprise. "I don't have it in here. Is there a record of it in the case file?"

"All I have is a transcript of a conversation between Burke and the Dulles manager for United," he says. *"Burke: Do you have a record of a Victoria Wright purchasing a ticket for January seventeenth from Dulles to Venice Marco Polo Airport? Manager: Yes, sir. Right here. Seat 2B on the nine-thirty flight on the seventeenth. Burke: Do you have another record for Patrick Wood? Manager: Yes, Seat 2A, same flight. Burke: Did both Wright and Wood board the plane that evening? Manager: Yes, sir. It was a full flight. Burke: Thank you for your time."* Liam looks up after reading the transcript.

"Son of a—" I say. "He never got visual confirmation! She might not have even gotten on that plane!" In fact, the more I think about it, the more likely it seems. If someone was going to kill her, it would be a lot easier to kill her before she got on an international flight rather than trying to coax her back over or waiting for her to return. Was that why she was killed, because she was leaving?

"C'mon." I grab my coat and head for the door.

"We're not driving to Dulles, are we?" Liam asks.

"If we have to. I want you to get on the line to them, see if they can email us the security footage from that night," I say. "In the meantime, I want to go over to this Motel Five. It's likely she met Patrick there before they were supposed to head out. For all we know, he ambushed her there and killed her, then got on the flight by himself."

"But the manager said it was a full flight."

"Right," I say, pulling my arms through the coat. "But who's to say it wasn't a standby passenger in her seat? Until I see footage of her walking through security and down that tarmac, we don't know she was on that plane. The motel could be the last place she was seen alive."

Liam heads out after me, going for the driver's seat.

"Uh-uh," I say, grabbing the keys from his hand. "You've got a call to make. I'm driving."

Chapter Sixteen

When we reach the Motel Five on the far side of town the sun has already dipped below the horizon and lamps from the overhead streetlights paint the street in bright circles.

Not surprisingly, the light in front of the motel itself is out, which means most of the cracked and deteriorating parking lot is bathed in darkness. I pull in, pretty sure if I could even see any paint lines, no one would care where I parked. There's one other vehicle further down the lot, in front of one of the doors, but the window is dark, despite the fact it's barely past seven.

"Yeah, okay. Got it, thank you." Liam finally gets off the call. "They're sending over everything from that day. All cameras, all angles, every airline. They said they don't have time to sort through it all."

"And we do?" I sigh, frustrated. Maybe this is better anyway. At least we'll have control of the data. And if Zara can come up with an image for Wood, we should be able to confirm whether he actually got on the plane or not.

When I get out of the car, my heart drops a little. It's not that I was expecting a fancy place, but Liam is right. If Janice had put me up here, I think I would have died of septic shock the first time I used the toilet. The building can't be up to code in this condition. Parts of the plaster are cracked along all the walls, one of the windows to an unoccupied room has a spiderweb crack at the corner, the concrete walk in front of the doors is crumbling and dilapidated. I can't even imagine what the rooms themselves look like.

"Why doesn't the town shut this place down?" I ask. "It can't look good to allow it to operate in this condition."

Liam shakes his head. "I think it's somewhere on the agenda, they just haven't gotten to it yet."

Or they don't want to, for whatever reason, I think. Their delays are our advantages, it gives us an opportunity to investigate.

We make our way to the front office, which is attached to the rest of the rooms, but sits off to the far-left side of the lot. I take in the entire place as we walk. "What do you think? You've been messaging with someone for a year, you've agreed to go to Europe with them, and they ask to meet you here first. What's the angle?"

"Looks like a place where you don't want anyone looking too closely at what you're doing," Liam says.

"Exactly. So why did she do it?"

As we round the corner, I see that the back of the motel butts up against a small drop-off, which leads to a forest of trees. But this motel is on the other side of town from the property where we found the body. Why kill her here and then risk taking her body all the way out there, potentially leaving a trail of forensic evidence behind? Unless you know you're not going to get caught. Because you've done this many times before and you've honed your craft.

The front door to the motel is metal with a small window inset. Honestly, it looks more like a prison door than a motel office entrance, but I give the door a yank and it screams its way open. Inside I'm greeted by the thick smell of cigarette smoke, combined with the lingering pungent odor that can only be old vomit.

To my surprise, the desk isn't separated with steel bars, which I'd half expected. This place has to be a prime target for anyone looking for a quick score of cash. Yet a man sits behind the desk, leaning on his arm and looking half asleep as a lit cigarette dangles dangerously from his mouth. I clear my throat to get his attention, but he doesn't move, and given that opening the door was a lot louder than me, I have to wonder if maybe he's deaf.

As we approach the desk, the eye on the side of his face closest to us arches up the tiniest hair and he pushes himself up, revealing his large belly only half covered by his stained collared shirt. I get the distinct impression the old vomit smell is coming from him.

"I'm Agent Slate, this is Detective Coll," I say, showing him my badge. He doesn't react, which already tells me a lot. "Were you working on the night of January seventeenth of this year?"

He scoffs, producing a cough deep in his lungs, causing him to take the cigarette and put it out. "Lady, I don't even know where I was last week."

"Are you the manager?" I ask. He just glares at me. "I realize this isn't news to you, but your establishment is in a sad state. When was the last time the Virginia Department of Health was out here? Hell, when was the last time you had a visit from OSHA?"

He shrugs. "Dunno. Maybe a year or two ago."

I exchange a look with Liam. "I think it might be time for another inspection, don't you?"

"Look, just tell me what you want and stop harassing me. Ain't no health inspector gonna come out here, not unless they looking to get shot."

"Is that a threat?" I ask.

"It's a fact. It's a good thing tonight's a light night, other-wise ya'll had to put up a firefight just to get in here."

I glare at him, daring him to push me. He's obviously just

trying to get a rise out of us, for whatever reason. Maybe he's bored. "Is this really how you want to play this?" I ask.

He drops the smirk and motions for me to continue. I point to the cameras up in the left and right corners. "Those work?"

He shakes his head. "Just so I don't get shut down."

"Oh so the health and safety inspector *has* been out here," I say, surprise in my voice. "We are definitely going to have a talk with him."

"Listen lady, I don't want no trouble. I just run this place. People come and go as they please. I don't ask questions, and I don't make recordings. Maybe that's why they keep coming back. But it's all I got."

"You're not concerned your guests are conducing illegal activity in your establishment?" I ask.

"How'm I supposed to know whether they are or not? It ain't like I'm in the room with 'em. Live and let live, I say."

"Do you at least keep records of who checks in and when?"

He reaches under the desk and pulls out a paper logbook. I haven't seen one of these since my training days. Then again, as I look around, I don't see a computer system either. Just an old laptop across from the man, playing some old TV show. He probably doesn't even use it for records.

I flip open the book while Liam walks around to the other side of the desk, keeping an eye on the proprietor. Judging by the variety of names in here, I'm willing to bet the vomit man doesn't do much as far as authentication of ID. There's no way Wood used his—

I stop short. "Here it is. Checking in on the sixteenth. Patrick Wood." I turn to Liam. "Why would he use his real name?"

"Seems like a dumb thing to do," Liam says. "And we know our guy isn't dumb."

God, why doesn't anything in this freaking case make

sense? If Patrick is the killer, then why sign in under his own name, the day before he's scheduled to meet Victoria here? "Were you here this day?" I ask, more pointedly.

"I dunno, probably," the man says.

I stare at the entry into the book. It says he took room three, staying two nights, checking out on the eighteenth. The day *after* they were scheduled to be on that plane. We need to find Patrick Wood. I turn and storm my way out the door, heading down the cracked walk toward room three.

"Em? What are you doing?" Liam calls behind me.

Right now, I don't even care. This case has twisted and turned me in so many different directions it makes me want to scream. And if Wood was in room three, I need to check. I need to make sure he didn't leave some shred of evidence behind. The way this place looks I wouldn't be surprised if rooms even get cleaned between guests. Maybe I'll find my crime scene right here, where no one has looked for three months.

When I reach the door with the number three attached to it, I realize it's next to the room that the vehicle outside is parked in front of. Further down I can hear the murmur of voices, but all the lights are still off. That should deter me; shock this out of my system. There's no way any evidence wouldn't be tainted given how long it's been.

It should make me stop and consider my actions. It doesn't.

"Emily?" Liam says again, trotting down after me, the manager is close behind.

I can't control myself. I feel like the killer is out there, laughing at my inability to wrap my mind around what's going on. At my failure to not figure out what's going on here. I need to see it for myself.

"Open this door," I tell the manager, standing right beside the entrance.

"What? No," he replies. "Get a warrant."

I step up to him, the vomit smell becoming more pronounced. "Do you *really* want me to do that? It's possible a murder occurred on your property. You can either let me in to look around and if I find nothing, we leave you in peace, or I can bring the full brunt of the federal government down upon this place and trust me, we in the federal government know how to take our time with things. We are very thorough, and we won't be searching just one room. We'll be searching *everywhere.*"

He exchanges a look with Liam, who offers him no help, then grits his teeth. "Hang on," he says, storming back to the office for the key.

"Full force of the federal government, huh?" Liam asks, an amused smile on his face.

"We've been known to be a pain in the ass from time to time." I look back at the door. "I doubt there's anything in there, but I need to see it for myself. Just in case."

The manager comes back, grumbling under his breath and uses the actual, physical key to unlock the deadbolt. I bite back a quip about still using a physical key in this day and age and wait until he's moved out of the way before I enter.

Inside it seems like a standard room, nothing special. There are two queen-sized beds, both made. A dresser with a small flat-screen and little else. I switch on the overhead light which bathes the room in a yellowish hue, illuminating the wood-paneled walls. Nothing seems out of place, or to suggest that any kind of struggle happened here, which doesn't surprise me.

"When was the last time anyone stayed in this room?" I ask.

"Maybe a week ago," the manager replies. "It's the slow season."

"Uh-huh," I reply, keeping an eye out for anything out of the ordinary. "And how many have stayed here since Wood?"

"Jeez, lady, I don't know," he replies. "I don't have the goddamn book memorized."

I turn to him, a too-sweet grin on my face. "Do me a favor and find out."

He huffs and is off again, stomping down the walk.

"You just like busting his chops, don't you?" Liam asks.

"Look at this place," I say. "No smoke detectors, no CO_2 detectors, a sprinkler system that is no doubt out-of-date, if it works at all…mold in the bathroom, dingy carpets, low security," I nod toward the door. "You're damn right I'm gonna bust his chops. I'm also going to call the Department of Health once we're done. Somehow this guy has flown under the radar, but this place is a real hazard."

"I'm sure the investigator will get to it in a few months, when his schedule clears up," Liam says. I look at him, not understanding. "We've only got one," he adds.

I nod, then get down on all fours to inspect under the beds. Shining the light from my phone under them, I don't see anything that's out of the ordinary. I notice Liam is inspecting the room as well, which I appreciate. He doesn't have to indulge me; he could just as easily stand outside and let me do this by myself.

"Four people," the manager's voice says from the doorway. "Since the eighteenth of January."

I stand back up. "Any of those for longer than one night?"

"Nope," he replies. He knows what kind of place he operates here and he's under no illusions of what happens in his rooms. To have someone stay more than one night would be unusual.

I take one more look around the room. It was a long shot, anyway.

After Liam and I exit, I realize the voices next door have gone quiet. They must have heard us through the walls and probably didn't want us to hear them. But it gives me an idea.

"Was there anyone in either of the adjacent rooms on the days Patrick Wood was here?" I ask.

The manager sighs, growing more frustrated by the minute. But he knows if he doesn't cooperate, we'll look a little closer here and find out what he's *really* got going on behind the scenes. Not that it's something I'll forget about after we leave. But right now I need to keep him just compliant enough to cooperate. We head back to the office where he inspects the book again.

"Someone in room four on the night of the seventeenth," he says, turning the book and pointing. I pull out my phone and take a picture of the record.

"Jo-Ann Langley," I say, turning to Liam. "What do you think, real name?"

"At least it's not Marilyn Monroe," he says. "I'll see if I can't dig anything up on her." He turns and heads back to the car.

"Do you know who this is?" I ask, pointing to Jo-Ann's name.

He shakes his head. "But she's been here before." He flips back through the book, and I see Jo-Ann's name pop up a few more times. It looks like she's a regular.

"Let me guess, she always pays with cash." It's unlikely we'll be able to track her digitally, but I want to get Zara on it.

The manager shrugs. "Most people do. Not a lot of people around here with good credit, if you know what I mean."

I flip through the rest of the book. Her name appears a few more times, always about five months apart. She hasn't been back since that night. I tap the book a few times. "Stick close. We may have more questions later."

"Like I've got anywhere else to go," he calls after me as I join Liam back outside. It's grown chilly again and I have to pull my coat up around my neck to stave off the cold.

"Yep, yep. Okay, send it over. Thanks, Jill," Liam says as I approach. I look at him expectantly. "Good news. Unless it's a coincidence, it looks like she used her real name. The woman is a local transient, she's got a rap sheet a couple pages long."

"Criminal?" I ask.

"Mostly trespassing, sleeping in public, that sort of thing. A friend of mine at the station is sending everything over on her, but she'll be tricky to find. No permanent address."

I look over my shoulder at the motel behind us, its neon lights blinking in the night. "Of course not. Why should it be easy?"

Chapter Seventeen

"YOU'RE TELLING ME YOU WEREN'T EVEN HERE THAT weekend?" I ask.

The man across from me gives me a smug smile. "That's right, detective. Out of town on business."

"It's Agent," I say, though I'm reasonably sure Fuller did it on purpose. After striking out at the motel, Liam and I called it a night before getting started again this morning. Though this time there'd been no meetup at the local cop bar. I'd wanted to be clear-eyed and at Fuller's office right when they opened, which we were, only to learn that Fuller doesn't normally make an appearance until around ten a.m. Sure enough, nine-forty-five rolled around and there he was, pulling up in his Bimmer.

There was no question someone informed him of our presence here yesterday, because when we came in to question him, he already had the same shit-eating grin he's got on his face now, having had plenty of time to prepare himself for our questions. He's also managed to comment on how young I look more than once, something that makes my skin crawl, though I didn't let him see it. It just makes me want to nail him to the wall even more.

His primary defense has been that he and Victoria never had anything but an appropriate working relationship over the past eight years and that he wasn't even in town the weekend she disappeared. I can feel myself getting as frustrated with him as I did with the manager last night. This case is pressing down on me, and I feel like there's someone else out there in danger, someone who will find themselves dead if we don't find a way to crack it.

And yet, Rex Fuller just sits there, behind his fancy desk, grinning and thinking he holds all the cards.

But I know something that he doesn't. Miraculously, this is the one part of the case where Burke put some legwork in. He discovered that Fuller had an alibi for the weekend, at a conference two hours away in the city. I reviewed what few notes there were, finding he was actually only there on Saturday and Sunday. There's no record of him being there Friday night, which was when Victoria was scheduled to get on that plane…also in D.C.

"You attended the semi-annual Mid-Atlantic Law Conference, is that right?" I ask.

His face falters a little; he wasn't aware that I had this information. But he recomposes himself rather quickly. "That's right. I told that other detective a couple of months ago. He came around asking all the same questions."

"And that took place January seventeenth through the nineteenth, is that right?"

"Yes," he says with a hint of impatience. "I told you, I've already answered all of this once."

I nod. "You have. And I seem to recall that the hotel has you on the security footage for the weekend."

"Yep," he says, looking from me to Liam. Fuller is a slim man, in his late forties, with expertly-trimmed hair and a suit that costs more than six months of my rent. He's a man completely confident in himself, which is strange considering how close he's come to having his business shut down due to inappropriate behavior. But I can see it in him, how he would parade around a place like this, flirting with anyone close to him. He's got that swagger, like any woman would be lucky just to get one night with him. He wears a gold band on his left ring finger, and I can't help but wonder how his home life is.

I look down, acting like I've been defeated before I hit him with the knockout punch. "Well, you see Mr. Fuller, Victoria went missing on Friday night, and as far as we can tell, the hotel doesn't have a record of you being there until Saturday."

The grin disappears and I can feel a subtle shift of the tension in the air. Suddenly, Fuller is on edge, even though he's doing his best not to show it. I exchange a glance with Liam; he feels it too.

"I don't know what to tell you, I was there," he says, though there is none of the prior confidence behind his words.

"Then why does the hotel have you checking in on the morning of the eighteenth, and not the evening of the seventeenth?"

"I probably got there and started at the bar," he says, beads of sweat appearing on his brow. It's the reaction of someone who knows he's been caught in a lie.

"Before you even checked in?" I ask.

"Sure, you know how it is," he says. "Away from home, from all your responsibilities. There's always some hot young thing hanging around these bars, waiting for a guy like me to buy her drinks. And I don't like to disappoint young ladies." He throws a disgusting smirk my way, trying to regain his swagger.

I glare at him, not reacting to the bait. "Mr. Fuller. You do realize that lying to the FBI is a federal crime and a felony, don't you? If I call down to the Montenegro in D.C. and ask them to show me the footage from their bar the night of the seventeenth and you're not there, I will have you arrested for making a false statement."

He goes pale, his confidence evaporating.

I glance at Liam again and he nods. "I think we need you to come down to the station with us," I say, putting on the pressure.

Fuller sits forward. "Wait, wait a second. If I give you the name of the person I was with, will you believe me? I wasn't here, I swear."

I purse my lips. "Depends on the witness and if they're credible."

He sighs and sits back. "Okay, but total honesty here. I don't know anything about Victoria. Last I heard she was off with some guy in Europe, at least that's what the cop who came here last time said. I didn't know she was missing."

"Actually," I say. "She's dead. We found her body a few days ago."

His mouth gapes open and for a moment he doesn't speak. But he manages to compose himself rather quickly. "Dead? That can't...and you think I had something to do with that?"

I note the lack of concern for Victoria. It seems Mr. Fuller's reputation is well-earned; he's always looking out for number one. "Tell me about this miraculous witness of yours."

He shoots a look behind me, out to where the rest of his office. "Okay, but look, it's not what you think. I was with one of my employees, Sarah Ellis."

Why am I not surprised? I knew there was something going on when I spoke with her yesterday; this only confirms it. I lean forward. "That's convenient. I'm sure she'll be more than happy to vouch for your alibi, considering you'll fire her if she doesn't."

He leans forward as well. "Look, it's not like that, okay? We weren't...it wasn't anything inappro—" He stops himself. "It was a business meeting. We had dinner that night. At Caldore's, it's in Falls Church. We were there late. I went to the hotel after, checking in around two a.m. or so."

"Long way away for a business meeting," I say.

"It's so no one would recognize us," he replies. "If it had been here, someone would have seen us together and made…assumptions."

"Kind of hard not to when you go out to dinner with one of your paralegals, especially when you don't want anyone to see you," Liam says.

"I know how it looks, but you have to believe me, it's not like that."

"Then tell us what it's like," I say, leaning even farther forward, doing my best to intimidate him.

"Okay, look. Sometimes I get a little…friendly…at work."

"Is this the appropriate conduct you were referring to earlier?" Liam asks.

Fuller casts his gaze to the side. "I just…I like women, okay? Is there anything so wrong with that?"

"There is when you use your position here to force people to do things they don't want to do," I say. "Especially when their job or job performance depends on it. That's called harassment and intimidation."

"No, no," Fuller says, waving his hands. "Look, one day a couple of months back, maybe five or six, I can't remember, we'd just won a particularly hard case. I took everyone who worked on it out to celebrate. And then I had too much to drink. I was coming out of the bathroom just as Victoria was going in and I…I took her to the side for a chat."

"A chat," I say.

He huffs. "Fine, I don't really remember all of it, okay? Like I said, I was drunk. But everyone knew she and her husband weren't getting along. It was all over the office, you know how people like to gossip. And I just thought I could make her feel better, you know? Like a favor?" I can't even describe my loathing for this man. But I allow him to continue. "I don't know exactly what happened, I just remember her pushing me off her and storming to the bathroom. But when I turned to go back to the party, Sarah was standing there. She'd seen it all."

"So what, did you threaten Sarah if she told anyone?" Liam asked.

Fuller gives him an incredulous look. "Man, have you seen it out there lately? They have all the power! No, she threatened *me*! She knew about the previous call to the State Bar and that if we had another the office would probably be censured and I'd lose my license. She said she'd keep quiet, but only if I gave her a raise and a bonus."

I exchange glances with Liam. "How did Victoria feel about that?"

"I don't know. Sarah told me to stay away from Victoria, so I did. Never spoke to her again unless it was in a meeting. I even made sure the other partners knew I didn't want her assisting any of my cases."

"And no one else found that odd?" Liam asks.

He motions to the office beyond. "Most people aren't paying attention to that kind of thing. We have over seventy employees here."

"What was the meeting on the seventeenth about?" I ask.

Fuller curses under his breath. "I know this looks bad, but…"

"Just tell us," Liam says, impatience creeping into his voice. "Stop trying to make excuses."

Fuller hangs his head. "We were meeting to update the terms of the…agreement. She wanted more money for her continued silence."

"So Sarah was blackmailing you for her silence regarding Victoria," I say. "And then it so happens that Victoria disappears, right when it becomes more expensive for you." I tap my chin a few times. "Doesn't look too good."

"I swear, I swear to God I was in Falls Church that entire evening," he says. "I left straight from work, drove the two hours to get there, met Sarah where we...bargained for a few hours, then I went to the hotel to check in."

"What time did you leave work on Friday?" I ask.

"I usually don't get out of here until six or six-thirty."

I turn to Liam, motioning to the door. "Stay there," I tell Fuller. "We'll be right back."

Keeping Fuller's office in eyesight in case he tries to run, we retreat to a quiet part of the office. "What do you think?" I ask, as we huddle close, keeping our voices down.

"Definitely gives him motive, and opportunity," he replies.

"We need to confirm his alibi. And I want to do it now, before he can slip out of our fingers. This guy is well-connected. We leave now and he'll be on the next flight to Portugal for an 'emergency' vacation."

"Yeah, that's a good point."

"See if you can't get any kind of confirmation from this restaurant he mentioned, Celedore's. Maybe they have a receipt on file. If Ellis was blackmailing him, I doubt she paid for her own food."

"Are you going to speak to her?" he asks.

"Yeah. We've already established something of a rapport. Don't let him out of your sight until I get back."

Liam nods and pulls out his phone as I head off in search for Sarah Ellis.

Chapter Eighteen

I HAVE TO GIVE HER CREDIT; SARAH IS SHREWDER THAN I'D originally anticipated. Still, she took advantage of someone else's misfortune and I need to confront her on that. I make my way around the stacks and into another part of the office, finally seeing her platinum-blonde hair at one of the workstations. As I approach, she catches sight of me and her eyes go wide, but she doesn't make a move to get up or leave.

I take the seat of the workstation next to her. "Hi," I say.

"Hi." Her voice is guarded, and her entire body is tense. She wasn't expecting me to come back to her, probably because she never expected Fuller to give us the truth.

"We need to have a talk."

"Okay," she says, still careful. I can see the fear in her eyes.

"Can you tell me where you were the night of January seventeenth of this year?"

She swallows, then glances to her computer, pulling up her calendar. She closes it just as quickly. "Um. I was at home."

"At home," I say. "On a Friday night?"

"I don't like the social scene," she says, which may or may not be a lie, but it's not important at the moment. "I stay in a lot of nights, watch movies, read books. You know." She makes a small gesture with her hand. It's shaky.

"Do you live alone?" I ask.

"No, I can't afford to. I have a roommate. We've been living together for about three years now."

I nod. "Was your roommate home that night?"

She hesitates a beat too long. "I...uh, I don't remember. It was so long ago."

Okay, time to cut to the chase. One way or another, I'm going to figure out if Fuller was involved with Victoria's disappearance before I leave this office. And if I have to interrogate every single employee, I will.

I lean forward, placing my forearms on my knees as I stare into her ocean-blue eyes. "Sarah. Here's the deal. I know what's going on. All of it. And I need you to be honest with me about it. Victoria isn't missing, she's dead." Sarah's face blanches. "We found her a few days ago. And if you're lying to me, then you are helping whoever killed her get away with it. I need to know the absolute truth."

"Victoria's...dead?" she asks, her voice shaking. I nod. "B-but...how?"

"We're not a hundred percent sure. Though it looks like she knew her killer. It wasn't random, we're pretty sure of that."

"She's supposed to be in Italy," the other woman says, tears spilling from the corners of her eyes. This is the part I'm not good with. I can handle my fair share of kidnappers, murderers, and rapists, but trying to comfort someone...I'm just shit at it. I never feel like what I'm saying is genuine enough. And sometimes keeping quiet is worse than saying anything at all.

I reach over and place a hand on her knee. She doesn't pull away; I take that as a positive sign. "Listen. I need your help. Are you completely sure you were at home on the night of the seventeenth?"

She shakes her head, her face pinched together. Her blonde hair flits back and forth.

"Where were you?"

"I was...oh, God. I was out at dinner with Rex."

"Where?"

"Um...Celedore's. It's a couple of hours from here. Close to D.C."

"What were you talking about?"

She wipes her eyes, staring up at the ceiling as she tries to get control of herself. "We had an arrangement," she says, her voice shaking. "I'd...seen something. I agreed not to tell anyone for a pay raise."

"What did you see?" I ask.

She tells me about the party, her details matching Fuller's accounting. "He was just there, pushing up into her," she says. "Holding her breast...like he was trying to dry hump her. It was...disgusting," she says.

I'm willing to bet Fuller remembers more of that than he's letting on. He just doesn't want to admit it. Pig.

"Then what happened?" I ask.

"She managed to push him off, and she actually slugged him, though he was so inebriated I don't think he even remembered," she says. "But he saw me. He knew I'd seen. After that Rex walked back to the party like nothing happened. His cheek was red for a few days."

"How did Victoria feel about your...arrangement with Rex?" I ask.

"I followed her into the bathroom and asked her if she was okay, I think she was just a little shaken. She said she wanted to go to HR and report it, but she was afraid of what her husband might say if she did."

"Her husband?" I ask. "Wouldn't he want her to report it?"

She shakes her head. "I don't know. She just seemed adamant that he not know. I told her if I could make it so that he never talked to her again, would that fix it and she agreed."

"She agreed, just like that?"

"Well, it was a longer conversation," Sarah says. "But yeah. She said as long as no one found out, she didn't care." She shakes her head. "I just can't believe she's gone."

I don't like where this is going. Victoria intentionally contributed to a coverup of sexual harassment, because of her *husband*? We'll have to take another run at him; I must have missed something the first time. When we met I didn't get anything from him other than sorrow and loss regarding Victoria. But I also have to consider all the information I've gotten about the problems between Victoria and her husband have all come from the same person. I need another source to confirm this for me.

"Why did you lie to me yesterday?" She said she'd seen them in an office together, not at a party. And not so graphic.

"I just...I didn't want to jeopardize the money. I thought if you found out, you'd make me repay it or he'd find a way to sue me or something. You don't understand. The only reason I'm still above water is because of that money. It's the first chance I've had since graduating to start paying down my debts."

"How long were you at dinner with Rex on the seventeenth?" I ask.

"It was at least a couple of hours," she replies, wiping her eyes again.

"And you had no problem sitting there with him for that long? Knowing what he'd done to your friend?"

"I never said I didn't have a problem with it," she snaps. "But the longer we were there, the more I could milk it. I ordered just about every thing on the menu then took a bite before ordering something else. All of it just to piss him off and leave him with a huge bill by the end. He knows he screwed up and he knew there was nothing he could do about it."

"Except," I say. "Victoria left. Without her, why would he continue to agree to the blackmail. From his perspective all his problems were gone."

"Yeah," she says. "He told me he wouldn't be paying me any extra when he learned she went off to Europe and that if I wanted to fight him on it, Victoria would have to come back and file the complaint herself. Otherwise, it's just hearsay."

"But he let you keep your job."

"He talks a big game, but I think he's afraid of what I might do if I leave. And he's paying me almost double what he was before. It's more than I'll get anywhere else in this town."

I sigh. "You know extortion is a felony in Virginia, don't you?"

"But...I was just trying to help!" she protests. "Victoria wasn't going to do anything about it, and I figured someone should at least benefit from that snake."

"Except now Victoria is dead," I say.

She casts her eyes to the side. "Did Rex do it?"

"I can't say at the moment. We don't know exactly when she was killed, only that the last time anyone saw her was on the seventeenth. It seems Rex was occupied that entire weekend. It doesn't put him in the clear, but we have other suspects." I stand up. "Until we can eliminate him as a suspect, there's a chance all of this will go into the official record. If that's the case, you might want a lawyer."

"But I was doing the right thing. He's the asshole who felt her up!"

"I know. And he's not going to be above retribution either," I say. "I'm just saying this from experience. Cover your butt. Get a lawyer you can trust. Because if he goes down for her murder, he's going to try and take everyone he can down with him."

She sniffs and nods, wiping her eyes again.

"Don't leave town. We may need to question you on the record," I say. "And you don't want this to get any worse."

"Okay," she says. "Thanks."

I head back to Liam, my head swimming with information. Fuller may have had the motive, but if he killed Victoria and knew there was no way she could come back and file the report, why not just fire Sarah and rid himself of this entire problem? It's seeming more likely to me that he was afraid she might come back to find the one other person who knew about the harassment had been let go, only then to rain down holy hellfire on this place. Fuller was protecting his ass, like always, by keeping Sarah close and happy. But now that he knows Victoria is dead, that might be in jeopardy. Which is even more reason for Sarah to retain her own lawyer.

"Anything?" I ask as I get back to Liam. He's staring daggers at Fuller through the plate-glass window to his office and Fuller only seems to be getting more nervous by the second.

"Celedore's has his credit card on file for that night. Processed at twelve twenty-two a.m."

"Damn," I say. "A four-hour dinner. She really did run him through the ringer."

"She confirmed his alibi?" he asks.

I fill him in on everything Sarah told me, including the details of Victoria's assault. Despite his earlier betrayal, he needs to know this stuff if he's going to help me on the case.

"So where does that leave us?" he asks when I finish.

"Fuller isn't off the hook. Not until we can get a definitive time on her death. And given how long she was in that box; I don't see that as likely. Based on what Sarah told me, we need to take another run at the husband. I want to figure out what was going on there."

"What about him?" Liam asks.

"We charge him with assault," I say. "Which should keep

him busy for a couple of days. Hopefully long enough that we can eliminate him as a suspect." I don't want Fuller getting away with what he did to Victoria, and since she's not here to defend herself anymore, we'll have to do it for her. Unfortunately, it means Sarah will probably face some retribution as well, depending on how the case goes.

We head back into Fuller's office.

He looks like he's about to pass out. "Well, did you talk to her? What did she say?"

"That you assaulted your subordinate," I say. "And we have a witness who is willing to testify to that."

"What?" he yells. "I never—" A look from me shuts him up.

"If I were you, Mr. Fuller, I'd get myself a good lawyer. You're already going to be facing a slew of legal troubles regarding this second strike. Not to mention you're the prime suspect in a murder investigation. I'm going to need you to stand up and put your hands behind your back."

Immediately he grows indignant. "You can't do this to me," he says.

Liam steps forward. "Do you really want to defy an order by the FBI?"

Fuller looks from him to me and back again. "But can't you just...this is your jurisdiction, and she's so—"

"Young?"

"Well, yeah. You're like my daughter."

I give him a sneer. "Mr. Fuller, don't make me sicker on the stomach than I already am. Now stand up, hands behind your back. You don't want to find out what happens if you don't comply."

He grumbles, standing up. "I'll use the entire legal force of this office to fight this," he says as Liam clasps his hands behind him. "I have the resources to do it."

"Of that I have no doubt," I say, taking him by the arm and leading him out of his office and down the hall. Everyone looks up as we parade him out. I really hadn't counted on arresting him today, but I can't ignore the fact he assaulted a co-worker, even admitting to it. He's going to have a hard time wriggling out from under that one and it doesn't make him look great for Victoria's murder either.

Fuller wisely doesn't say anything else as we get him outside and wait on the black and white Liam called in. We follow them back down to the station where he's processed into the local lockup until he can get his lawyer to secure a release, which will probably be tomorrow. Regardless, I'm going to suggest confiscating his passport just in case he tries to run while he's out on bail. Before leaving we briefly return to the detectives' office so I can grab anything I might have missed before.

"What the hell is going on here?" Burke bellows from down the hall. I share a look with Liam. I should have known I wouldn't be able to get out of here unscathed.

Burke appears in the door frame to the office. "Why do you have Rex Fuller in custody?"

"Because he assaulted Victoria Wright and paid off one of his employees to keep quiet about it," I say. "Or didn't you figure that out from your original investigation?"

His eyes burn with rage. "Now listen here, young lady—"

Before I can lay into him for belittling me, Liam steps in. "You knew, didn't you? That Fuller had assaulted her. And you let him go anyway. What kind of a cop does that?"

"Careful, Coll. Otherwise, you'll find yourself on leave. I may not be able to do anything about the agent here, but don't forget who you work for."

I can see Liam is working himself up to lay into Burke, but I put a hand on his shoulder, stopping him. "Not now," I say. Then I turn back to Burke. "And as for you, I don't know why you closed this case so fast without properly investigating it, but you can bet I'm going to find out. And if you call me anything other than agent one more time, you're going to be looking for a new set of teeth."

His entire face and neck have gone a shade of deep crimson and his nostrils flare a few times, reminding me of a bull that's about to charge. "I regret to inform you the resources of this office are no longer available to you."

"Fine by me," I say, pushing past him.

"And I'm reassigning Detective Coll to another case," he calls.

I stop. While it's his right to do that, I was finally making progress with Liam. Doing all of this by myself will be harder and take longer, but if that's how it has to go, then I don't have much of a choice. "That's your call," I say.

"You can't just—" Liam protests, but before he can finish, Burke puts one finger up.

"Say another word back to me and you're fired." I shake my head at him. It's not worth him losing his job over.

"Very well, Chief," I say. "If this is how you want to do things. I'm just sorry you're such a worthless cop you can't see the bigger picture here." I turn and storm out of the precinct, heading back to my car. Damn that man. But hopefully I already have all the files I need. Still, without Liam's assistance and contacts, this job is going to be much harder.

Angry with myself for letting things get this far, I head back to the motel.

Chapter Nineteen

NOW THAT I'M ON MY OWN, I'VE SPENT MOST OF MY TIME reviewing the footage from Dulles to see if I can find any evidence of Victoria or Patrick Wood actually coming into the airport and getting on one of the tarmacs. It's long, thankless work and at some point I become so bleary-eyed that I have to turn everything off and lay down. My stomach is grumbling as I've barely had anything to eat today, but after facing Fuller and then Burke, I'm burned out. I just need something quick and fatty to curb my body's need for food, then maybe I can get some sleep.

My eyes snap open as I hear the rapping on the other side of my door. My first instinct is to grab my sidearm, which is on the table beside me. Though part of me knows if someone wants in here, they're probably not going to knock. Still, I keep it in my hand as I approach the door.

"Yeah?" I ask.

"It's me."

"Alone?"

"Yeah." I look through the peephole to confirm. When I open the door, Liam stands there, his jacket wrapped tight around him. Outside it's grown dark again. I'll be glad when the time changes back over so the sun will stay out a little longer. It's barely seven p.m.

"What are you doing here?" I ask.

"Come to help with the case," he says. "If you still need it."

"What about Burke?" I ask.

He shrugs. "I'm off the clock. This is my free time; he doesn't get to control every aspect of my life." I step aside and invite him in. "Made any progress?" he asks.

"Barely. Been reviewing the footage from Dulles you got for me. Thank you for that."

He takes a seat in the chair, leaving his coat buttoned up around him. "No problem."

"And thank you for standing up to Burke today, even though it could have cost you your job."

"I've been going over it in my mind all day," he says. "You've been like the biggest wake-up call for me. I don't know if I just ignored it before or if I really was that blind. If I was, what does that say about me as a detective? And I'm just not sure I can keep working for a man like that. He's just so—"

"—Arrogant."

"Right, and entitled. He expects whatever he says to be taken as law, like we're all there to enforce his decrees, not the other way around." He shakes his head.

I take a seat on the bed. "Sometimes it's hard to see what's right in front of us."

"Want me to go through the video files with you?"

I motion to the computer. "Have at them. I'm less than a quarter through."

"Great, just what I love," Liam says, rubbing his hands together. "Surveillance footage. You know what I like to do sometimes?" I shake my head. "I'll throw on some epic music, you know, like the stuff they use in those really intense scenes in movies and play it while I'm watching. It makes things a lot more exciting. You start anticipating people to begin doing backflips any second. It's kind of a rush."

I crack a grin. "I'll have to give that a try." He's a little bit of a free spirit, with a lot of humor in him. I feel like some of that's been tamped down by the job, but it's still there. If he's not careful, this job could end up consuming him, leaving little behind. I've seen it before and I know I'll see it again.

Liam spends about forty-five minutes on the surveillance footage while I review other aspects of the case. I need to re-interview Gerald Wright, but I want to hold off on that for now, at least until it's absolutely necessary. I may only get one more shot at him. More importantly, I want to find this woman who was in the hotel that night. Maybe with Liam here we can come up with a way to find her. Surely he knows all the homeless shelters in town.

And then there's our mystery man, Patrick Wood. It bothers me how little I've been able to uncover of him so far. But thankfully, Zara is on the job. She'll figure out a way to track him down, I'm sure of it.

"Hey," I say, causing Liam to look up. "Any developments on Fuller after I left?"

He shakes his head. "Arraignment tomorrow. Burke gave me hell over that, said I never should have let you arrest him. I halfway thought he was going to drop the charges, but given what Fuller said himself about what he did, I don't think that would have looked too good. Especially not for the press."

That seems odd. "Is he that egotistic that he can't even allow *one suspect* in this case?"

"I have no idea. It's like he's…" he trails off, then turns to me. "What if Fuller paid Burke off to cut the investigation short?"

I scoff. "Burke's corrupt, but is he *that* corrupt? Accepting a bribe on a missing person's report?"

"Is it any wilder than what he's already done?" Liam asks. "We both know he's capable."

"Capable, yes. But stupid enough to put himself under Rex Fuller's thumb? I don't know."

Liam stands. "Think about it. What if Fuller paid Burke off so he wouldn't find out about Sarah?"

"And because he thought Victoria had left the country, he didn't have any reason to keep the file open," I say. "It's a definite possibility. But there's no proof, is there?"

"Maybe there could be, if Fuller's lawyers are willing to cut a deal."

I smile. Taking down Burke would be icing on the cake. But I can't let that be my focus at the moment. We still have a killer out there who may or may not have another victim in their possession. Until we find them, I can't allow myself to get sidetracked. "It's a good idea. Something that we can come back to. Right now, we need to stay focused."

He nods. "He wants to take my job? I'll take his job," Liam mutters as he turns back to the computer.

My stomach rumbles again and I realize I still haven't eaten and it's nearly eight o'clock. "Know of any good grease traps around here?" I ask.

Liam eyes me. "You sure you want me to divulge my secrets? I figured you more for a vegan."

"Tried it once, didn't stick," I say. "I'm a sucker for some fast food. It only gets worse when I'm out of town."

"There's a great place called *Lou's*, just off Albemarle. They serve nothing but burgers and hot dogs until midnight."

"Sounds perfect," I say, grabbing my coat.

He stands, setting the computer aside. "So is this another one of those 'date-ish' things?"

Immediately my mood turns sour. "You know what? Never mind. I'll just grab something from one of the vending machines."

"I wasn't being serious, I just thought it was funny," he

says, looking genuinely hurt. But I can't help that. His feelings aren't my responsibility.

"I know," I say. "I just didn't realize how tired I was."

"Emily, even if I weren't a detective, I know a line of bull-shit when I hear it." His candor strikes me almost as if was a physical blow. I've been tiptoeing around Matt for three months, which, given the situation, I feel is appropriate. "I'm sorry," he says. "It's just…I usually don't have such a hard time reading people, and you keep a lot of yourself close to the chest. There's probably a good reason for that. But I like you, Em. You're a good cop, one of the better ones I've ever met. And you're a crusader."

I arch an eyebrow. "A crusader?"

"Yeah, someone who fights for those who can't. Look at everything you're doing for Victoria Wright. You're not just working the case; the case has become your life. It's inspiring."

I'm not sure what to say. It's a lot all at once and takes me a moment to process it all. Maybe Zara was right, I can't expect Liam to be sensitive to my situation if he doesn't know what's going on. And this just confirms that I'm not crazy when I feel that spark between us. I thought for a while there it was just a fluke, but the more and more time I spend with Liam, the less I think that's the case.

"I was married," I say. "For almost five years. We met in college." He's watching me intently, but not probing, not expecting. I'm not sure what's causing me to open up like this; it's not something I do. But for some reason it feels okay, now. "He…died, a few months ago."

Liam's face transforms into one of sorrow, which does nothing but make me want to break down, but I hold it together. "Unexpected," I add. "I just…and he was there…" I shake my head and look elsewhere, trying to stem the tide of tears.

"I'm so sorry," he says. "I didn't know."

I look down at my finger to where a ring should be, but isn't. "We had wedding rings, but I only wore mine occasionally. Because I was undercover so much, and because I was playing someone a lot younger than I actually am, I couldn't risk having it look like I wore a ring all the time. I hate I had to give that up."

Silence stretches between us for a few minutes until I'm sure he's trying to figure out how to get himself out what he considers an awkward situation. "Tell me about him," Liam says.

I look up. "What?"

"Tell me about him. What did you love most about him?"

Now I can't help the tears from falling. Everyone who knows has avoided the subject, except for Zara, of course. But even she only occasionally mentions his name. Everyone else just doesn't talk about him, and I guess I've become used to that. I know thinking about him while I'm at work isn't a good idea; it's how I screwed up in the first place. But maybe now that I've had some distance...

"He had this way of looking at me," I say, softly. "And I could just tell in that moment he loved me for exactly who I was. He didn't expect me to be the perfect agent, the perfect wife, or the perfect person. Whatever I was in that moment was all he needed. I just remember him giving me those looks from time to time and feeling...fulfilled."

Liam holds out his hand to me. "Come on. Let's go eat. I want to hear all about him."

"Why?" I ask.

"Because the best way we can honor a person's memory is to tell their stories to others. So that they won't be forgotten."

"I haven't really talked about him since..."

"You don't have to talk about that part," he says. "But you've got five years of good memories. I want to hear them all."

I look at his outstretched hand. Part of me wants to just stay in this dark room and stare at the drawn curtains until it's time to get up again. But another, stronger part of me wants to take him up on his offer. Maybe he's right. Maybe talking will help.

"Okay," I say, taking his hand. "But you're buying."

Chapter Twenty

I WAKE UP TO THE BUZZING OF MY PHONE ON THE NIGHTSTAND. Grunting, I turn over and look at the caller ID with bleary eyes trying to make my brain work. I was in a deep sleep, deeper than I've had in a long time.

"What?" I say, putting the phone to my ear and closing my eyes again to shut out the bright light.

"Morning!" Zara says on the other end.

"Don't you sleep?" I ask.

"I prefer to keep my own hours, thank you," she says, way too chipper for four-forty in the morning. "But hey, I let you sleep an extra thirty minutes."

"Twenty-five," I grumble.

"You know, for someone who likes to be places early, you sure don't like getting up."

I rub one eye and push myself out of the bed. It's chilly in the room, like I forgot to turn on the heater overnight. I also realize I slept in my clothes from last night. "What can I say? My body is at constant war with my mind."

"Well, anyway, I've gone as deep as I can on Patrick Wood."

My eyes snap open. "What did you find out?"

"First, are you alone?"

I frown, turning back to the bed and looking around the room. "Of course I'm alone, why wouldn't I be?"

"I dunno," she says, her voice too mischievous for my liking. "I just thought I'd check before I delivered some sensitive information."

"Zara, what's that supposed to mean?"

"Just that last time we talked it seemed like you were being intentionally obtuse. Like you didn't want someone to hear our conversation," she says.

"Yeah, well he heard it anyway. So thanks for that."

"What'd he do?" she asks. I can practically see the excitement on her face.

"Look, I don't know what you think is going on, but nothing is going to happen with Liam. I'm still grieving."

"No, no, I get that. It's just I can hear something in your voice when you mention him. And have you noticed you've gone from using his last name to his first?"

Have I? I'm not sure when that happened, but it concerns me I didn't notice. "I told him about Matt last night."

She goes quiet on the other end. "How are you feeling about that?"

I shake my head even though she can't see me. "I don't know. Okay, I guess. I haven't openly talked about him before with anyone else other than you. It was...nice."

"See? I told you. You can't just compartmentalize your husband off like you do with your job. It's not gonna work."

"Seems you were right," I say. "But he's still a big presence in my life. And I'm afraid if I open that door, I'll never get it closed again. You know what happened last time."

"That's different," she says. "It was only a few days after... you never should have been at work."

I push away the bad memories. She didn't call me to reminisce about worse times. Taking a deep breath, I reset myself. "What do you have on Wood?"

"Okay," she says. I can almost imagine her pulling together a bunch of files and straightening them on her desk before beginning. Of course that's not how it is; Zara works exclusively in the digital realm. "First off, I got in contact with Interpol. They have no record of this Patrick Wood anywhere in Europe, including Italy."

"So then he never got on the plane," I say. "We're still reviewing the footage from Dulles, but so far we've come up empty."

"You're not going to find him on any surveillance footage," she says. "This guy is too smart for that. He's managed to go eight years without being positively ID'd. I doubt he'd slip up with an airport security camera."

"Eight years?" I ask. "What was eight years ago?"

"As far as I can tell, that's when Patrick Wood popped into existence," she says. "Like he was created out of thin air."

I straighten. "He's a ghost?"

"Seems to be. His history, what I can find of it, only goes back to 2012. Before that, nothing. But he managed to get assigned a social security number, built a credit line, even owned a house in Stillwater for about a year."

"Where is he now?" I ask.

"Dropped off the grid three months ago," she says. "After the eighteenth of January, I can't find anything on him. It's like he disappeared into thin air."

I flop back on the bed, trying to work out the implications. "Jesus. Do you think we're working with an overseas operative here? Or is this domestic?"

"I couldn't say," she replies. "But in my experience, people only create a second persona if they're coming from some-where else and are planning to return to that place once the job is over. Whoever this was, he appeared eight years ago, lived his life, then disappeared at the same time as Victoria Wright."

"After he killed her," I say, even though that's still conjecture. "But what was the motive? That seems like a lot of resources to go after one woman, a woman who has no important connections, as far as I can discern. Except maybe her husband."

"Maybe he was the real target and she got in the way?" Zara asks.

"No way. This guy was targeting Victoria specifically. He cultivated a relationship with her online. Apparently in order to lure her out into the open." I sit up again. "What was so special about eight years ago? And why did he wait so long if the plan was to take her out? Surely it would have been easier to do it before she was married with children."

"I wish I could answer," Zara replies. "But this is all I found."

"Did you get a picture?"

"Unfortunately not," she replies.

I screw up my features. "Then how the hell did he get a social security number? Or buy a house without a picture ID? Something about this isn't right."

"I've got his last known address in Stillwater if that will help," she says.

"I've already got it, but send everything over anyway. Maybe I can find the realtor who sold him the house. Someone has to have seen this guy. Victoria wouldn't have just gone to meet someone she'd never seen before."

"Sounds like she was catfished," Zara says.

"It does, doesn't it?" I rub my forehead, trying to figure out just what's going on here. "Anything else on the second victim, Laura?"

"I guess it's possible this person was under a different identity when they killed her," Zara says. "Maybe that's the M.O. Pose as a person for a specified period of time, kill the victim, then destroy the persona so they can't be traced. It's hard to accuse someone when the killer doesn't really exist."

"Oh, they exist alright," I say. "They've just done a good

job of covering their tracks. "Someone killed this woman. And they aren't going to get away with it. Do you have a work history on Wood? How did he sustain himself for eight years?"

"That's the strange thing. He had bank accounts with regular deposits, but I can't figure out where they were coming from. Cash deposits, every time. Someone was paying him for *something*, but I can't seem to find what or who."

If there was any part of me left that wasn't fully invested in this case, it's completely disappeared by now. I *have* to find whoever was masquerading as Patrick Wood. Once I find him, I'll find my answers and the person who killed Victoria Wright. But at this point, it could be anyone. I need to find someone who actually met the man.

I hear her sigh on the other end. "What's wrong?"

"I just wish there was more I could do. I don't feel like I'm being very effective here."

I can't help but scoff. "This isn't even your case! If Janice finds out you're helping me on company time—"

"Oh, she's not going to do anything," Zara says. "She may not seem like it, but she's a big softie. Plus I'm not sacrificing any of my time on any other cases to help out. Let me take over the airport surveillance feeds. I can run through those a lot quicker than you can."

"Are you sure?" I ask. "Based on what you told me I don't think they're going to show up."

"Yeah," she says. "But we need to make sure. It'll make me feel like I'm still helping." I can still detect the hesitation in her voice. "I just..."

"What?"

"I need to get out of this office, Em. I want to be out where you are, on the ground, working the cases directly, rather than stuck here in the data analysis center."

"Then go to Janice and ask for fieldwork," I say. "Trust me, you don't want to be where I am, barely hanging on to your career by a thread."

"You're gonna catch this guy, I know it, Em. It may not feel like it, but you'll get him. Janice will realize she made a mistake, and you won't have anything to worry about."

I look around the dark room, the silhouettes of the sparse furniture staring back at me. "I sure hope you're right. And it may not seem like it, but this is a huge help. Thank you."

She gives me a mirthless laugh on the other end. "Well, I'm glad it's something. Because from this end it looks like another dead end."

"Nope," I say. "Just a wrinkle. One I plan on ironing out."

Chapter Twenty-One

AFTER A SHOWER AND FRESH SET OF CLOTHES, I FEEL MORE like myself and am ready for the day. I can't believe I slept in my clothes from last night; I never do that. Mostly because whenever I do, I never sleep well. I can't stand the thought of putting clothes that have absorbed all the dirt of the day under clean covers. But then again, the Nite Owl isn't the most discerning of establishments. I'm sure these sheets have seen worse.

When I open the door to head out, Liam is sitting in his vehicle out front, yawning. He sees me and gets out of the car, a steaming cup of coffee in his hand.

"You are a god," I say, reaching for the cup he's offering.

"Nah. Just a demigod. Or maybe nothing more than a mythical figure. They still sing stories of the man who died from getting up too early three days in a row."

I chuckle. "I have to give you credit. Didn't think you'd be able to handle it."

"I used to pull the night shift when I was on patrol," he says. "My body adapts to time changes pretty quick."

I check the time. It's almost six. "What are you doing there? Aren't you due at the station in an hour?"

"I took the day off," he says. "It seems Burke doesn't want me around any more than I want to be around him."

"Doesn't he suspect what you're doing in your spare time?" I ask, taking a sip of the coffee. The blend is glorious; I think I'm starting to like the local flavor.

"Probably. But I've built up a large buffer of off-time. He just doesn't want to look like he's not approving it for the other officers. It wouldn't look too good if someone like me, who never takes time off, is suddenly *forced* to be in the office." He pulls out his cell phone, wagging it in the air. "Still on call though, just in case."

"You don't have to do this, you know."

He levels his gaze at me. "I want to do this. For you, for Victoria, and especially to nail Burke to the wall."

I laugh again. "That's as good of a reason as any."

I walk around to the side of the car, checking my phone to go over all the notes Zara sent on Patrick Wood. "I received a call from one of my colleagues at HQ," I say. "She's pulled some interesting info on Wood."

"Yeah?" he asks, slipping into the driver's seat. Inside the car is already warm, which is a nice change from the chill outside.

It only takes a minute to fill him in on all the details Zara provided me on Wood. And by the time I'm done his eyes are the size of saucers. "What the hell is going on here?" he asks. "Was this a hit?"

"It doesn't have the hallmarks of organized crime," I say. "This feels more personal. Like it was important for Wood to get close to her. Though I don't know why. Why draw her in just to kill her? It seems like a lot of extra work for nothing."

"I don't know, but our main priority is to figure out who this Patrick Wood person really is. He can't have just dropped off the face of the Earth."

"You think he's still in Stillwater?" Liam asks.

I grit my teeth. "Seems unlikely, doesn't it."

"Probably went back to Russia to train with all the other assassins," he says, taking a sip of his own coffee.

"Still. We have to work the case as it's presented. Which means going over every bit of evidence we have. If it's this personal, it's someone from Victoria's past. But without a detailed list of her friends and acquaintances, we could spend forever and a day going over everyone she's ever come into contact with. We need to focus on identifying Patrick before he takes another victim. I want to talk to the realtor, see if she remembers him. If nothing else we could bring down a sketch artist and get a composite on this guy. And I still want to find Jo-Ann Langley. She might be our only eye-witness."

Liam revs the engine. "Which one first?"

I check my watch. "Let's start with Jo-Ann. The realtor won't be accessible for a few hours, but there's a good chance Jo-Ann is already up, probably trying to find breakfast."

"I don't know," he says. "Some of them have learned to hunker down pretty good."

"One of the first things you do when it's this cold is to keep moving. You stop and you risk freezing," I say. "If she's not at one of the shelters, she's out walking around. Either that or she's dead."

"Okay," he says, pulling out his phone. "The shelters it is." I prepare for him to back up but he doesn't put the car into gear. I look at him and he's got a sad sort of smile on his face.

"What's wrong?"

"I just wanted you to know I appreciated last night," he says.

"All we did was talk."

"I know. But I enjoyed it. I hope you did too."

I swallow, trying not to let my emotions breach the wall. "It's not an easy thing to talk about. But thanks for listening."

"Anytime," he says.

It's close to ten a.m. by the time we reach our third shelter. The first two were complete busts, one of them not even knowing who Jo-Ann was, while the second hadn't seen her in a few days. I'm starting to wonder if she's a block of ice under a bridge somewhere. Who's to say she didn't skip town for someplace warmer or that she didn't succumb to the cold one night between January and now.

Liam pulls up in front of a dilapidated brick building, with a colorful mural painted on the front depicting some kind of abstract landscape. The building doesn't look very big; the plot can't be more than thirty feet wide. But it goes back a good distance, the building expanding in the rear. Back when the building was built, street-front property was at a premium.

"Cute place," I say, getting out of the car.

He follows suit. "Yeah, it's run by the local Presbyterian Church. The building looks as old as the town itself."

I make my way to the front door and enter into a large foyer that's little more than a laminate floor with crosses and pictures of Jesus on the walls. There's a staircase to the left that goes up to the second floor and the rest of the hallway narrows to accommodate it. But beyond the staircase I can see what looks like a cafeteria in the back. We head back to find the place bustling. It's much more crowded than the last two places as people are lined up for food along the back wall. The cafeteria-style tables are almost all full and people are talking, laughing, and generally enjoying themselves.

Back in the kitchen a line of volunteers helps to serve the food. I look around for someone in charge who might be able to help us, until I lock eyes with an older man who looks like little more than a skeleton with skin. He's clearly a drug addict, and his white, stringy hair falls around his face in clumps, only adding to his wild appearance. His tray of food sits untouched in front of him as he slowly stands, keeping his eyes directly on mine.

"Liam," I say, alerting him to the situation. In my peripheral, I can see him tense as we both try to figure out how this is going to go. Some people, especially those whose minds have been warped by years of drug use, tend to react badly when they notice a cop, federal or not. They've spent their whole lives learning how to detect them because they're the people that make their lives harder, despite that's the opposite of what we're trained to do.

I hold up one hand to calm the man and the room goes quiet as more and more people notice us and the excitement going on.

The man mutters something under his breath; it sounds like one long string of words instead of actual sentences, but it's too low for me to understand. But I can read his body language perfectly. He's preparing himself for a fight.

"Bill," a soft voice says from across the room. I turn to see a man in his mid-fifties approach the wild-eyed patron. He's dressed in jeans and what looks to be a comfortable hoodie, and he's got an easy smile on his face, though he looks like he's built like a tank. If I didn't know better, I would say he fit the physical description of a bouncer. "Billy, just calm down, y'hear?"

"Them's demons," the wild-eyed man says, pointing at us.

"Now we've talked about this. There are no demons," the bouncer replies. "Besides, they're not here for you." He turns to us. "Are you?"

I shake my head. "Nope."

"Don't trust 'em," Bill says, beginning to shake like a leaf.

"Bill, now if you don't calm down we're gonna have another incident like we did back at Christmas. You don't want that, now do ya?" the man asks.

Bill's eyes flit to the man for the first time, breaking contact with mine. Suddenly he looks more scared. "No, don't want that."

"Good. Now take a seat. Those people, they're not even here, understand?"

Bill slowly lowers back to his seat, watching the bouncer. "They's ghosts," he says. A chill runs down my spine. I don't know if it was because of the way he says it or if it's because of the man we're hunting. Either way, I don't like it.

The man nods. "Right. Now you just eat, and you don't pay them any mind. Hear?"

"Yessir. Thank ya, reverend."

I have to contain my shock. I shoot a glance at Liam who has a big grin on his face, like he knew this was coming.

As soon as Billy seems more interested in his meal than anything else, the reverend leaves his side, makes a motion to the room, and everyone goes back to what they were doing. I still catch a few furtive glances our way though. People are wondering who we're here for.

The man approaches us, extending a large hand. "Sorry 'bout that. He's always a little skittish. Reverend Michaels."

"Agent Emily Slate, FBI," I say, taking the hand.

He gives it a good shake and then turns to Liam. "Don't tell me they drafted you into the FBI too? A man with your temperament? I'd never believe it."

Liam smiles and reaches out, pulling Reverend Michaels into a hug. "Caleb, how've you been?"

"Better, now that I don't have to play with you anymore," the man laughs.

"Am I missing something?" I ask.

"Liam and I used to play on the same local soccer team," the reverend says. "Until he got kicked off for aggravated conduct on the field."

I turn to Liam, an amused expression on my face.

"It was nothing," he says. "I just kicked a few chairs."

The reverend gives him a pitiful look. "And knocked over a water cooler and destroyed one of the goalposts as he was stomping away. This boy does not like to lose."

"Really?" I say, staring at Liam. "And here you were the one comparing me to a dog with a bone."

He's gone a little red in the face, which really flushes his cheeks. "It's not the same thing, it was just one game."

I turn back to Reverend Michaels, eager to hear the rest of this. "So he's banned from ever playing again?"

"I wouldn't say forever, but at least until a few seasons pass. You gotta give people time to get over their trauma."

"Ha, ha," Liam enunciates, clearly embarrassed. I like this side of him; it's something I haven't seen before.

"All joshin' aside, he's okay." Michaels winks at me. "But I'd keep my eye on him. Now, what can I do for you two on this fine morning?"

"We're looking for someone," Liam says, relief coloring his words. I know he's glad to be off the subject of his own *incident*, but I plan on investigating fully later.

"I gathered that much," Michaels says. "I doubt you came here for the food. But you'd be missing out. This morning we're having buckwheat waffles. I can grab y'all a plate if y'like."

"No thank you," I say, though they do sound mouthwatering. I think this place is beginning to turn me. Maybe I *am* a breakfast person after all. "We're looking for Jo-Ann Langley. Do you know her?"

"Sure, Jody is one of our regulars," he says.

"Jody?" I ask.

He smiles. "Real name is Jody Taylor. She likes to go by Jo-Ann though, thinks it makes her sound more regal."

"Is she here today?" I ask.

"'fraid not," he says. "I haven't seen her in a couple of days. Let's see…today's Saturday, she usually shows up around Sunday or Monday, comin' down from whatever high she's been on all weekend. She'll stay a couple days, then disappear again until the following week."

"Have you ever tried to get her into rehab?" I ask.

"Once. But I learned a long time ago you can't help people who don't wanna help themselves. So mostly here we just make sure they have good food and a warm bed if they need it. No requirements, no judgments."

"Wow," I say, surprised. "That's kinda progressive for the Presbyterian Church."

"Not our job to judge," Michaels says. "That's for the big man upstairs. I'm happy to give ya'll a call if she shows up though. She's not in any sort of trouble, is she?"

"No, nothing like that," Liam says. "But she might have seen something. We just need to ask her about it."

Michaels' face turns grim. "If you're hopin' to use her as a witness, I'm afraid she's not gonna be much help. Half the time she don't even know what year it is, much less what she was doin' last week. She's the kind of person who lives more in the moment, if that makes sense."

"Shit," I say, then realize where I am and offer Reverend Michaels a sheepish face. "Sorry. Force of habit."

"'s all right," he says. "Sure I can't offer you some breakfast?"

"Thanks, but we have to go," I say.

"Thanks Caleb," Liam says, tapping him on the shoulder as we pass. "Let us know, huh?"

"Sure will. Y'all have a good day."

We walk back out into the sunshine. Despite the brightness, it's still cold as Everest out here. I get into Liam's car, rubbing my hands together. "Soccer tantrum, huh?"

He faces me. "Don't start. I've been trying to live that down for nine months."

"Didn't take you to be a soccer fan," I say as he starts the car.

"Yeah, well when you grow up watching nothing else on TV 'cause your dad's obsessed, it kind of gets ingrained in you." He shakes his head. "Even if we find Jo-Ann—Jody, there's no way we'll get a positive ID from her. No prosecutor in the world would bring her up in front of a jury."

I shift in my seat as the heat comes on. "Maybe not. But I still want to talk to her. I want to know what she saw."

Jody is a long shot; that's obvious. But we can't leave any stone unturned in this case. There has to be something… somewhere. People only have so much control. I don't care how much time, experience or luck you have doing something, eventually it runs out. Eventually things don't go your way. There has to be some part of this that can give us a clue as to this guy's identity.

"So. Where to now?" Liam asks.

"Realtor," I say. "It's our only good lead on Patrick. Maybe she can help us figure out who he really is. Then I want to go talk to the husband again."

Liam turns back to me. "I thought you said we needed another source—someone else who knew their marriage was on the rocks."

"We already got it," I say. "Fuller. He said there had been rumors going around the office about it. Remember? It was his excuse for his…behavior."

"Rumors that could have been started by Sarah Ellis," Liam points out.

He's not wrong. "Still. I want to take another run at Gerald Wright. I need to make sure I'm not missing something."

"Okay then. Realtor first. Husband second."

Chapter Twenty-Two

"You've got to be kidding me," I say, staring at the sale document before me.

"No, actually, it's becoming more common," the realtor says, her voice light and airy. Her blond bob bounces along with her words. She introduced herself as Marcia and despite the fact she's probably fifteen years older than me, she's still as happy and bubbly as you would expect of an airline attendant. I can't even imagine how jaded and cynical I'll be by that age.

"So he contacts you online, you send him pictures of the house, and he purchases over the phone," Liam says.

"Well, it's a little more complicated than that," she replies, pulling the property sale document back and placing it in a folder. "But those are the broad strokes, yes."

"You never met him?" I ask. "Even when he sold the property?"

"Not once. When he contacted me telling me he was ready to sell, I had assumed he was flipping it, since he'd only owned the property for a year," she says. "But when I came with the inspector to do our walkthrough, it looked the same as it did the day I sold it to him. Maybe a little cleaner, but otherwise, exactly the same."

"Did you ever come by, after you sold it? To see how he was liking the place?" I ask.

She nods. "I tried a few times. I like to follow up with my clients right after a sale, make sure they're happy with their purchase. But I could never catch him at home. Eventually I just called, and he told me everything was going great."

"So then, you never even saw him in the house. Did he ever move anything in?" I ask.

"Well, I assume he did," she replies. "But can't say for sure. I wasn't peeking in the windows if that's what you're asking." She gives us a nervous laugh like she doesn't like what we're implying.

I turn away in frustration, racking my brain.

"I don't understand," Liam says. "How can you approve someone to buy a house with no photo ID? Without meeting them in person?"

"The couple that lived at this house prior to Mr. Wood were empty nesters, and motivated to sell. They'd been sitting on the property a few years too long and were eager to get out. Got themselves set up at a nice retirement facility. But they couldn't move without the money from the sale itself. And Mr. Wood didn't need to be approved for a loan, he paid cash."

I whip back around. "He paid *cash*? For a *house*?" I lock eyes with Liam and I know he's thinking the same thing I am: the jewelry. Untraceable.

She nods. "First and only time it's happened to me," she says. "But I know other agents who've seen it before too. I received a wire transfer from the bank the day of sale and everything went through beautifully. He mailed in all the legal forms required, notarized."

"Can I see those forms?" I ask.

"Don't you need a warrant of some kind?" Marcia asks.

I give her the politest smile I can muster. "Marcia. I am doing everything I can to find this man because he is wanted as a possible murder suspect. Now getting a warrant will take time, which is that much longer he is out there, free. Not to mention I'll have to disclose the name of the company and agent who sold the house, along with all the pertinent information. It's a lot less paperwork if we can just take a quick look at the forms." I can hear the exhaustion in my own voice. Part of me expected this, anticipated it even. Of course he wouldn't buy a house in person, not if he's trying to hide his identity. He would have done everything possible to stay anonymous.

She bristles and I can see the gears turning in her head. How will it look if her name pops up implicated in a murder investigation? Will anyone buy a house from her ever again? My approach may have been somewhat heavy-handed, but in situations like this I feel its warranted. Plus, I am running out of patience.

Finally, Marcia turns to her computer and taps a few keys, then swivels the screen around so we can see it. "Here's the purchase agreement. His signature is on the final pages."

I scroll through the pages until the end. And when I see the last page, my heart skips a beat. "Liam."

He looks at the document. "Whoa."

"Can you print these out for me, please?" I ask. "Just the final two pages."

Marcia huffs, then taps a few more keys. A printer on the other side of the room warms up, then spits out two pages, which I retrieve. "Thank you," I say, gathering them together. "Is the house occupied now?"

"Yes, a family moved in about a month and a half ago. Two small children," she says.

There goes any chance for any forensic evidence, I think. It's the hotel room all over again. If we had found Victoria right after she'd died, all these places would have still been fresh; there might have been salvageable evidence. But it's been too long.

"Perfect, got them," I say, holding up the pages.

"Mm-hm," she says, gathering up her briefcase. "Now if you don't mind, I have three showings left today and I'm already going to be late."

"Of course," I say. "Thank you for your time." She escorts us out and locks the door to the realtor's office behind her, before disappearing into the back. Liam and I make our way back to the car.

"So," he says. "What is Victoria Wright doing notarizing purchase documents for Patrick Wood?" Liam asks.

"I don't know," I say, looking over the pages again. But there it is, in black and white: Victoria's signature, along with her notary commission stamp which doesn't expire until later this year. "Could this be how they met?"

"If so, she's the only person who saw him face to face," he replies.

"That they knew of. But how would Patrick have ever met her in the first place? Normally you go through a bank to find a notary, not a lawyer's office."

"Maybe she did it on the side," Liam suggests. "Like one of those mobile pet groomers. Except, instead of coming to your house to wash your dog, they come to your house to witness signatures."

I ponder this as we get into the car. It's a good theory. And it fits with the assumption that Victoria knew her killer. This more or less proves it. "It gives us something else too," I say. "An actual signature from Wood. We need to get copies of signatures from Fuller, the husband and anyone else who might have been a suspect. Then I want to send all of them down to Quantico to the forensic lab where they can compare them."

"Do you really think he would have been stupid enough to not pay attention to how he signed his name?" Liam asks. "He's been so careful everywhere else."

"Maybe not, but everyone slips up eventually. We can pull Fuller's signature from his arraignment, and I'm sure there are public documents online that could give us Wright's."

"Why purchase a house if you're not going to use it?" he asks.

"To leave some kind of imprint that you were here," I reply. "He's trying to establish Patrick Wood as existing. Or having the appearance of existing. I doubt he even spent one night in that house."

"So why not kill her there? Why the motel?"

I shake my head, unable to make sense of it. Maybe it was too easy to trace it back to him; I don't know. The house was already sold before Victoria disappeared, so we know that couldn't have been where the murder took place. And even though we don't have forensic evidence on the motel, I still believe that's where she took her last breath.

As I'm racking my brain, I hear the vibrating of Liam's cell in his pocket. My first thought is it's Burke calling him back to the station, finally on to us. But when he looks at the phone he gives me a positive sign.

"Caleb? Yeah. We'll be right there."

Chapter Twenty-Three

"AND YOU'RE ABSOLUTELY SURE?" I ASK, STANDING BACK outside the Presbyterian shelter with Reverend Michaels.

He nods. "I've been askin' around ever since ya'll left. A couple of ladies saw her down at the Freemont last night. As far as they know, she's still there."

I look to Liam for more info. "The Freemont is what they call one of the drug houses in the run-down part of town," he says. "Lots of abandoned buildings around there. Easy places for someone to hide out." He turns back to Caleb. "Did they say anything else? About her condition?"

He shakes his head. "Nah, but you know how it is. If you find her, let her know we've got a warm bed and meal for her here, if she wants it."

Liam nods. "Thanks, Caleb, I owe you."

"Nothin' worth owin'," he says with a smile. "Just as long as you stay away from my goalposts."

"No promises!" Liam calls out as we get back in the car. Five minutes later we're heading into a part of Stillwater I haven't seen before. It's not exactly urban and it's not rural either, instead it's stuck somewhere in between. It's an older part of town that looks like it might have thrived in the fifties or sixties, but now has just been abandoned.

"Lovely," I say.

"This is where I end up spending a lot of my time," Liam says, scanning the streets as we drive. "Most of us do."

"Drugs," I say, without even needing to ask. It's as much an epidemic in Stillwater as it is anywhere else.

"It can get pretty bad out here," he replies. "Laborers get hurt on the job and get hooked, or kids with not enough to do find their way into something they can't get back out of. The mayor has tried to stamp it down with more police, more patrols, more arrests; none of it does any good."

"Never does," I say.

"The real heroes are the ones like Caleb," he goes on. "Him and those like him are the only thing keeping a lot of these people alive; keeping them from slipping off the edge. Though the way Burke talks, he'd just rather be rid of the lot of them."

It's a sentiment I'm familiar with. Having grown up during the mid-nineties and living through the "War on Drugs", I saw what a heavy-handed, military-level response did to a country that needed social help. It's led to places like this; carved out areas of cities that are havens for those who have nowhere else to turn.

"You make a lot of arrests down here?"

"I try not to," he says. "If they're non-violent, sometimes I'll give them a lift to Caleb's or one of the other places. Sometimes they don't want to go. It's the shame they feel, I think."

I nod. I've never had a substance abuse problem, so I have to believe that however bad I imagine it, it's probably three times worse than that. These people have it hard, and they're fighting biochemistry. That's just not something you're going to fix with deterrents and arrests.

"Okay," Liam says, pulling the car up to an abandoned

house. There's a chain-link fence around it, but it's been bent and warped in so many places that it's effectively worthless other than a lawn decoration. I look up at the street sign. Freemont and Haven.

"The local community center?" I ask.

"As close as you're going to get," he says. "If we're lucky, she'll be inside."

Once we're out of the car I follow him through yard, though once you see the way it's relatively easy to avoid the fence. We duck under a bent portion and make our way to the wooden porch, which is crumbling from age and rot. Liam walks over to what was once a bay window, peering inside. He hesitates, then motions for me to follow as he ascends along the side of the porch where it hasn't completely fallen apart. The door to the house is already partially ajar and he steps inside, slowly.

I follow behind, my adrenaline kicking up. I can't help but want to draw my weapon, but I know in a place like this, it could only add to chaos. So I have to keep my cool. Liam leads me through the front hallway. Off to the left is a great room, in which four or five people are splayed out over dirty blankets and pillows. Each of them is either asleep or on the verge, their eyes and minds blank.

"Jody?" I ask, but none of the women look up. "Jo-Ann?" Still nothing.

Liam is further down the hallway, staying quiet, not moving very fast and he makes the same inquiry on another room before turning back to me and shaking his head. We have no choice but to go upstairs.

The stairs themselves look like they might collapse at any moment, so I hold Liam back. Instead, I begin going up, carefully. He's probably got fifty pounds or more on me, and I don't want these things to fall with him on them.

When I make it to the top I signal for him to stay down there. He nods and moves off, checking some of the other rooms. I notice it's a hair warmer up here than downstairs. There are three bedrooms, each with various bodies in them. The first is a group of all men. I take notice of the discarded needles in a small dish beside the dirty mattress. One of them rolls errantly on the floor.

The next room is empty except for one older woman who looks like she's in her fifties but is probably late thirties. "Jo-Ann?" I ask. Her eyes lift up to me and I see they're green, but then she drops her head again. Possible.

When I reach the last bedroom, there's two couples, all on the younger side. None of them are probably any older than me and my heart breaks for them. To get caught up in this so young…

"Jo-Ann?" I ask.

A blonde girl raises her head, her eyes glassy. She looks like she's not long out of high school, though in the dim light I make out strands of pink and purple in her hair. "Wha?"

"Are you Jo-Ann Langley?"

"Who's asking?" one of the boys asks, also sitting up. He's got tattoos on his cheeks and below his lower lip and his hair is darker than mine. But I can already see the distrust in his eyes. All he has on is a leather jacket over his naked torso, and he's skinny as a rail. He probably weighs less than I do.

"I just need to ask her a few questions," I say.

"Cops!" the boy yells out and all of a sudden it's like someone has turned on a switch. I see that same look that I saw from the old man at Caleb's mission this morning, those distrusting eyes, looking for any reason to fight. "Cops!" he yells again and the whole house begins to rumble. I look out into the hallway to see the men from the other bedroom scrambling down the sagging stairs as fast as they can manage, each of them holding what little they can carry.

"Just calm down," I say with my hands out. All four of them are up now, though Jo-Ann—Jody—has backed up into the corner. The other boy is larger than the first, and he looks like he knows how to handle himself. The other girl that was with them has a mean look across her face and I notice a knife in her hand.

"Gimme that," the skinny boy says, yanking the knife from the second girl. She seems unperturbed as he brandishes it at me.

Shit. I pull my weapon, but keep it pointed at the ground. "Look, I'm not here for you," I say. "I don't care what you're into or what you're doing. I just need to ask Jody some questions and then I'm gone. Like I was never here." Below I can hear scrambling and yelling as people struggle to find a way out of the house. I hope Liam is doing okay on his own.

"Nah," the kid says, showing his rotting teeth. "Cops always lie." He holds the knife out in front of him sideways, like he's going to flick it at me. I guess I should be grateful he doesn't have a gun.

"She's gonna shoot your balls off, Nathan!" The other boy yells in a high-pitched squeal. It's all the skinny kid needs to ignite his courage. He's completely off balance as he attempts to charge at me with the knife, only to end up falling flat on his face before he can get two steps, the knife scattering across the wooden floor. I holster my gun again and plow my knee into his back to hold him in place. The drugs have made him groggy; he's got the strength of a kitten, but it doesn't stop him from whimpering as he attempts to free himself from my hold. But I don't take my eyes off the other three.

"Now, I need to speak to Jody," I say, pinning Nathan to the ground with my knee.

The other boy looks at me with disbelief for a moment before charging me himself. Inwardly, I sigh. This is not how I wanted this to go. I'm forced to get off Nathan and put my hands up as he comes at me with a flurry of punches, his timing and attacks uncoordinated and slowed by the heroin. I manage to keep him off balance, and sweep his leg out from under him, sending him crashing to the floor on his back. He hits the back of his head then immediately rolls over and retches all over the hallway.

I see a fist coming at me in my peripheral and manage to dodge quickly, grabbing Nathan's arm and twisting it back around him so I've got him in the same hold again. I apply a small amount of pressure and he goes down to his knees, crying out. I pull a zip tie from my coat and slip it around one arm, before wrestling the second down behind him and zipping it down. I then push him over close to his friend, both of them splayed out.

"Is there going to be any more trouble?" I ask the two girls. The meaner-looking one, peers around me, then makes a dash past me and down the hall. I hear her footsteps hit the stairs until I don't hear her anymore.

I look at the scared, trembling girl before me and kneel down. "How old are you?" I ask.

"Twenty-two," she replies. The drugs have already begun to prematurely age her.

"Four years out of high school," I say.

She glances around, maybe hoping for some more help from somewhere else, but we're all alone in here. "I'm not going to jail."

I shake my head. "No, you're not. That wouldn't help anyone, would it?" I check for any obvious wounds, but to me she seems relatively healthy. "How long?"

She shrugs. I'll take that to mean a while, at least.

"I hear sometimes you like to stay over at Motel Five," I say.

She scoffs. "No, I don't."

"Your name is in the book."

"So? Someone could've forged it."

"Someone forged your pretend name?"

"It's not pretend!" she yells, startling me. She takes a second to get herself under control. "It was the name my dad called me, before he left."

I smile. "I used to have a secret code with my dad too. We'd use it whenever we didn't want my mom to know what we were talking about. Plan surprises for her, or just to talk."

"Yeah? We used mine so that my mother wouldn't blow up and throw bottles at us." I can see the energy coursing through her. The adrenaline is burning off her high, which is good for me.

"Sounds like you've had it pretty hard."

She crosses her arms, just looking at me. Not responding, but she's stopped shaking.

"I know you go to the Motel Five regularly," I say. "Once every…five months or so?"

She looks away, out the dirty window to sun that has already begun to make its march toward the horizon. "What's with the schedule?"

"It's when my boyfriend comes into town," she says. "He's a trucker. Gets one night every few months off, when he's close. He's gonna get me out of this shithole."

"I thought I was your boyfriend," Nathan calls from the hallway. It's a pitiful sound.

I nod. "Sounds like a plan. The last time you were there, it was back in January, yeah?"

She shrugs again.

"Do you remember if anyone was staying in the room next to yours?"

"I dunno, maybe," she replies.

"This is very important, Jo-Ann," I say. My legs burn from hunching down for so long, but I'm not about to move and spook her now. "I need to know if you had someone staying in the room next to yours."

"Yeah, we did, okay?" she yells. "Pissed me off. There's never anyone staying there. We've usually got the whole place to ourselves."

"But not that night. Did you ever see them? See what they were driving?"

She shrugs. "Some kind of fancy car, I don't know. I don't know much about cars."

My pulse picks up. "A fancy car." I pull out my phone and recall a picture of Fuller's Beamer, or at least a close enough version. "Like this one?"

"Maybe," she says.

I pull up another picture, this time of a Mercedes, like the one Wright drives. "Or this one?"

She squints. "I dunno. They both look the same to me. Could have been one of those."

"But you never saw anyone leave the room?"

She shakes her head. "We weren't there that long, get it?"

"Did you hear anything through the walls? Anyone speaking? Do you know if there was more than one person in that room?"

She kind of shrugs again. "We don't pay attention to that kind of stuff. We had our own thing goin' on if you know what I mean."

I take a deep sigh. Liam was right, I'm not going to get anything from this girl. She's got too much else going on at the moment. "Do you know Caleb, down at the missionary? He says he has a warm bed and food for you if you'd like to stop by."

"Yeah," she replies, "I might."

"It has to be better than this," I say, looking around. There's no heat or electricity in here, just a bunch of dirty mattresses, spray-painted walls with peeling wallpaper and a bunch of open or broken bottles littering the stained floor. Not the kind of place I'd ever want to wake up.

"Yeah? What do you know about it?" she asks, sullen.

Not much, I think. Having come from privilege, I can't sit here and tell this girl she has better options; I've never been where she is right now. "Just know the offer is there. He asked us to tell you personally."

She turns to the side and I stand back up.

"Em?" Liam calls from the floor below.

"Yeah," I call back pulling Nathan up by the backs of his arms. He whines and flinches. I look for the knife, and find it leaning up against one of the door frames. I fold it closed and slip it into my pocket.

"You okay?" he asks.

I pull Nathan back to me and unclip the zip ties, allowing his arms free. He holds his place for a minute before turning and backing away from me. "Yeah," I call back. I address Nathan. "Like I said, I'm not here for you. Little tip, don't go after cops with a knife. It's a good way to get shot."

"It was Skylar's anyway," he replies through tears. His half-hearted attempt to attack me technically constitutes attempted assault, but with as spaced as these guys are I was never in any real danger, and I doubt they'd remember it anyway. Taking them in would be a waste of resources and time as they'd just end up back here in a few days, no better off. I nod down to his friend who is half-conscious on the ground.

"Take care of your friend." I give him one last pointed look, then head back down the creaky stars to find Liam. When he sees the expression on my face he knows he was right, but it doesn't give him any pleasure.

We head back out into the afternoon sun together.

Chapter Twenty-Four

As we slip back into Liam's car, I can't help but reflect on Jody Taylor.

"Did she say anything useful?" he asks, starting the engine.

"Just that she remembers a fancy car there that night. Though she doesn't know what kind. She never saw him."

"Great," Liam says. "So he could still be anyone."

"She also couldn't confirm he was in there alone or not." I hit the center console, but not with very much force. "I was really hoping that would pan out for us." It takes me a second before I realize he hasn't said anything. I turn to him, only to find his eyes locked on mine. I feel that familiar surge of energy, but I don't look away. "What?"

"I'm not sure I've ever met anyone else like you before," he says.

Now I can't help but look down. "Don't say that."

"I'm not trying anything here, Emily, I swear. I just...I wanted you to know."

"I know you're not, and that almost makes it worse because I can't just dismiss it out of hand," I say. "Let's just..." I look at the clock on his dash and realize by the time we get to Wright's house it'll be dark. "Let's just find something to eat. I missed lunch again."

"What about Wright?" he asks.

"Tomorrow. I don't want to go over there at night. I want him fresh. We'll do it first thing in the morning."

"Tomorrow's Sunday. What if he's at church?"

"Then all the better. He should be a in a giving mood."

Liam chuckles. "You're the boss. Any idea of where you want to eat?"

Something in the back of my head says I should just go back to the motel and order in. I've been out with this man alone two nights now. Another part of me wants to know what nunnery I'll be going back to when I return home. I'm equally torn; unsure what's the right move. I don't want to dishonor Matt's memory any more than I already have, but at the same time there is something there with Liam. Usually I'm too busy, stupid, or arrogant to see it, but this is as clear as a sign gets. I'm not sure if I want to give it up; it isn't every day someone like this comes along in your life. For me, it's only happened once before.

"I...uh." I'm stalling, trying to buy time but for what? He chuckles again and I give him an indignant "What?" in return.

"I've just never seen you so flustered. Even just now, in there with those druggies, you were cool and collected the whole time. I could hear everything you said to those boys. But the mention of dinner throws you into chaos."

"It's not the dinner," I say, trying to broach this carefully. "It's the dinner with you."

"Is this the trust thing again?" he asks. "Because——"

I wave him off. "No, nothing like that. I'm pretty sure you're not going to rat me out to Burke again. It's just...it's only been three months since——"

"——since your husband died."

"Yeah. And I feel this...this...inexplicable pull. It's almost visceral, like someone has stuck a magnet inside my body and it's getting harder to resist. Does that make any sense?"

"I think I know what you mean," he says, though I detect a subtle shift in his voice. Is that nervousness?

"Do you? Because I'm having a hard time understanding this emotion. I was only ever with Matt, we met in college and were on and off some, but never far from each other. I don't know the rules of something like this. I don't know how it works."

"I don't know that there are rules," he replies. "You just kinda…go with it."

I sigh again. Never in my life have I felt so unsure about something. I don't know if it's the case, Liam, or the fact that my job is on the line, but it's all a little too much right now. I need to decompress. "Maybe it's better if you just drop me off. We can pick back up in the morning."

He hesitates a beat before putting the car in gear. "You got it." I wait for the inevitable backlash, the accusations I've seen in so many domestic violence cases before. Women who dared to make their own choices and their husbands couldn't deal with it. Or girls who said no on a date and the guy wouldn't take that for an answer. Not that I expect that level of a reaction from him. But I do expect annoyance, or disappointment.

But as I watch Liam drive, I don't see any of that silent judgment coloring his features. He's not whistling happy or anything, but he's also not putting off negative vibes, and I certainly don't feel anything like that coming from him. I wonder what it must be like for him, since he all but admitted to feeling it too. All of a sudden, I realize I don't even know a thing about his relationship status.

"Do you have a girlfriend?" I ask.

He arches an eyebrow. "Why? Looking for someone who knows all my dirty little secrets?"

"Just in case you get out of line," I say.

He shakes his head. "The problem with a town this small

is you either already know everything about everyone, or you're related to the people you want to date," he jokes. "There aren't many single girls my age left in town. And those that are, aren't the kind I see myself spending my free time with. So it's the single life for me."

I think back to Jody Taylor. How, despite her insistence, she'll probably never leave Stillwater. It happens to the best of us. It's expensive to move, and if you can't even take care of your basic needs, you're not going to be moving somewhere you don't know.

Some deep part of me is screaming that I shouldn't be letting something like this slip through my fingers. But I know what will happen if we go out one more time. I'm going to start losing my resolve and I can't afford to do that. Not now. I can't afford to get sidetracked when we're this close to making a break. Gerald has to be the key, I know it.

"You've got that determined look in your eye. The crusader is back," he says.

"Keep saying it." I'm trying to keep the tone light between us, but I can feel the emotional weight of our proximity.

Finally he pulls up to the motel just as the sun is dipping behind the horizon. "Get a good night's sleep," I tell him as I get out. "I want you fresh tomorrow."

"I'm supposed to be at a barbecue at eleven," he says. "Think we can make it quick?" The look on my face must be priceless, because he bursts into laughter.

"Funny," I say.

"I'll be here, bright and early, as always," he says, then gives me a loose salute.

I throw it right back to him then watch as he drives away. This is why I have such a problem with relationships. How am I supposed to focus on anything with this turmoil going on inside me?

After he's out of eyesight, I pull up the nearest take-out place to the motel and input the address before I get in my rental. I want to go over everything I have on Gerald Wright again before tomorrow. I want to be prepared for any eventuality, no matter how extreme.

And to do that, I'm going to need some Mandarin Chicken.

Chapter Twenty-Five

As we make our way to Wright's house, I reflect on our small breakthrough yesterday. Even if Wood conspired to cover up the true nature of his signature, he doesn't know how much those guys down in the analysis lab love doing their jobs. They spend *hours* toiling over the smallest details in a person's signature. And it feels good to know that I was right; no one is perfect all the time. Eventually everyone screws up, we just had to find it.

But I can't let the excitement of the case override my better judgment. I need another look at Gerald Wright. I need to look deep into his soul and see if there is anything I missed. Because I can't afford to be wrong about this case. I can't let something obvious slip through my fingers. And I'll do whatever is necessary to make sure I bring in the right person.

Liam pulls up to the curb and shuts off the car. It's midmorning, we're looking at a tasteful, white craftsman-style house, with a black roof which matches the window frames and door and it's as cold as the arctic circle out. The house is more subdued than I'd expected from Gerald Wright, given what he does. I'd half thought he'd have a massive stone mansion out in the middle of the country somewhere. But this house is set close to the street, in an older part of town where most of the other homes are of a different era. A few have been updated, like this one, but it's easy to tell this is definitely the most expensive house on the block.

As we get out of the car, I notice Wright's Mercedes in the driveway. Beyond the car, the drive heads down to a separate garage building behind the house. I can't help but wonder if Victoria's car is in there.

The front walk is lined with gorgeous landscaping; something I wouldn't have expected in Stillwater. Still, I'm not surprised to see some nicer houses here. A fair share of the residents commute into D.C. for their jobs, even though it's a haul. But the trade-off is they get to live in large houses with lots instead of tiny condos or buildings squeezed only feet from each other.

"How do you want to play this?" Liam asks as we approach the door. He showed up this morning, right on time and with coffee yet again even though I've never once asked him for it. I feel better after last night, today that pull isn't so strong. I feel more like myself again.

When we reach the door, I look up to see a camera pointing down on us from the upper corner of the porch. Not surprising in this day and age, these doorbell cams are becoming more and more commonplace.

"Straight," I say, ringing the doorbell.

A moment later a little boy runs up to the other side of the door, smiling at us through the plate-glass. He's got dirty-blonde hair like his father and gives us a small wave. I wave back, though my hands have turned clammy. I haven't been around many kids since I was suspended, and seeing him just brought the memories flooding back. And here I thought I was out of the emotional rapids.

"Hey, you okay?" Liam asks. "You look a little pale."

"Fine. Let's just get this over with."

Finally, Gerald Wright appears from the far end of the hall

and approaches, his face drawn with worry. He eases his son out of the way as he opens the door and I hear the soft beep of a security system. "Agent. Detective. Has there been a break in the case?"

"We were hoping to ask you a few more questions," I say.

I see something flicker across his features, but it's gone too fast for me to tell what it could have been. He's as guarded as I am with his emotions, that much I can tell. I know how to recognize when someone has tucked their emotions away, if only to continue operating in a semi-normal manner. If I had to think about Matt all the time, I doubt I'd get out of bed. So I can empathize with Wright. Having just found out his wife was murdered…it must be a hell of a shock.

"I don't understand. What further help could I be?" he asks.

"We just need to clear up a few details," Liam says. "But we are making progress."

He nods, opening the door further. "Come in. This is my son, Jacob."

"Pleased to meet you," the little boy says, sticking out a hand. I can't help but be impressed with his manners.

"Jacob, this is Agent Slate and this is Detective Coll." I take the boy's hand first. He's got a firm grip for a seven-year-old and gives me an exaggerated shake. Then he does the same for Liam.

"Hi," I say. In my mind's eye images from that night at the warehouse start to squeeze their way in, but I manage to push them back. I knew there would be kids here. I prepared myself for this and I can get through it.

A young girl comes screaming through the hallway, going from one side of the house to the other. "And that's Emma," Wright says. Her voice is like a siren as she tears through the back half of the house. "Sunday is our play day where we do everything we can to wear ourselves out before lunch." He turns his attention away from the kids. "Can I get you some coffee? Or tea?"

"That'd be great," I say as we follow him through the foyer and into the main living room, which is open to the kitchen in the back. I notice Jacob stays right with us, looking up at Liam as we walk.

Wright pulls a couple of cups from the cabinet and starts the coffee machine. I take note of how clean everything is, especially for a house with two kids. The living room is a mess, with toys strewn everywhere, but every other surface doesn't show a speck of dirt or grease. The counters in the kitchen are empty of clutter and everything seems to have a place.

"Wish I could keep my kitchen this clean," I say as the coffee maker bubbles.

"I'd take credit," Wright says. "But I have a cleaning service come in once a week, which is about the time it takes us to mess everything up again."

Emma goes screaming past again, completely oblivious to the two strangers in her house.

"So, how can I help?" Wright asks as the first cup fills.

I look down at the boy, who has nearly attached himself to Liam.

"Perhaps we should do this in private," I say.

"Of course. Jacob, take your sister upstairs to play for a few minutes, okay?"

"But dad, I want to hear," he says.

"I'll tell you all about it later. Now please. This is important."

Jacob grumbles something that I don't catch and as Emma makes her way around for another lap he steps in front of her, redirecting her to the stairs. She makes a screeching noise and turns, hitting the stairs with full force and climbing them like she's in a race for her life. Jacob follows directly after and a second later we hear a door close.

"They seem like good kids," Liam says.

"They're a handful," Wright says. "Now, what's all this about?" He hands me and Liam our mugs.

"Can you tell us if you and Victoria were having any marital troubles?" I ask, letting the coffee warm my hands.

Wright frowns. "No. I mean, things were stressful here. But aren't they for everyone? Two careers, two kids, very little alone time? It's hard to stay connected. But I didn't think we were in trouble. At least, not in that sense." He sighs. "Then again, what do I know? Turns out she was seeing someone else on the side and I never picked up on it."

"So you hadn't had any more arguments than usual, say over the year up until she…left?" Liam asks.

He shakes his head slowly, as if he's trying to remember. "Not that I recall. Why?"

I shoot Liam a glance. "We've been hearing that she was complaining about the state of her marriage. That she wasn't happy."

Wright scoffs. "Clearly." He leans back on the counter and stares at the ground. "You know, it's hard. Part of me is furious with her for going behind my back…for doing this to us. And at the same time, I miss her. Knowing she'll never come home again…it's…it hasn't been easy."

"You feel like things will never be quite right again," I say, not really meaning to. But somehow it just slips out.

Wright looks up. "Yes, that's it exactly." He crosses his arms. "Maybe it was my fault. Maybe I just hadn't been as attentive lately. My work…it takes a lot of my time and concentration." He hesitates. "We hadn't had sex in over a year."

I take note of his body posture. He's back to being defensive, like it hurts him to tell us this.

"Was that a conscious decision?" I ask.

"No. I didn't even realize it until after our anniversary passed. But I guess I was just oblivious to what was really going on behind my back. She wasn't missing it because she had someone else."

I furrow my brow. "Mr. Wright, how much do you know about your wife's relationship with Patrick Wood?"

He shifts his gaze, uncrossing his arms. "I know I'd like to kick the shit out of him," he says. "Strangle him with my bare hands. He's the one who did this, you know."

"Have you had any contact with Mr. Wood?" Liam asks.

He shakes his head. "No. Just what they showed me the first time from her computer. All the records of messages, emails. Phone calls." He stares off into the distance. "I don't know how I could have been so blind."

I shoot Liam a look. *We see what we want to see.*

"And you were here the entire weekend beginning January seventeenth of this year?" I ask.

His brow forms a "v". "Yes, of course I was. I already provided that information," he says, raising his voice. "Am *I* a suspect here?"

"We're just verifying our information," I say, though the change in his demeanor is notable. Sometimes when people face a soft accusation like that they become more compliant. Other times, they push back, mortified to find out they're under consideration. Wright's reaction isn't extraordinary, but it is worth examining. "Do you have cameras on all your outside doors?"

"Yes, front, back, one side and garage," he says.

"And do you still have the footage from that night?"

He shakes his head. "They only record when they pick up something on the motion detector. If I get a notification at night, it's usually it's nothing more than a stray cat walking through our yard. But unless I see something weird, I delete them the next day."

There goes that possibility.

"You said you were with your children, correct?" Liam asks.

"Right," he says, the word clipped.

"Would you mind if we spoke to them a moment, please?" I ask. "With you in their presence, of course."

"Is that really necessary? I still haven't broken the news to them; I don't know how. They still think she's off on an adventure across the ocean."

"We won't mention anything about your wife," I say.

He scoffs. "You just want to make sure I was where I say I was." He shakes his head like he can't believe he has to put up with this and rounds the kitchen island, heading for the stairs. "Kids, come down here please."

A moment later Jacob comes down the steps with Emma bounding shortly after. She's got a stuffed frog in one hand and a stuffed bear in the other. "Can we listen now?" Jacob asks.

Emma seems to register us for the first time and pulls back behind her brother.

Liam gets down on one knee and peeks around the boy to her. "Hi," he says. "I'm Liam. And that there," he points to me, "is Emily."

Her eyes widen. "That's like Emma," she says.

"Yep, exactly."

I can't even begin to express my gratitude to Liam for taking point on this. If I had to get down there with those kids I'd be a bubbling, shaking mess. I'm doing good to hold it together as it is.

"Do you remember the very first weekend your mommy was gone on vacation?" Liam asks.

"Yeah," Jacob says. "That's the weekend dad got us a new Playstation."

"Wow," Liam says, "That's a great present."

"Yeah," he continues. "We spent the whole weekend playing."

"No we didn't, Jacob, you lie," Emma says smacking him with her bear. Suddenly my heart is in my throat, and I have suppress the urge to spin around and stare at Wright, looking for a tell. "We went to the park too," the little girl adds.

"Oh yeah," Jacob says. "I forgot."

"Did you guys do anything else fun that weekend?" Liam asks.

"We had pizza!" Emma says.

"Yum. Okay, this is very important. Were you with your dad all weekend? Did he ever leave and get you a sitter?"

Jacob shakes his head.

"What about when you went to bed? Is it possible he could have left then?" Liam asks.

"This is ridiculous," Wright says, clearly frustrated. "He's answered the question." His entire posture has changed. Whereas before he was more complacent, now he looks as though he's gearing up for a boxing match. I can't tell if it's because he's hiding something or if he really is just frustrated with us needing to question his kids.

"Mr. Wright, please. He's almost done," I say. Wright makes a motion to continue.

"What do you think Jacob? Is it possible your dad left after you went to bed?" Liam asks.

The boy shakes his head *no* emphatically.

"Why not?"

"Cause of the house shield."

I look over to Wright. "The security system," he says.

"Yeah, it always makes a noise whenever anyone opens one of the doors in the house," Jacob says. "And it always wakes me up."

I look at Wright. "I've called them to come fix it but they tell me they can't turn off the door chime without getting us a brand-new system. I know they're just trying to bill me for something I don't need."

"Awesome," Liam says, holding out his fist for Jacob to bump, which he does with gusto. "Thank you both very much."

"Do you want to pet my frog?" Emma asks, holding out the stuffed frog.

"I'd love to," Liam says.

"Is that it? Are we done now? Can you please get back to work finding—" Wright cuts his sentence short, looking at his kids. "—at doing your job?"

I nod. "Thanks for your time," I say. I turn to the kids and give them a little wave. Suddenly Emma comes running up and hugs my leg. It nearly startles me so much I fall over.

"Whoa there, Em," Liam says, taking hold of my arm to keep me upright.

"Emma, please let go of Agent Slate's leg," Wright says. "It's not polite to grab people without their permission."

The little girl backs away. "Sorry," she says.

"It's all right." I push past Liam for the door. "We'll be in touch, Mr. Wright. Have a good day."

I'm outside in the cool air before the hyperventilating starts. Thankfully I manage to keep from doubling over. Liam comes up beside me. "Hey, what's going on? Are you okay?"

"Fine," I say. "Just needed some air." Though I'm taking big, heaping gulps. I head back to the car. "C'mon. We need to go."

Chapter Twenty-Six

"SO DO YOU WANT—"

"No," I say, interrupting him. I focus on the scenery going by as he drives.

"Okay, I'll take a guess. You were an only child growing up so you never really learned how to interact with other kids. You were shunned from the playground as a pariah, content to live out your days—"

"Liam, stop," I say, heat in my voice.

He pauses. "Okay. I'm sorry. I didn't realize it was a sensitive spot for you." I don't say anything. "But at the same time, you might have given me some warning too, especially when you knew there would be two of them in there."

"I handled it," I reply.

"Not without freaking out Wright. I'm not entirely sure we can eliminate him from the suspect pool. I don't want to spook him."

"Fine, I'm sorry, okay?" I shout, not meaning to. I pull it back, tuck it under a neat little box in my brain, and draw a deep breath. "I had a case with kids go bad. I'm...dealing with it."

"Was that the case that got you suspended?" he asks.

I nod.

"That's rough. I'm sorry. I just wish I'd had a heads up."

I rub my temples. A headache is coming on, but the breathing helps. "I should have told you sooner. After all, you are doing this on your second day off in a row."

"Damn straight," he says. "Which reminds me, I need to go pick up my dry cleaning. You don't mind, right?"

I arch an eyebrow at him.

"I'm just kidding. Obviously, I don't even get my clothes dry-cleaned." He opens up one side of his jacket to reveal his button-down. "See? It's a wrinkle-free shirt. Isn't that great?"

I can't help but notice how the shirt form fits him well. Even back at the house when he grabbed me, I still felt that electricity surge through me. It was probably the only thing that kept me from completely losing my grip.

"Thank you," I say, "for taking the lead with the kids back there."

"It was no problem," he says. "I have three older brothers. I had to do a lot of conniving growing up." He pauses. "What was your read on Wright this time?"

"He's hiding something," I say without even thinking about it.

"What gives you that impression?"

I shake my head. "I don't know. He's doing all the right things. Saying all the right things. But there's just something I don't like about it."

"Would that be the infamous 'gut instinct' of the FBI kicking in? Giving you *sight beyond sight*?"

I glare at him. "What does that even mean?"

"I dunno. I heard it in a cartoon as a kid," he replies. "I didn't feel like anything was off, but his alibi is a problem."

"You mean he could have coached them?" I ask.

"Sure. Or he could be lying about the security system."

"I didn't think to get his signature," I say. "I meant to, while you were talking to the kids, but I was just…frozen."

"That's okay," he says. "I'm sure there are more than enough examples where we can find his signature on public documents. Especially if they concern land deals."

I tap my finger on my lips, thinking. "I wonder if the data from those security cameras is backed up anywhere?"

"Like in a home server?" Liam asks.

"Like to an offsite location. I know he said he doesn't keep the videos for more than a day or so, but I wonder if the company who runs those things keeps a backup of everything in their files?"

"Wouldn't that be illegal without his knowledge?" Liam asks.

"All it would take is a paragraph or two buried deep within the contract when he signed," I reply. "I'll contact the camera company, see if they have any of it backed up. At least then we could verify his alibi without the need of a seven-year-old's word."

I pull out my phone and see I missed a call from Zara. She must have called while we were in with Wright and I just didn't notice. She left a message and I tap it, listening to the entire message.

Liam glances over when I put the phone down. "What is it?" he asks.

I pull up the message again to let him hear it.

Hey Em, it's me. I finished going over all that footage. I know what you're thinking, it's impossible, right? Well, no, because not only do I have multiple screens, I wrote a quick script to locate anyone who had a similar build and complexion to Victoria Wright. And after going through all the candidates, I got nothing.

Timber says hi, by the way. He's being a very good boy.

As best I can tell from the footage I did see, they were originally scheduled to get on the plane bound for Venice, but they never arrived.

Instead—and after cross-checking with the airline to confirm this was true —it seems their seats were given away to standby passengers. So when they said it was a full flight, that was the truth.

What's really strange though, is when I called the airline to confirm, I spoke with a woman who said they'd talked to the police regarding this matter. She said they'd told him the same thing; that Wood and Wright had never showed up for the flight and she couldn't understand why I was looking for the same information. Said the guy's name was Burke.

Anyway, hope that helps! Call me if you need anything else! Bye-eee!

I save the message and put the phone away. Even after hearing it twice it's taking me a minute to process. This proves that Burke intentionally covered this investigation up. Which officially makes him a suspect.

"We need to look into Burke," I say.

"You'll never find anything," Liam says. His knuckles have gone white gripping the steering wheel, and we've picked up speed.

"Liam," I say. "Calm down. Nothing good will come from getting in a wreck." He slows but doesn't take his eyes off the road.

"All this time, I can't believe he knew. You were right. Ever since the beginning you were right," he says.

"The question is why? Why put himself at risk like that?"

"It's not really a risk if the case was closed," Liam says. "He probably figured he was in the clear, and that Victoria was long gone."

"Or he knew she wouldn't be coming back and there would never be a reason to reopen a missing person's case because it had been 'solved'," I say, thinking. "Plus, hasn't Burke lived here his entire life? Doesn't he know the area well?"

Liam grits his teeth. "Yeah. He does."

"Then I think it's time we had a talk with Stillwater's police chief," I say.

"He won't take it lying down. He's going to fight us the whole way."

I stare out the window as Liam takes a turn that will lead us back to the center of town. "I don't care what he does; he doesn't have a leg to stand on anymore."

Chapter Twenty-Seven

WE STORM BACK INTO THE STILLWATER POLICE STATION. Since it's the weekend, Trisha isn't behind the main desk. But the officer who is sees Liam and buzzes us through without a question. I told Liam I'd handle this since he was technically off the case already, but he insisted on coming along.

We bypass all the other offices, with a few officers looking up as we head to the end of the building where Chief Burke's office is situated. I don't even bother knocking before going in, I just open the door to find him sitting behind his desk, going over paperwork.

"Well, well, Agent Slate. Catch your killer yet?" His voice is full of derision until he looks up and sees Liam. "Coll? What are you doing here?"

"Chief Burke," I say, stepping between him and Liam, though it does little good considering Liam has about three inches on me. "You have knowingly and intentionally obstructed justice. I want to know why I shouldn't arrest you right here."

His face breaks into a grin and he has to stop himself from laughing out loud. "You feds are all the same. Think you can come around wherever you want, flashing your big badges and everyone is going to kneel to your authority. I'll not have an agent who has been on the job less time than I've had heartburn to storm into my office and accuse me of breaking the law!" He reaches over for the phone on his desk. "I'm calling your supervisor. Pack your bags, Ms. Slate."

"It's Agent," I say, staring him down. "And before you make that call, you might want to figure out how you're going to explain to my boss that you closed the Wright case when you were fully aware she wasn't out of the country. Something you neglected to mention when I took the case."

His hand stops before it reaches the phone. "What are you talking about?"

"I'm talking about the fact that you spoke to the airline Victoria Wright was supposed to be on and they told you the same thing they told us: she and Wood never showed up, so they gave their seats to standby passengers. A detail that was curiously missing from the case file."

"So?" Burke asks. "It was clear she was with this Wood guy whether they flew overseas or not. It was an open and shut."

"The body in the morgue says otherwise," Liam says.

"Well guess what, I didn't have a body. I had nothing, except a bunch of messages and emails between the two lovers. Can't you see what happened here? Bored wife finds some excitement online, decides to leave her husband. It's not that complicated."

"Except," I say. "Had you done some *actual* police work, you would have figured out Patrick Wood is an alias. A ghost. Up until eight years ago, he never even existed. And the minute he was supposed to get on that plane, he vanished, just like Victoria. Now does that sound like a closed case to you?"

His face has gone beet red. It's obvious Burke isn't used to having people challenge his authority. Having been the chief in this area for so long has gone to his head. "Do you see this, Slate?" he says, pointing to a stack of folders on the side of his desk. "These are real cases. Domestic abuse charges, theft, burglary, property damage, arson. All real problems that real people in this community have. And we're getting more every day. I don't have the time to—"

"What? Do your duty?" I ask, pushing him even harder. "Curious that when an actual murder happens in your town you seem content to just let it disappear, just like the case you closed. Makes me wonder what you have to hide."

"That is enough," Burke says, standing, attempting to use his size to intimidate me. "This is my precinct, my town. And you will not come in here and tell me how to run it."

"You're not fit to run it," Liam says. "If you're willing to let things like this slide."

"That's enough, detective," Burke says. "I've already pulled you off this case. Do you want a suspension as well?"

I glance behind me and see we're drawing a crowd. Faces are peeking down the hallway since we left Burke's door open.

"I used to look up to you," Liam says. "I always heard good things about you growing up. But you've compromised the integrity of your badge and you have failed the victim of a murder."

"That's it," Burke says. "You're on suspension. Without pay. Hand in your badge and your weapon."

"Chief," I say, trying to stave off Liam's consequences. "Are you seriously going to make me call in backup? You have knowingly obstructed this case."

"You know what, Slate? You do what you have to. I obstructed nothing. What I did, was make a judgment call based on the available evidence. Maybe it didn't turn out to be right. And it wasn't as if Victoria Wright had any relatives hounding me to solve the crime anyway. We all made the same assumption. So before you come in here all high and mighty, think about what you're really doing to your career if you decide to try and prosecute me."

I glare at him, not willing to give him the pleasure of me

breaking eye contact first. But he has a point. It's shaky, at
best. Given the right circumstances, one could make a reason-
able assumption Victoria ran off with Wood, which is probably what happened. Then, somewhere along the line, things
went bad. But proving that Burke knowingly obstructed this
case would be close to impossible. Not without more evidence.

Finally, he turns his gaze from me to Liam. "Badge.
Weapon. Right now."

Liam sneers, placing them both on Burke's desk. "Dunwaite!" he bellows. Another patrol officer comes in from close
by, looking at both of us. "Escort Coll off the property. He's
not to be given access to this station until his suspension
hearing."

"Yes, sir," Dunwaite says.

"And make sure Agent Slate knows the way out as well,"
he adds.

"You can't forcibly remove me from this station," I growl
at him. "You don't have authority over the FBI."

Burke sits back down, folds his hands together and glances
up at his patrol officer. "Dunwaite, do you work for the FBI?"

"No, sir," Dunwaite says.

"That's what I thought. See, Agent Slate, this is my town
and it's my rules. Now if you want to come back here with a
platoon of FBI agents and raid a little police station in the
middle of nowhere, you can be my guest. But my bet is your
boss won't think it's worth the trouble." He nods to Dunwaite.
"Get her out of here."

My hand goes to my weapon as Dunwaite reaches for me.
There's a tense moment when he freezes, unsure if I'm going
to pull it on him or not.

"Don't do anything stupid, Agent," Burke says. "You can
still walk away from this." I hate that he's right. Escalating a
conflict now would only get people hurt or killed, and spark an
incident the FBI can't afford, not right now. Not to mention
my career would be over for pulling a weapon on a local offi-

cer. I have to find some other way to nail Burke, as it seems his cronies will do whatever he tells them to.

I hold my hand out, showing I'm not going for the weapon. But before Dunwaite can reach me, I turn and leave the same way we came. As Dunwaite escorts us out, I notice almost everyone in the station is looking at us, including the criminals that are undergoing processing. It's like someone had sucked all the sound out of the room and the only thing I can hear are my boots against the linoleum.

When we're back outside, Dunwaite stays at the door while we head out to the parking lot. Liam turns, addressing the man. "Micah. You can't think this is right."

"Right or not, I got a family to feed. I can't afford to go on suspension," Dunwaite says. "Some of us got responsibilities."

"Even if he's using the office to his advantage," Liam says.

Dunwaite shrugs. "Maybe they'll appoint someone else. But I doubt it. You know how things are here. Nothin' ever changes. Sorry you got caught up in it." He turns and heads back inside.

"Yeah," Liam says after him.

I place a hand on his shoulder. "You didn't have to do that. He can hurt you a lot more than he can hurt me."

"I think I kinda did," he says. "This wasn't why I became a cop. To play all these power games. I just wanted to help people. But not if it means covering up the truth."

"Don't worry," I say, heading back to the car. "He won't get away with it. When I get back to D.C. I'll talk to the Attorney General's office. Let them know there's a seed of corruption in the town of Stillwater. They'll look into it."

"And if Burke has everyone under his thumb?" Liam asks.

I try not to think about it. But just like this case, it all comes down to the little details. What did Burke forget about, and what did he miss? "We'll find a way," I say. "We'll have to."

Chapter Twenty-Eight

My first thought after being summarily dismissed from the Stillwater Police Station was to call Janice and inform her of what's going on down here. The only problem with that is it flies directly into conflict with what she told me to do. And it doesn't deal with the real problem of finding Victoria Wright's killer. Whether Burke goes down or not makes no difference to this case, unless he was somehow involved in something other than obstruction. Given how cavalier he's being about it, I feel like something else *is* going on, but I have no evidence for it.

Not to mention calling her would only reinforce that I can't handle the assignment out here and I'm letting the local cops walk all over me. Neither of which would be conducive to getting back into the Bureau's good graces. I need to put Burke aside for the moment and focus on the case.

Which means we're right back at square one: finding Patrick Wood.

Except how do you find someone who created a fake persona and lived as that person for eight years? It could be anyone.

We have no solid evidence pointing to any one suspect and

I'm starting to give up hope. Our one lead is the signature from the housing document, but it could take the analysis lab weeks to come up with something. And even then it won't be much more than an educated guess. But still, it's better than nothing. I pull out my phone and give Zara a call.

"Hey! Did you get my message?"

"Yeah, I did." I shoot a glance at Liam. "It was a big help. I need you to do something else for me."

"Anything."

"I'm sending over an image of Patrick Wood's signature from the sale of his property. And I'm going to email you a couple of other signatures as well. I need you to get them down to the analysis lab and have the techs start doing some comparisons."

"Sure," Zara says. "Though there might be a backlog; I heard Simmons talking about some big fraud case down in Florida that just come through. If they've got priority on that—"

I lean my head back against the headrest. "—then it might take a while." I shake my head. "I'm sending them over anyway. If there's anything you can do…"

"Sure thing. Are you getting enough to eat out there?" she asks.

Inwardly I wince because I know I'm probably not. Whenever I get hooked on a case like this everything else, including food, tends to go out the window if I don't actively think about it. "I'm working on it."

"Okay," she says. I know she's just worried, but it grates on me some. This is why I don't like getting close to people. Because then they get involved in my life and all of a sudden I start to feel like I have to answer to them. A silence hangs between us for a moment. "Send those over whenever you're ready. I'll run them downstairs."

"Thanks, Zara. Talk to you later." I hang up and begin

scrolling through my phone, and send the image of Patrick Wood's last page of his property sale. I'll get the others to her when we get back.

"Everything okay?" Liam asks.

"Fine," I say, hearing the lie in my own voice.

At least I'm not alone here. We head back to my motel so we can pull those other signatures and to go back over what little evidence we still have. Given what just happened at the police station, any remaining suspicions I had about Liam have evaporated. I think I finally see the real person underneath that Burke had tried to bury with all his talk about *unified fronts* and *the chain of command*. Despite the fact that those are important parts of police work, they aren't the end all and be all of the job. Liam was the only one at the station to stand up to Burke's bullying, and it may have cost him his job. But here he is, still working the case with me, even though he technically isn't even a detective anymore.

Once we're back in the room, I flop back on the bed, trying to work the case over in my mind. So far it feels like we've been spinning our wheels. We can't eliminate anyone, and we can't charge anyone. It's like nothing we've done has made a difference, and it's driving me insane. I let out a frustrated breath.

"Sounds like a train engine over there with all that huffing," Liam says, tapping away on his phone.

"Yeah, a train that's been on the wrong track this entire time," I say.

"Let's wait and see what comes back on the signature," he replies, putting the phone to his ear. "Hey Jill, yeah…no, yeah I know. It's…look I need a favor." I listen to him go back and forth with this Jill, who I never had the pleasure of meeting. But it's easy to tell they're good friends, though right now it sounds like that friendship is strained. Probably because Burke is putting pressure on anyone in the station to sever all ties with Liam.

"I get that, I do," he says. "I just need one document. From Fuller's arraignment." He pauses. "He did. Okay. Can you get me his signature? No, a photo will be fine," he says, looking to me for confirmation. I nod in approval. "Great, thank you. I know. I owe you the biggest stack of cupcakes when I get back." He ends the call.

"That sounded strained," I say.

"No, everything's fine," he replies, parroting my own word back to me from my conversation with Zara. He slips his phone back into his pocket. "Actually, that's not true. Fuller made bail this morning, and apparently, he's gunning for us. Coming after us with a wrongful arrest suit."

"Lawyers," I say. "I guess he figures once he loses his license, he'll have no reason not to do everything he can to punish the ones he feels are responsible. But it doesn't matter. Now that the charges are out in the open, he's ruined."

"If he did kill Victoria Wright, then we might want to be cautious," Liam says. "Especially you, since the killer seems to have something for women."

"If he wants to come after me, he's more than welcome," I say. My phone buzzes with the image of Fuller's signature. "Thanks," I say, holding the phone up. I forward it on to Zara.

"You got it. At least it's better than nothing, right?"

"Barely. Who knows how long that will take and even if it will result in anything? He could have signed those documents with his non-dominant hand for all we know, making identification nearly impossible. In fact, given what we know about this guy, I think that's a certainty."

Liam looks up. "So you do think it's a guy."

"I'm almost certain he is," I say. "Medium build, early thirties to late forties, probably white. Clever, more than likely college educated or above. Someone who has patience but is also driven. A pure and utter narcissist, someone who is so good at lying that they wouldn't have a problem passing a polygraph. He's devious…a tormentor, this guy. He likes to get close to his victims. And they never see it coming."

The room is silent for a moment. I usually don't lay out my profiles like that; they're something I keep close to the chest. But Liam has shown himself to be more than trustworthy.

"Wow," he says. "That's…specific."

I sit up. "That's what we do."

"Anything else?" He asks. "Maybe a full description of the guy, name and social?"

I laugh. "I wish that was how it worked. But this is just going off the data we have. Maybe if we had—" I pause, realizing I've missed something.

"What?"

I pull out my phone, going back over my messages from Zara. "More data," I say. I scroll back through my emails until I find what I'm looking for. "Hand me my laptop."

Liam grabs it off the chair and hands it over. On it, I pull up the encrypted files Zara sent over on the second victim: Laura Allen. Or maybe I should call her the first victim. "This other woman," I say, "that was found in a similar condition, we need to talk to the people who worked her case."

"What do you mean? That was in a different state," he says. "We don't have—"

"—jurisdiction?" I ask and he smacks his head.

"Right. Too many years thinking as a local. But if they never had an ID on the killer and he changed his identity anyway, what good will it do?"

"It gives us more data points," I say. "And it allows us to flesh out his profile. Maybe there's a commonality between the two cases we haven't seen because all we're seeing is the bare bones information. They didn't know they were working with a serial; it even says here they're not sure if she died from natural causes or not." I scroll through the information. "We need to go to Soft Bend."

"Maryland?" he asks. "That's at least an hour-and-a-half drive from here."

"Yeah," I reply, "it is. So make sure you pee before we go."

Chapter Twenty-Nine

EVEN THOUGH HE OFFERED, I INSISTED ON DRIVING OUT TO Soft Bend. It isn't often I get to drive out of the city so it's a nice change of pace for me, and to be honest, it makes me feel more in control, even though logically I know that's an illusion. I could have a wreck just as easily as Liam or anyone else, but there's a certain serenity that comes over me when I get behind the wheel. And after re-reading the case notes on Laura Allan, I'm feeling more invigorated.

I think because I was so intent on identifying Victoria, Laura's case fell to the back of my mind. But I should have seen it before: a similar case, similar M.O....if it is our killer, maybe he made a mistake with Laura—something the Soft Bend police didn't know to look for. Something that taught him how to dispose of Victoria in a way that we'd never be able to find his identity. Maybe Laura was the "test" case. Regardless, it opens up a whole new host of possibilities for us.

"And you accuse me of driving fast," Liam says, grabbing on to the "oh shit" handle above his window as I bank a sharp turn on the country road.

"This car has a low center of gravity," I say. "It can handle it."

"Do you really think there will be anything useful there?" he asks. "It was six years ago."

"You'd be surprised what people remember, even after six years," I say, banking another turn. The route from Stillwater to Soft Bend takes us through West Virginia and then into Maryland's upper arm, nestled deep into the Appalachian Mountains. There are no interstates up here and people play fast and loose with the speed limits.

We crest a hill and the town of Soft Bend comes into view in the valley below. It's probably half the size of Stillwater and looks like a railroad town from what I can see of the multiple lines running through its center. The valley is surrounded by thick woods and rolling hills. Easy for someone to disappear up here, stay out of the limelight.

"Should we have let them know we were coming first?" Liam asks.

I shake my head as the road takes us down the switchbacks into the valley. "I didn't want to spook them or give them a heads up. Better to not give them a chance to hide anything."

"Why would they hide anything?" Liam asks.

"I don't know. Why did Burke try to cover up Victoria's case?"

"Good point," he says, glancing at his phone. "I have service again."

"Good," I say. "I was afraid we'd have to rely on landlines out here."

We pass by a lot of old homes, houses that look like they've been there for a hundred years or more, and a large factory off to the east that looks closed and abandoned. But as we get closer to the center of town, I can tell a lot of effort has been put into revitalizing the community. Lots of green spaces, newer buildings, apartments even. It's something you don't normally see in smaller towns like this one because they just don't have the jobs to support it.

Having re-acquired the signal, the GPS points us right to

the main police station near the center of town. I'm struck by just how similar this town is to Stillwater, and wonder if there's something about a town like this that is attracting our killer.

I pull up to the station, parking right on the street. There are no meters to feed and no designated parking times, so I don't bother looking for another spot. Liam and I make our way up and through the front doors of the station where a small desk sits off to the side while a partition with an open door separates out the rest of the station.

"Afternoon," the man at the desk says, looking up. He's in his late fifties, with graying hair. But he's trim and his rolled up sleeves expose arms that look like they've seen their fair share of labor over the years. "What can I do ya for?"

"I'm Agent Slate with the FBI," I say, pulling out my badge. "And this is—" I hesitate, not wanting to reveal Liam in the event word gets back to Stillwater. "—a civilian contractor we've hired to assist in a case I'm working. Liam Coll." This produces a beaming smile from Liam.

"FBI?" The man asks with an amused grin. "What on Earth could you want up here?"

"We're investigating a case," I say, "regarding the death of a young woman. We understand you had a similar unsolved case from about six years ago."

The amusement leaves his face. "Laura Allen."

I nod as he stands, putting out his hand. "Sheriff Willie Parks. Pleased to meet'cha." He shakes both our hands, then leads us through the open door to the back.

"Is it normal for the sheriff to be covering desk duty?" I ask.

He throws me an amused look over his shoulder. "It's Sunday, ma'am. Most people are out with their families, enjoyin' the day. We don't run into too many problems 'round here. Plus I got a couple deputies on call if I need 'em."

He takes us back into his office and I'm reminded of

sitting down in front of Burke. Is this going to be another fight? Does Sheriff Parks have something to hide as well?

"So. How can I help?" he asks, much to my relief. At least he's not openly hostile.

"We were hoping to talk to the officer—or deputy—who investigated the case."

He scoffs. "It was a dead girl. We *all* investigated it."

"You were here at that time?" I ask.

"Sure. I've been here since 'ninety-six. B'fore that I was sheriff over in Hardy, you know it?" I shake my head. "Well, anyway. Been here a while. Long enough to know we don't get too many murders."

I take a seat in one of the ones in front of his desk. "So then you do think it was a murder. The file was unclear on that."

"Well," he says, his accent becoming a bit more pronounced with the word. "I have to put that in the case file, 'cause we got no evidence to the contrary. But the way that girl was boxed up...wasn't no accidental death I can tell you that. And the way they fixed her eyes...I mean, someone could make an argument that it was a death ritual I'spose. Kinda like two coins for the ferryman, but I never thought so." He hesitates. "If you've already read the file, what do you need from me?"

"We need to know as much about Laura Allen as you do," Liam says. "Anything that wasn't in the file, or that you might think could help us."

He squints at us, confusion in his face. "Why?" He emphasizes the last letter.

I take a deep breath. "Because a second woman was found, in almost the exact same condition," I say. "Down in Stillwater."

"Jesus," he says, bringing a hand to his mouth. "I'd hoped it had just been a fluke thing...someone passin' through or somethin' in the heat of the moment. I'd resigned myself to believin' we'd never figure out who killed her." He gets up and heads over to a filing cabinet beside the desk, rifling through files until he pulls one with the name ALLEN across the top tab. Parks returns to the desk and opens the file. I recognize the same pages from what Zara already sent me.

"Laura was well known and well-liked by everyone 'round here," he says. "Which is why it was such a shock when she went missin'. Then her body turnin' up three years later? Her poor parents...they just couldn't take it. Her momma moved out to California and her daddy stayed around for a year or two before headin' to Florida."

"Did she have any brothers or sisters?" I ask.

"Sure. Two sisters, both livin' somewhere out west I think. They were gone by the time her body turned up. Said they didn't want anything more to do with this cursed town. Can't say I blame 'em."

I glance at Liam. Victoria didn't have any living family, which marks a departure between the two victims. Was that what Patrick learned?

"And you never came up with a suspect?" I ask.

"Nothin' concrete," he says. "Never could nail down her exact date of death, which made gatherin' suspects difficult. Best we could do was a two-month window. Can't account for everyone for a time period that long."

"We've run into something similar," I say. "But fortunately it's only been a few months. Have you ever heard the name Patrick Wood before?"

Park shakes his head. "Don't believe so. It's not ringin' a bell anyway. Is that your suspect?"

"The best one we have," Liam says.

"Got a picture? I could take a look," Park says.

"Unfortunately we don't," I reply. "Right now he's unknown to us." I rack my brain. "Is there anyone else we can talk to who knew Laura? Friends? Boyfriend? Anyone who might have some insight into her personal life?"

He nods. "She did have a boyfriend. Now we looked at him, close, the weekend she went missin'. But he was off in Boston, goin' to school out there. We had pictures and witness statements testifying he was there. He didn't know she was missin' 'till we called him in, thought she was out with friends."

I exchange another glance with Liam. Similar to Gerald Wright.

"Where's this boyfriend now?" I ask.

"Name's Brian Becker. He lives here in town. Works at the farm up on the hill." I give Park a confused look and he squints a minute then snaps his fingers. "Ya'll must have come down Route seventeen, over the mountain, comin' from Still-water. You wouldn't have seen it. Soft Bend is the hub for a new wind turbine farm, just on the other side of the ridge. Most of the people runnin' and buildin' them live here."

"That explains all your urban development," I say, though I'm really thinking more about this Brian. He might be the only lead we have on Laura.

"Yessum. It's done wonders for this town. Brought a lot of jobs back here. Brian's one of the supervisors on the project."

"Do you have his address?" Liam asks.

Park opens up his laptop and types a few things. "Sure. Right here," he turns the laptop around to show a map of the general area with a little gray dot on one house. "I can never remember the number, but I know where it is. Memory's funny like that sometimes."

I check the time. It's closing in on two p.m. But based on where the house is on the map, it shouldn't take us more than fifteen minutes to get there. "What did he have to say about it, at the time?"

"Oh, he was heartbroken," Park replies. "They'd been together for a while when she disappeared. He always thought she ran off with another guy but when we found her buried under that building...well, that was all she wrote on that."

I stand, making sure I have the address in my phone. "Thanks Sheriff. This has been a big help."

"Always happy to help," he says. "It's kinda our motto here. The energy generated by those turbines will help power half the east coast one day. And it'll all be due to Soft Bend." He smiles. "Ya'll let me know if I can do anything else."

We head back out to the car, and once again I get into the driver's seat before Liam can. "What are you thinking?" he asks.

"That Brian might know something. Might remember something," I say. "His situation is too similar to Gerald Wright's to be a coincidence." It's a long shot, I know. But at the same time, I'm hoping that the killer messed something up along the way with Laura. Brian might not have the answer; instead, he might be the key to a clue. And he'll be able to point us to her other friends, anyone else who is still in the area who might know something about what happened.

"C'mon," I say. "Let's go see what he has to say."

Chapter Thirty

WE PULL UP TO THE MODEST HOUSE ONLY ABOUT TEN MINUTES later. Despite what the map says, the traffic in Soft Bend is virtually non-existent.

Becker's house is a small one-story ranch with some plants along the front underneath a large bay window looking into the living room. As we make our way up the walk, we can hear children playing in the backyard. I motion for Liam to follow me around the side of the house where the driveway leads to a large wooden fence that seals off the backyard from the street. Embarrassed that I have to get on my tiptoes to look over it, I see a couple of kids playing on a new plastic playset shaped like a multi-story log cabin. A man and woman sit close by, the woman reading a book while the man sips from a Budweiser can. Both of them have on heavy jackets.

"Excuse me," I say, holding up my badge so they can see it over the fence. The kids pay me no attention, but the man shoots a glance at who I assume is his wife and gets out of his plastic chair, headed in our direction.

"What's this about," he asks, growing closer.

"I'm Agent Slate with the FBI, this is Liam Coll. Are you Brian Becker?"

He stops when I say who I'm with. "Yes. What's going on?" The woman gets up, wrapping her arms around herself as she approaches.

"May we have a minute of your time, sir? I need to ask you a few questions."

"About what?" he asks.

I sigh, wishing there wasn't a locked fence between us. "About Laura Allen," I say. From a distance Brian didn't look much older than forty, but as he walks toward us I can tell time has taken its toll on him. His blonde hair is beginning to thin and established wrinkles sit at the edges of his eyes. But he's not refusing.

"Why do you want to know about her?" the woman asks over Brian's shoulder.

"Mrs. Becker?" I ask and she nods. "We're here because there might have been a break in Laura's case and we're following up."

"A break?" Brian asks as he reaches the fence. "I thought…well, Sheriff Park said…"

"It was," I reply. "May we please come in? Or at least can you open the fence so we can speak?"

Brian undoes a latch on the other side, allowing a section of the fence to swing in. I nod my appreciation, as Liam and I step into his backyard.

"You're just a child," Mrs. Becker says, hugging herself even more tightly. "Is this some kind of joke?" She's looking at Liam like he's going to let her in on it.

I hold my badge out to her. "No joke, ma'am and I know I look young. But I've been with the Bureau for four years now. My specialty was infiltrating street gangs and places that needed young-looking women."

Becker's wife takes a look at the badge then purses her lips, returning to watching the children. I can't express how grateful I am they're staying over on their playset.

"Sorry about her," Becker says. "She can be...blunt. What's going on with Laura's case?"

"Mr. Becker, what can you tell us about the case that you remember?" Liam asks.

He scrunches his face up in concentration. "Laura and I had been together for a few years, but it was always off and on. But I knew she loved me. When I left for college, we decided to try and make it work. She couldn't afford to go but wanted to move in with me when I was done with school, wherever I ended up. Kinda funny that I ended up back here."

I nod, trying to encourage him to continue.

"I didn't even know she was missing. They called me at school, said they needed me to come down and provide a statement. By then it had already been two or three days. I think they were just looking for anyone who might have had something to do with her."

"Did anything about the case stand out to you?" I ask. "When she disappeared?"

He shakes his head. "Back then things between us hadn't been great. I mean, they weren't terrible either, but it's hard when you're six hundred miles away. I knew it wasn't fair to ask her to wait on me. I just figured she'd gotten tired of me and run off with someone else. I mean, everybody liked Laura, so the fact that some guy could have convinced her to go cross-country with him wasn't out of the realm of possibility."

"Until the body showed up," I say.

He nods. "I was in my senior year when I got the call from Laura's mother. By then I was already dating Melanie," he motions to the woman back on the porch, watching us carefully. "I had to go back over everything with the police. Account for all my movements from the three years before and that same week she was found. But by that point I hadn't left Boston in over two years."

"What brought you back to Soft Bend?" I ask.

"Opportunity. My major was in engineering and when this turbine project came up right next to the town I grew up in, I couldn't pass it up." He turns to look at his family. "It's a great place to raise a family."

"I don't suppose you've ever been to Stillwater?" I ask.

"Over in Virginia?" he asks. "I don't think I ever have. Why?"

I shake my head. I don't get the feeling Becker had anything to do with Laura or Victoria. He doesn't strike me as the type. "You mentioned you thought she ran off with someone else. Did you have someone in mind? Maybe an old boyfriend?"

He shakes his head emphatically. "Laura only ever had one serious boyfriend before me, and she sure as hell wasn't going back to that psycho."

"What do you mean?" I ask. I notice Liam lean in.

"The guy was a real piece of work. They were together for few months when he broke up with her one day out of the blue. She couldn't understand why, and maybe got a little obsessive about trying to figure out why he didn't like her anymore. So this…guy, he shows up on her doorstep a week later with flowers and an apology, saying he made a mistake. They get back together, and things are going great between them. He's kind, attentive; the perfect boyfriend. I mean the whole nine yards, he's having dinner with her parents, they're talking about plans after high school and he showers her with gifts, dinners, everything. It's like a fairytale. Then exactly one year after they got back together, he breaks up with her again, telling her that the entire year was nothing more than an act. Just to show her he could do it. To undermine her trust in any future relationship. It completely shattered her."

"Jesus," Liam says.

My heart is racing. He fits my profile exactly. A narcissist who is only concerned with his own emotions and has no compunction about hurting others is, by the book, a psychopath. And from what we know about Victoria's experience, it fits. This guy must have taken on the persona of Patrick Wood when he came to Stillwater and lain in wait. But eight years is a lot longer than one. What could he have been doing that entire time? "This guy, did the police look into him when Laura disappeared?"

"That was just it," Becker says. "He disappeared himself a few months before she did. Completely gone, empty house, no trace of where he could have gone to. Sheriff said they never could find where he went or what happened to him. But he was what they called a person of interest."

"Damn," I say. "What was his name?"

"Joe Lewis," Becker replies and there's an undercurrent of hate there. Something beyond what he did to Laura. It's something Becker feels between him and this Lewis character; a level of disgust I'd missed before.

"You knew him, didn't you?" I ask.

"We were all in school together," Becker replies, his eyes welling up with tears. "And I never saw it. He was just like anyone else. Normal guy. Maybe if I'd realized what he was back then, I could have warned her off, stopped her from ever dating him. He just hurt her so bad…"

"…and you were there to pick up the pieces," I say, thinking. "You wouldn't happen to have a picture of Joe, would you?"

He wipes his eyes with his sleeves. "There's probably one in my old yearbook. He was a grade ahead of me."

My heart rate picks up. "Could you get that for us, please?" I ask.

He looks back at his house. "Yeah, sure. Just…uh…just give me a minute." He heads back to the deck where his wife is waiting and he speaks to her, but they're too far away for us to hear. Though from her body language I can tell she doesn't like what we're asking. A moment later he disappears in the house and Mrs. Becker stomps down the deck stairs again, heading for us.

"Ah, shit," I whisper. Liam nods.

"Just what in the hell do you think you're doing?" Melanie Becker asks. "My husband has been through enough regarding this woman. Yet every few years it seems someone else shows up to hound him about her."

"We're trying to find her killer, Mrs. Becker," I say.

"So has everyone else in this county. Don't think I don't hear about it from time to time from the local gossip vines. Not a month goes by since we've moved here that someone will mention Laura Allen and poor, poor Brian Becker and that wife of his. And how they can't believe we moved back."

"I take it you don't like Soft Bend," I say.

She narrows her eyes. "It's not my favorite place, let's just say that."

"Mommy!" one of the kids yells, sending a spike of adrenaline through me. I have to steady myself and will my body to calm down. I don't know if Mrs. Becker notices, but Liam certainly does. "Come watch!"

She waves to the little girl then turns back to us. "Please, just leave my husband alone. Allow us to move on with our lives." She turns and heads over to the playhouse.

"You okay?" Liam asks.

"I just want to get this picture and get out of here," I say, forcing my heart rate to slow.

"You think Joe Lewis really killed her?" Liam asks.

"I'm sure of it," I reply. "Think about it. Only a truly deranged person would date someone for an entire year just to hurt them for it. That's what we call the long, long game. To pretend for that long, to be that practiced and not have it wear you down so that one day you can just flip a switch...we're dealing with an emotionally vindictive person here, capable of anything. Someone who is a practiced liar. As I said."

"Found it," Brian calls out, coming back through the

sliding door. He comes down the steps toward us, his face less flushed than before. "Sorry that took a minute, it was buried under some stuff in our junk room." In his hand is a thin hardback, bound with a glossy green cover and gold highlights. He opens it up, flipping through the pages until he comes to the right one. "Yeah, here he is. Prick." He turns the book to us, and my mouth drops open when I see the picture.

"Holy shit," Liam says.

I snap a picture of the page with my phone. "We gotta get back to Stillwater. Right now."

Chapter Thirty-One

"I DON'T GET IT," LIAM SAYS AS I PRESS ON THE ACCELERATOR, squeezing around the turn. I glance over and see he's got the picture of Joe Lewis pulled up on his phone and he's comparing it to the picture of Gerald Wright in the case file. There's no mistaking it; they're the same person, about fifteen years apart in age. "What is going on here?"

"I'm not sure," I say. "All I know is that Joe Lewis's girlfriend and Gerald Wright's wife both have ended up with their eyes sewn shut, stuffed in a box. The fact they are the same person is no coincidence." I'm trying to figure out how I missed this. I went through Wright's background info; it was all there. Birthplace, schools, college, etc. There was nothing about him living in Soft Bend under a different name for eighteen years.

"But what do either of those people...or that person, I guess, have to do with Patrick Wood?"

"What if they're all the same person?" I ask, banking the next curve and sending the car lurching to the side.

"The same person?"

"Think about it," I say. "Joe Lewis grows up in Soft Bend, but he's insane, so shortly before he's ready to make his first kill, he 'disappears', making it seem like he's skipped town, when in reality he may have established a completely new identity in Stillwater, as Wright. He comes back, kills Laura, then returns to his life in Stillwater, where he spends the next decade setting himself up as a real estate mogul. He marries, has kids, and then, decides to set up *another* identity, to get rid of his current wife. He creates Patrick Wood out of thin air, then sits on him for eight years. Until one day, he's ready."

"But he didn't disappear this time," Liam says. "He's still in Stillwater, three months after Victoria died. If this was his pattern, wouldn't he have left by now?"

I shake my head. "It's different now. He's got kids. They're his legacy and he needs to protect them. He's not going to disappear and leave them all alone. Creating a new identity with kids is a lot harder than alone. Emma might not be old enough to remember everything about her old life, but Jacob is. Taking him and trying to explain to him the need to use a new name in a new place would be a big risk.

"Plus, Wright has this real estate empire now. He's not just going to walk away from millions of dollars. But what creating Patrick Wood has done was give him the ability to kill his wife without needing to make a new life for himself somewhere else. He just reversed it."

"But why go to the trouble of creating Patrick Wood at all?" Liam asks. "And why do it so long ago? Did he know what he was going to do eight years ago?"

I shoot him a glance. "Remember what Brian said. That Joe pretended to be a loving boyfriend for a full year before revealing his true self. What if this was just an extension of that? Like he knows that one day he'll get rid of her, but not until he's ready."

"That's one twisted individual," Liam says.

"That's why I need you to get on the phone, get Burke or somebody over to Wright's house. Our visit this morning probably spooked him. I don't want him running." My heart is pumping so fast I can feel it in my chest. My hands are practically shaking, but keeping a death grip on the wheel is helping. I just can't believe I didn't see it. It takes a master of deception to be able to control all the little involuntary things the human body does when it lies, and Gerald passed that test with flying colors. It was as I predicted, he would have no trouble passing a polygraph. The perfect liar.

Liam presses the phone against his ear. "Hey Jill...yeah, I know," he says. "No, I know, okay? Look, you need to get someone over to the Wright house, make sure he doesn't leave. No...just, will you please listen? I don't care if Burke fires all of us, Wright is our main suspect!"

I don't envy Liam; this won't end well for him. But if we can nail Wright on this, then all will be forgiven. The only problem is we have little more than circumstantial evidence and speculation right now. But if we can figure out how to connect Wright to Wood, then I think there's a good chance we can make it stick. The picture enough is proof Gerald Wright used to be Joe Lewis, we just need to find that connective tissue.

"Okay, yeah, thank you," Liam says, hanging up.

"Well?"

"She's going to send over the next patrol she can to keep an eye on him. But if Burke finds out, she'll likely be right where I am," he says.

"I'll be sure she gets a hearty thank you from the FBI once we nail this guy," I say.

"How are we supposed to do that?" he asks.

"I don't know. But we need to get him into an interrogation, a *real* interrogation," I say. "Somewhere I can sit face to face with him, confront him with what we know. He's never been caught before. He might break under the pressure."

"I hope you're right," Liam says, looking at his phone. "And I just lost my signal. Great."

"You'll get it back once we get over the mountain," I say,

taking another hairpin turn. I know I'm pushing the limit of what this car can do, but I want to get back to Stillwater as soon as possible. I can't believe I was staring the man in the face just this morning and I didn't see it.

Or maybe I did. I remember seeing a flash of something cross his face when we showed up and not being able to tell what it was. It was because we'd surprised him by coming back around. He hadn't expected us again. And he'd grown short with his children. I thought it was just impatience and frustration with us because he'd seemed so normal in every other respect.

It just goes to show, you never can tell.

"So are you going to tell me about it, or what?" Liam asks.

I slide my gaze over for a second. "What?"

"That's the second time in the same day you've been freaked out by a kid. If we're about to go into a potentially hostile situation, I need to know what's going on."

I huff, focusing on the road. "Can't we just let it go?"

"No. Because if you freeze up out there, you could get yourself, me or someone else killed. Tell me what's going on so we can plan for it."

I grit my teeth, trying hard not to think about that night three months ago. But I can still feel the heat of the machinery above us, the sweat dripping down my back as I ran, too hard, trying to catch him. Zara is right, I never should have been there in the first place.

"I almost shot a kid," I say, letting the words hang in the air between us. I take the next turn, allowing the silence to stretch out until the car heads up and back down a short hill which bounces us both up in our seats.

"What happened?" he asks, quietly.

"Bust gone bad," I say. "I was…too emotional. It was right after Matt…" I have to take a second and steady myself. "Anyway. I wasn't paying attention and this kid just comes out of nowhere. I actually pulled the trigger. If I'd been a better shot,

I would have hit him. I probably would have killed him." I let out a ragged breath. Only Janice and Zara know the full details of what happened that night, and if it's up to me, it's going to stay that way.

"Have you…talked to anyone about it?" he asks.

I shake my head. "I don't talk about it."

He slowly bobs his head. "And you haven't been around any kids since."

"Not until today," I say, recalling the near-disaster at Wright's house. I'm not sure I can even trust myself to apprehend him with those kids around. I feel like everything is on a hair-trigger. Like one false move and I'll do something to endanger their lives. Kids are so small, so…fragile.

I shake my head. "Can we not talk about it, please?"

"Fine," he says. "But when we get to Wright's house, I'll take the lead, just in case. The kids will probably still be in the house. Maybe if we're lucky, we can catch them unawares around dinner time."

I look at the clock on the dash. An hour and a half back to Stillwater—I can shave maybe fifteen minutes off that if I push it. But that's still going to put us there past six, after the sun has gone down. I just hope that Wright is cocky enough to think he can still get away with this. I don't want to think what could happen if he gets scared or tries to run.

"Emily?" Liam says. I can hear the worry in his voice. "Have you ever dealt with anyone like this before?"

I wish I could tell him I have. I wish I could say that I've made my career catching serial killers; that I'm an expert on knowing what they'll do next. But the honest truth is we don't deal with many cases like this. Most of my cases have involved infiltration of drug rings, kidnapping organizations, even something as banal as tax evasion. This feels like it's on another level. We're dealing with someone who has the capacity to convincingly become another person, and who can kill without remorse. Someone who lacks any kind of true empathy, but is a master of playing the role, of pretending so they'll fit in; go unnoticed. It's honestly the scariest suspect I've ever had to deal with, even more so than when I've had a gun pointed straight at me. Because even in those situations, I knew who I was dealing with.

I looked Gerald Wright dead in the eyes and saw nothing wrong. And that scares me most of all.

"No," I finally reply. "Not like this."

Chapter Thirty-Two

IT TAKES ANOTHER HOUR TO GET DOWN THE OTHER SIDE OF the mountain and back into cell range. As soon as we're out of the sticks, Liam's phone rings at the same time it buzzes intently.

"Shit," he says, looking at the screen. "I've got six messages; this is Jill now."

My stomach drops. I know that can't be good, given their last conversation. My mind is flooded with the possibilities: did the cops show up and Wright went nuts? Did he kill someone else?

"Jill, hey," Liam says. He's silent for a moment while I can hear the woman on the other side of the phone. I can't pick out the words, but her tone is urgent, but professional. "Okay. Thank you. We're on our way." He hangs up. "Wright's gone."

"What?" I ask.

"By the time she got over there with the patrol, his car was missing from the driveway and there's no one home. Kids are missing too."

"He's running," I say. Which means he knows. He knows we're on to him and now he's in panic mode. Given how prepared he's been up until this point, I can't believe he doesn't have an exit strategy. "Do they have any idea how long he's been gone? Which way he went?"

He shakes his head. "Nothing to indicate."

"Damn it!" I hit the steering wheel. "If I'd just seen who he was when we were there, we could have just...at least we could have waited around to see what he did. He could have left right after we did, which gives him—" I look at the clock again. "—what, four hours head start on us? Five? He could be halfway through Pennsylvania by now, or down in North Carolina."

I pull my phone out of my pocket, and tap on my one and only quick contact, putting the phone on speaker. "Grab the case file for Wright," I tell Liam as it rings.

"Hey there," Zara says, picking up. "How's the hunt?"

"Zara, we have a problem," I say. "We suspect Gerald Wright is the killer, but he's in the wind. Can you get us traffic cam info for the greater area around here?"

"What? It's the husband?" she asks. "Wow, yeah...um, go ahead." I look at Liam.

"Virginia plate, Adam-Robert-Frank-four-one-nine-two," he says.

"Got it. This wouldn't happen to be Detective Coll, would it?" Zara asks. I catch Liam's cheeks go red.

"Zara, not now," I say. "Get on it, going back to eleven a.m. this morning. He could have left any time after that."

"Right," she says. "I'll see what I can do. Do you want me to inform Janice?"

I grit my teeth but at this point I don't think I have a choice. I've lost control of the situation. We might need some backup if by some miracle we end up finding him. Not to mention there's a good chance he's already crossed state lines. "No, I'll call her. We're still twenty minutes out from Stillwater. I need to inform her of what's going on."

"Got it," she says. "I'll keep you updated. Be safe."

"You too," I say out of habit, and hang up. I turn to Liam. "Would it do any good to tell Burke to put out an APB on this guy?"

"He won't listen," Liam says, "But we can try." He dials the number, putting it on speaker for my benefit.

"Stillwater Police, how can I direct you," a bored voice says on the other end. I assume it's the same man I saw this morning, still watching the front desk.

"Jerry, let me speak to Burke," Liam says.

"Coll? I'm not supposed to put you through. He said for you to leave a message."

"This is important. We've got a suspect on the loose," Liam says. "I don't have time for his bullshit."

The man on the other end sighs. "Fine. Hang on." The line goes quiet for a minute before he picks up.

"Burke." Clearly Jerry didn't give him any warning otherwise I doubt he would have taken the call.

"Chief," Liam says. "We have a situation. A suspect is—"

"Coll, what the hell are you doing? You're on suspension. And not even six hours! Get off my line."

"Do you want another dead person on your conscience, Chief?" I ask, unable to help myself.

"Slate, what—are you...is Coll with you?"

"I've kept him on as a civilian contractor," I say.

"That's it, I've had enough of this," he replies. "You are not the police chief around here, and you are not going to be absconding with my officers!"

"An officer you put on suspension," I say. "As far as I'm concerned, he's a free agent. You can't stop me from using him for a case where I feel he has some value."

"You better get ready for a world of pain, Agent Slate. Don't think I'm going to—"

"Before you threaten me any further," I say, cutting in. "You should know that we've identified Gerald Wright as a possible suspect in Victoria Wright's murder."

He's silent for a moment. "Motive?" he asks.

"Unsure yet. But we've connected him to a similar case in Maryland, using an assumed name. Our theory is he created another identity when he arrived here and used that to lure Victoria into a false sense of security."

"That's ludicrous," Burke says. "And makes no sense. Why would he have to lure his own wife into anything? He had full access to her anytime he wanted."

I shake my head. "That I'm not certain about. He's clever; we need to bring him in and question him."

"Agent Slate, I don't know how they do things up there in D.C., but here we have something called procedure. You can't just go around accusing citizens of crimes just because you have a theory. Do you have any actual evidence connecting Wright to either the crime scene or the body itself?"

I shake my head. "This guy is too smart to leave evidence behind. He's practiced, which is what I'm trying to tell you. He knows how to get away with it."

He harrumphs on the other side. "And you call me a sloppy detective. Once you get your head out of your own ass and have something concrete, maybe then we can talk. Until then, I have actual work to do." The line goes dead.

"That was productive," Liam says.

I hit the steering wheel again, pressing down on the accelerator. I should have known Burke wasn't going to listen, but it's just so infuriating to try and tell someone the truth and they do everything in their power to put up barriers and excuses that keeps them from hearing it. "Thanks anyway," I say.

"Well, I'm pretty much fired," Liam says. He looks over at me and shrugs. "The funny thing is I don't feel very bad about it. In fact, I don't feel much of anything."

"I guess you were in the wrong job," I say. "But you're still a good detective."

He smiles. "Thanks. I just wish we could have nabbed Wright this morning when we had the chance."

"Me too," I say. "Burke's not wrong though. If he really was Patrick Wood, why go to all of the trouble just to get his wife to go somewhere?"

"Well," Liam says. "It does give him a layer of insulation. If everyone is looking at Patrick Wood, no one is looking at him."

"True," I say. "But if Patrick Wood isn't a real person, wouldn't that be more difficult? Why not just tell her to meet him somewhere? If he's the same person, he has to commit the murder either way." I tap the steering wheel as I drive. Why do all the extra work? What's the benefit?

I run through the profile again in my head. Wright is smart, but he also lacks empathy. From what we know about Laura Allen, he was more than cruel in his treatment of her. Maybe that's the answer. Maybe he gets off on the cruelty, of seeing the shock and betrayal in someone's eyes. "Imagine," I say. "Your spouse of eight years starts acting cold toward you. Recall the Wrights had marriage troubles."

"Allegedly," Liam says.

"Right. So after a while of trying and getting nothing in return, you go searching for…something. Companionship." I'm trying to put myself in Victoria Wright's shoes, to under-stand what she might be thinking. "And you meet someone… online. It turns out this person says everything you've been craving. Everything you're not getting from your spouse at home." I turn to Liam. "There's no documentation showing Victoria and Patrick ever met up before the day she disap-peared, is there?"

Liam grabs the case file out of the back, flipping through all the notes, messages and emails. "Not as far as I can tell."

"See, that's the kicker. If he's Patrick Wood, he can't let her see him. Not until he's ready to enact his plan."

"So…what? He's catfishing his own wife?" Liam asks.

I nod. "That's exactly what he's doing. Because he knows that look on her face, when she realizes she's been betrayed, that's what he needs. That's what all of this is about. And for him, waiting for eight years to do this, it would have to be a massive release for him. The best high he's ever had. He's meticulously planned this out ever since the day he met her."

"Jesus," Liam says. "The marriage, the kids...all of it just to feel this one sensation?"

I nod again. "Remember, people like Gerald, people who are true psychopaths, are wired different. Whereas you and I couldn't do that because we are able to feel another person's pain, to him, it doesn't register. All that matters are his own feelings. If someone else gets hurt along the way, it's like a non-event for him. And he'll hurt as many people as he needs in order to get what he wants."

Suddenly, I make a realization, pushing the accelerator to the floor as we see the first houses of Stillwater dotting the landscape around us.

"What?" he asks.

"The kids," I reply. "He's not protecting them. He's going to use them. The same way he used Victoria."

"You mean he's going to kill them," Liam says.

I look over at him. "What could be better for a monster that feeds on cruelty and betrayal than to receive that from a child? His own child, in fact. It's the ultimate violation." A wave of emotions threatens to spill over the dam I've built within myself. Those kids are going to suffer, he's going to make sure of it. No matter what, we can't let him do this. We have to find him.

Chapter Thirty-Three

THE TIRES OF MY RENTAL SCREECH TO A HALT AS I PULL UP IN
front of Wright's house. Outside sits a black and white with
two officers inside. They both scramble out of their vehicle at
the noise but I hold up my badge before they can react.

"I'm the one who called it in," Liam says and one of the
officers relaxes while the other remains rigid.

"You're not supposed to be here, Coll, Chief's orders," he
calls out.

"Get back in the car," I tell Liam as I run up to the door.
"You two, with me!" Despite the fact Wright is already gone, I
need to check his house, make sure he hasn't left something
incriminating behind. And since Burke won't lift a finger to
help, I can't count on anyone else to do this job.

As I get up to the door, I ring the bell even though I know
there's no one there. I look up at the camera mounted above
the frame, the blue light is on. Which means more than likely
Wright knows I'm here. Good. I want him to see me, to know
that I'm on his trail. Maybe he'll panic and just dump the kids
and run. At this point I'd take that option, even though it would
mean he could disappear. As long as those kids were safe…

"FBI," I call out, sure that the camera is picking up my words. "Open up if you're home. I'll count to three."

"What are you going to do?" one of the officers asks. "You can't enter without a warrant."

"Exigent circumstances," I say as I unlatch my service weapon from its holster. Then I stand back and kick at the door, causing the glass inside the frame to shatter. An alarm blares inside the house. I kick it again and the frame breaks, sending the door flying open.

"Emma! Jacob! It's Emily from this morning! Are you here?" I motion to the officers to begin searching the house. Just in case I pull my weapon out, keeping it pointed to the ground as we begin searching, the wailing siren echoing through the space. A quick inspection of the main level reveals nothing, though I notice all the toys that were scattered on the floor this morning are missing. They're not in buckets or holders anywhere I can see.

"Clear!" one of the officers yells from upstairs.

I head through the back door and out into the yard, my attention on the garage in the back. Like the house, the access door is locked and it's dark inside. I step back and kick at it again until the lock finally breaks. Flipping the light on inside, I'm surprised not to see Victoria's car. I was sure it would be in here, but it's mostly just a storage unit full of tools, paints and various other household goods. But around the side of the car there's a small, recessed area...large enough for a child to crawl into.

"Anything?" I look up to see Liam at the door. "I saw you coming around from the street."

"Get in here and help me look." I get on my hands and knees, crawling into the recess and see that it leads into what looks like some kind of cubby hole on the side of the garage. Images of dead children stuffed inside flood my brain, but when I flick on the light on my phone, all I see are a few boxes. But it's what is written on top of the box that catches my eye: the initials *PW*.

"Screw it," I say, reaching for the box. I don't have time to go through proper procedure, not with those kids' lives on the line. Inside are more financial documents, except all of these don't have his name on them. Instead they're emblazoned with the name *Patrick Wood*.

"Found you," I say. "Call Burke. Tell him we've got his evidence!"

"What'd you find?" Liam asks. I drag the box back out into the main part of the garage, to give us a better look. "Em." He reaches into the box as I'm extricating myself, producing a small key with the number three carved into it, along with a spool of thick, black thread. "Look familiar?" he asks.

"It's the key from the Motel Five," I say. "He kept a memento. And what he uses on their eyes." I can't be sure, but it looks like the same thread to me. It all makes sense. Everything about Patrick Wood is in this box. He wanted to keep it so he could always remember and come back to it whenever he wanted. "Wait," I say. "What if he didn't run? When he killed Laura Allen, it wasn't like he moved across the country to start over. He came to a town an hour and a half away! He was right under Soft Bend's nose this entire time."

"A power move," Liam says. "Knowing that he could get away with it."

I nod. "Exactly. What if he's doing the same thing now?" I hold up the key. "What if he's still right here?"

We look at each other a beat longer before we run out of the garage. One of the officers is standing on the back lawn. "Seal that building up!" I yell. "And get the CSI team down here. Call Burke, tell him we need backup at the Motel Five hotel. Possible armed suspect, highly dangerous with hostages!"

The officer's eyes flash and he nods, pulling his walkie

close to him and rattling off the orders to the dispatcher. Liam and I reach the car and I'm pulling out before we even get our doors closed.

"Do you think they're still alive?" he asks.

"They better be," I reply. "For his sake." I'm regretting my decision to be so brazen on Wright's cameras, but that was when I thought he was halfway to Memphis.

As I'm driving, my phone rings. I pull it out and glance at the screen, hitting the accept button.

"Em, good, glad I caught you," Zara says. "I got the guys to pull the camera data for Stillwater, though Janice wasn't happy about it. I thought you were going to call her?"

"I ran out of time," I say. I can deal with Janice later. Right now all that matters are the lives of those two kids.

"Well, it only came up with two hits in the time period you specified," he says. "One is on a camera at fourth and Blakewell."

"Do you know where that is?" I ask Liam.

He nods. "Near the center of town, not too far from the station, actually."

"The other is on Route nine, headed out toward the interstate," Zara adds. "But I checked all the interstate cameras and got nothing."

I floor it. "That's because he didn't get on the interstate," I say. "The motel is on Route nine." Our hunch was right. "Call the motel. Get that manager on the phone, I wanna talk to him. Thanks Zara!"

"Go get 'em!" she yells, then hangs up.

Liam makes the call, but I can tell no one is picking up. "Not good," he says.

My heart is pumping so fast I feel like it's going to explode. The streetlights give way to the darkness of the road, our headlights the only thing illuminating anything in front of us, other than the occasional house on either side.

Some part of my brain thinks now is the best time to do a

worst-case scenario. A deer could jump out in front of us, which would total the car and possibly kill us. Wright could have killed the manager before taking the kids into the room to kill them too. He could already be done, and maybe even offed himself in a murder/suicide. Any of those possibilities is in front of us and I have to navigate a way through. I have to force fate to bend to my will, to keep Wright from doing the one thing I know will give him pleasure above everything else.

"You got this," Liam says, next to me. He must be reading my facial expressions, which are probably all over the place. I don't reply; instead, I focus on the task ahead. No matter what it takes, I *will* stop this man.

Chapter Thirty-Four

THE FLICKERING SIGN OF THE MOTEL FIVE COMES INTO VIEW and I push the car to its top speed until we're right on the turn, swinging the vehicle around into the entrance. I curse when I see the parking lot: there are five cars there, including Wright's Mercedes, which is parked right in front of door number three. He's not hiding, not now, which only sends the pit in my stomach somewhere deeper. I don't like the implication of him being so brazen like this; he's not even trying anymore. Like an animal backed into a corner, he's unpredictable.

"We need to wait on the backup," Liam says.

I shake my head. "He knows we're coming; I can't risk those kids' lives any more than I already have. Look, he's in the exact same room where he killed his wife. You know he's doing it right now. We wait, they don't have a chance."

I've slowed the car considerably, as to not announce our presence. At least, that's my hope. I don't see any movement at room three's window, which is both good and bad. I don't want him to know we're coming, but at the same time I don't want him to be hurting those kids either. I park the car a few feet away, leaving the engine running and quietly open the door, taking out my service weapon again and making sure the safety is off.

My pulse is so loud I can barely tell if the sounds of the lot are coming from somewhere else, or my accelerated breathing. My hands are slick with sweat, though I have a strong grip on my weapon, keeping it down and to the side as I walk slowly up to the door. The room next to number three is occupied again, which means I must be careful of collateral damage. If Wright has a gun in there…he could end up shooting anyone.

When I reach the door, my hand barely touches the handle, but I can already tell it's locked. I motion for Liam to hand me the key from Wright's garage, which I slowly insert inch by inch. Inside I can't hear a thing, which only makes me want to forgo this and kick the door in. But there's no guarantee I'd get it on the first kick, and I can't give Wright a second's advantage. Once the key is all the way in, I press down on the handle and it gives way. I push open the door, leveling my weapon inside the room.

Wright sits on the floor, on his knees. In front of him is Jacob, who is looking up at his father as Wright holds a plastic bag in his hand. "Freeze!" I yell.

In an instant Wright spins Jacob around and has a knife to his throat. I don't even know where that came from. But my gaze is locked on both of them. Jacob's eyes are red-rimmed and his face is flushed like he's been crying, a lot. I sneak a glance to the bed to see Emma there, a plastic bag taped over her head around the neck.

It's like a spear through me. She's not moving.

"Wright, it's over!" I yell. "Let him go." He's got the boy by the hair, holding up his head as the knife is up against his skin. My mind goes back to that incident three months ago and I seize up.

"And deny myself what I've been waiting all this time for?" he asks. "I don't think so. Even if you kill me, I'll have already experienced it. And so will he. His last memory will be that of his father, the man he's looked up to for seven years, hurting him worse than anyone else ever could."

"Then what?" I manage to ask, glancing at Emma again. How long has she been like that? Is she already dead? "What good is betraying someone like that unless they feel it their entire lives? You're robbing them of the pain of life. Of never trusting someone again, isn't that right?"

"You're surprisingly intuitive, Agent Slate. They said that about you. It took me a while to figure out who you were; you stopped going by your married name." His comment throws me off, but I keep my focus on Jacob, trying to communicate to him that it's going to be okay. I don't know how Wright knows anything about me and I don't care. All I know is that if I don't do something, this kid is dead. "The fact is, I don't need them to live a life after betrayal. I saw what that was like. People are more resilient than you'd expect."

"With Laura Allen, right?"

There's a flicker in his eyes and the hint of a smile on his lips. "I was right to run. They said I was over-reacting, but they don't know what you're capable of," he says.

"Who is this they?" I ask, shooting another look at Emma. As long as he keeps talking, Jacob is safe, but Emma isn't. I need to find a way to disable him.

"I tried to let Laura live, I did," he says, ignoring my question. "I kept tabs on her. But then I saw how she was thriving. How despite everything I'd done to her, she had turned things around. It was like she'd forgotten me. And that wasn't acceptable."

"Because you needed her to be as miserable as you were," I say.

"Because I needed her broken. I wasn't going to give Victoria the chance to go off and make a better life without me. I made that mistake once. Never again. So you see, Agent Slate. First it is luring them into a sense of safety. Then betrayal, then death. And I make sure they can never open their eyes again. I seal the experience in, robbing them of any peace in death. It's the only way. But seeing as I'm sure you have reinforcements on the way, I think I'll be done with this." I see it a split second before he makes the move with the knife. He's already committed.

In my mind's eye all I can see is the scared little child in the corner that I almost killed the last time I fired a gun. He's there, shaking as the room reverberates with the ringing of the shot and I stand less than five feet from him, mortified that I think I've actually hit him. But at the same time, I see Jacob's pleading eyes; the boy knows these are his last moments. Something inside me steadies and I pull the trigger.

Wright's body wrenches back as the bullet plows into his upper shoulder, the knife flying from his hand. I rush forward, grabbing Jacob as Liam runs in behind me picking up Emma and taking her from the room. As I take Jacob's hand, the world seems to move in slow motion and I notice the flashing of red and blue lights outside. With all my strength I pull Jacob toward me though he can't get his feet under him. More tears flow down his face and I finally get him into my arms. I spin and push him back out the door, knowing he's still not safe. Not until Wright is restrained.

As I turn back, things speed back up.

I raise my weapon again to train it on Wright, but he's scrambled away from where he was on the floor to behind the second bed. Before I know it, he vaults the bed on his good arm and slams into me, knocking me back against the dresser, which digs into my back. I cry out, bringing my knee up into his sternum, which sends him back down to the ground. He's on all fours and I notice the bullet went straight through, though he's losing blood. I train my weapon on him again, but he has the knife in his hand once more and jabs it right into my thigh, leaving it in place. I don't even feel it. I pull the trigger again and the bullet tears through his mid-section. He grunts, then falls to the side.

The adrenaline keeps me from collapsing on my leg, and I manage to get out a zip tie band and pull his two arms into it, clasping them together behind him.

Liam appears at the door along with another female officer. "I've got him," I say, looking up. "The kids?"

"Jacob is fine," Liam says. "The EMTs are working on Emma now." I limp over to the door, pushing my way past him to see the EMTs have Emma on the ground, administering CPR. I have no idea how long that bag was on her head or how much CO_2 she inhaled. Stillwater police are everywhere on the scene, keeping people back, securing the area. I limp over to the EMTs, watching them work on the little girl.

The worst case flashes across my mind again. I wasn't quick enough. If I'd just figured it out a few minutes sooner, she'd still be here, not lying on some cold parking lot as the life drains out of her.

Miraculously, I hear her cough. I look up and see she's got an oxygen mask on, but her eyes have fluttered open and she's trying to cough. One of the EMTs pulls the mask back, helping her head to the side so she can get a good breath.

I feel a small hand slip into mine and I look down to see Jacob, standing beside me. "Is she going to be okay?" he asks, his voice small and scared.

I look back at the little girl, who seems to be breathing on her own now as the EMT's check the rest of her vitals. "I think she is."

Jacob wraps himself around my good leg and I realize the knife is still sticking out of the other one. "Thank you," he says. "Thank you for saving us."

I place my hand on his back, wincing as the pain in my leg becomes real. "You're welcome," I say. And I mean it.

Chapter Thirty-Five

THERE WERE ONLY TWO AMBULANCES AT THE SCENE AND despite my injury, I insisted the first one take Emma and Jacob both to Stillwater Medical to get checked out. The other is reserved for Wright, who is in worse shape than me.

In the meantime, I have two people from the local rescue squad inspecting my injury. But my eyes are on the open doorway to room number three. After I came out, more officers and EMTs rushed in, no doubt attempting to save Wright's life. At this point I don't care if they do or not. As far as I'm concerned, he can die in that room, just like he deserves.

"Okay, Agent?" the man to my left with the dark blue uniform says. He's young, probably not much older than twenty-one. But he's got a kind disposition. I turn back to him. "Based on where this knife is embedded, I'm going to recommend we don't remove it until we get you to the hospital."

"How bad is it?" I ask.

"It's close to your femoral artery," he says. "If we pull it out now, we could accidentally nick the artery and you could bleed out before we can get it under control." He takes a breath, inspecting the area where he's cut away my jeans. "But at the same time, I don't want you moving either. Any movement of the leg one way or another could do the same thing. Sit tight, we're going to get you strapped into a gurney, and get you over to the hospital, as soon as the other ambulance gets back, okay?"

I nod. They already made me sit down, so all I have to do is make sure not to move and I'll be solid.

More people have gathered, and even the local news has shown up, no doubt by listening to the police scanners. I notice Liam off to the side, speaking with the same officer who helped him earlier. I can only assume this is Jill. From the way they're talking, and their relaxed body language, it's easy to tell there's something there. Or at least, there was at some point in the past. He finishes his conversation and walks over, inspecting me. "So? What's the damage?"

"Fatal, I'm afraid," I say, looking down at the wound. "You lied to me."

He goes still. "What?"

I nod to Jill. "You do have a girlfriend."

Relief spreads over his face. "Oh, no, just a family friend. We thought there might be something there once upon a time...just didn't work out."

"I can understand that. What's the story on Wright? Is he dead in there?"

Liam shakes his head. "They're just trying to get him stabilized. He actually won't shut up. Wants to talk to you."

"I don't want to hear anything else he has to say," I reply.

"Give me one moment," the EMT says. "I'll be right back." He runs off for the ambulance. I look down and see he's given me a makeshift bandage to keep the knife in place. The area around the wound is bloody, but it's not enough to cause me a lot of concern.

"You saved them, you know," Liam says, indicating my wound. "I overheard some of the other techs. They said if

Emma had been in that bag any longer, she would have succumbed to hypoxia and died."

I sit there, letting the waves of emotion wash over me. I know how close we came. And how badly this could have gone. Thankfully we were able to figure it out in time. "I think that's how he killed Victoria. Suffocated her."

"Makes sense," Liam says. "It's not going to leave much of a trace after a while."

"And it's cold, detached, yet still personal. Exactly what someone like Wright would do to his victims. I'm sure Laura Allen was the same way. He's obsessed with making sure he is their last memory. Enough that he sews their eyes shut so there is no chance they could ever see anything else." I flash another look at the door as they wheel the gurney inside.

"You know," Liam says. "I'm glad you *are* a crusader. Otherwise we'd be looking at another murder scene."

"Couldn't have done it without you," I say. "You found the box."

He sits beside me, pulling his legs up to his chest. "Yeah. That *was* pretty heroic of me. I literally gave you the key to solving the case."

"Let's not get carried away," I say, wincing. A sharp pain runs up my leg as the EMT returns, applying some gel around the wound. "What's that?"

"Super glue," he says. "To help hold everything together until we can get you over there."

"You're kidding," I say.

"Wow," Liam says, leaning over to look at the wound. I take in the scent of his musk and bite my lip to keep from making a comment. "You'll be just like the bionic woman when you get done."

"The bionic what?" I ask, righting myself.

"Never mi—oh, shit." I follow his gaze out to where another police car has showed up. Burke gets out, surveying the area and barking orders at his officers. He gets them to push the growing crowd back and to further tape off the area. Another officer runs up and he berates them for a moment before pausing, then locking eyes with us. My whole body tenses as I prepare for the fight I know is coming.

"Agent, please," the EMT says. "It'll be better for you if you relax." I can hear the siren of the second ambulance in the distance, already on its way back.

"So," Burke says, hooking his thumbs in his belt as he approaches. "I see you found your man."

"No thanks to you. You might want to retain legal counsel, Chief, because you are looking at a host of obstruction charges by the time I'm done. You're just damn lucky those kids survived otherwise I'd be adding accessory to murder to the list."

His face remains impassive. "We'll see." He turns to Liam. "I should have you arrested for misappropriating police resources."

"Mis-*appropriating?*" I say, attempting to get to my feet, but the EMT nudges me back down. "All he did was protect the public interest and try to hunt down a killer! If not for Liam, this could have gone very badly. Keep threatening us, see how well that turns out for you."

Burke narrows his eyes at me before turning and walking away, heading for the news cameras. "Typical," Liam says.

"Oh, no," I reply. "He's not getting away with this. He has impeded this investigation at every step, and I'm going to make sure he pays for it." I fish for my phone out of my jacket pocket. But before I can dial, I see them wheel Wright out of the room. He's strapped to the gurney with a face shield over his mouth, delivering him oxygen. Two officers, including the one Liam was talking to earlier, escort the gurney out with the EMTs. I can tell Wright is mumbling something but can't make out what it is.

He sees me and his eyes go wide.

With one hand he reaches up and pulls the mask off.

"Emily!" His voice is hoarse, but there's still a lot of power behind it. I'm surprised he's not sedated. "I need protection! You agree to give me the protection of the FBI and I'll tell you everything."

"We already have everything we need," I call back. "Enjoy prison."

He shakes his head and pushes away the hand that tries to put his mask back on. "No, I'm serious. They'll kill me. I can tell you everything."

I shake my head as they wheel him away.

"Your husband!" He yells. "Matthew, right? I know about him. I'll tell you how they killed him! Protect me!"

I feel like my heart has stopped. In an instant I'm back on my feet. There's a din of sound coming from somewhere behind me, but all I can focus on is Wright and the gurney that's being wheeled into the ambulance. Someone has me by the arm while someone else is yelling something else at me, but it's like the entire world has gone dark and all I can see is Wright, still yelling something under the mask as they strap him into the vehicle. His eyes are wild, but pointed, and they stare right into my soul. Before I know it, the doors are closed, and the ambulance is off.

I look down to my leg and see the gush of blood pouring out from the wound. My head feels faint, and the world begins to spin. The last thing I see before I go down is Liam's face in my peripheral vision.

Then it all goes to black.

Chapter Thirty-Six

THE FIRST THING I'M AWARE OF IS MY HEAD POUNDING, EVEN before I open my eyes. It feels like someone kicked me in the back of the skull and I really don't want to open my eyes, but I do anyway. Thankfully, I'm somewhere with subdued lighting and I realize that I'm chilly. My arms are exposed and there's barely anything of a blanket over me. Movement to my right catches my eye and I look over to see a man dressed in light green scrubs check a bag hanging off a hook. I open my mouth to ask him what's going on, only to find it's dry and I can barely get a word out.

He looks at me, smiling, and hands me a cup of ice water, which I drink as fast as I can, relishing the coolness of the liquid as it coats my throat. I hand him the cup back. "Thanks," I croak out. "What's—"

"You're damn lucky, that's what."

I look to the foot of my bed where a woman stands, her imposing stature drawing a shadow across my bed, even though it's not very light in here. Her hair is silver and pulled back into a bun and she wears dark-rimmed glasses.

"Janice?" I ask. I blink a few times, trying to orient myself.

I'm in a hospital room. Before here I was...it all comes

rushing back to me. Confronting Wright at the motel, barely saving the kids, the knife in my leg. I pull back the thin cover to find my leg is wrapped in a bandage that goes all the way around my thigh. The hospital gown barely covers everything and I pull the covers back over. "Can I get another blanket?" I ask the nurse.

"Sure," he says, giving me a wink. I narrow my eyes as he heads out of the room, and I turn back to my boss.

"What's going on?" I ask.

"You almost bled out, that's what," she says. "Had the ambulance not been right around the corner, you would have died in that parking lot." She pulls out a vape pen and sucks on it, blowing the vapor up and away.

"I don't think you can use those in here."

"They took my cigarettes, they're not gonna take my goddamn vape pen," she says, pulling one of the chairs up beside the bed and taking a seat. She slips it back inside her coat as the nurse returns with a blanket that he spreads over me. It feels a little better, considering I'm practically naked under the sheet. What is it about hospitals that they have to be so…clinical?

The nurse leaves us, and I turn to look at the machine monitoring my vitals. As far as I can tell, everything looks to be in the normal ranges. "How long have I been out?"

"About twenty hours," she says. "They had to repair the artery and stitch up your leg. They also noticed you were suffering from vitamin deficiency, so they gave you a drip." She indicates the transparent tube running down to a needle under the skin of my right hand.

I try to reach up with that hand, but the tube keeps my hand from moving too far. Instead, I rub my face with my other hand. "I feel like I've been hit by a truck."

Janice pulls out the pen again. "They tell me you'll be back on your feet tomorrow."

I take her in, really this time. She's got on the normal

black suit I always see her in, white blouse, no purse. Janice isn't one who needs a lot of accessories. Anything she can't carry in her suit coat she doesn't take with her. "What are you doing here?"

She takes another puff. "When I heard one of my best agents might die, I figured I'd better make an appearance. You know, in case you kicked it."

That produces a smile. "We got him. Just in time, but we did it."

"You sure as hell did," she says, smiling herself. "As much as I hate to do it, I think I'll have to recommend you for a commendation."

"I assume this means I'm back in the Bureau's good graces?"

She scoffs. "Please. You're like a movie star. Breaking this case was no easy feat. I've already spoken to Detective Coll. He's got nothing but good things to say about you."

I lay my head back. "That's nice." Then it hits me. Wright's final words to me. I can't believe I'd forgotten. But they wash over me again just like the first time.

I'll tell you how they killed him.

Matt died of a heart attack. Or at least, I thought he had. That's what the medical examiner told me. But somehow Wright knows about him, knows what I went through. How is that possible? I sit back up. "Where's Wright?"

Janice shakes her head. "They've got him in surgery again, trying to repair all that damage your bullets did," she says. Before I can protest she holds up a hand. "Don't get me wrong, I would have done the same thing. But I want this son of a bitch alive so he can stand trial. With the evidence you found at his house along with his actions at the motel, there's no way a jury won't convict. I've got Zara working on connecting him back to Laura Allen's death as well. Regardless, you nailed the bastard."

I open my mouth to tell her about what he said about

Matt but hesitate. I'm not sure now is the best time to bring it up; plus, I want to see what he says first. Make sure this isn't some kind of trick. Wright has connections, maybe he's trying to use those to get me to go easy on him. But the evidence will speak for itself. Once I tell him there's nothing I'll be able to do to stop him from going to prison I'll see if maybe then he changes his tune.

Instead, I change the subject. "Right before my...accident...I was about to call you."

"Oh?" she asks, a twinkle in her eye.

"I'm bringing charges against Chief Burke," I say. "He knowingly and intentionally obstructed this investigation every step of the way. He curtailed resources, covered up the fact he had information that could have helped us in the case, not to mention the obvious abuse of power."

She takes another puff. "I've heard some rumblings. Didn't like that dick from the moment he tried to tattle on you."

Relief floods my system. Some small part of me thought he might find a way to get away with it. Fortunately for me, Janice might be tough, but she's always fair. And she's not about to let someone like him stay on the Stillwater police force. Suddenly I'm feeling more invigorated, like I've been given new breath. "When are they discharging me?" I ask.

She shrugs. "Didn't say. Probably today or tomorrow." She checks her watch, standing back up. "I need to get back to D.C. But trust me when I say you have the full authority of the FBI behind you. Close things up here and get back. We need you."

Those are the words I've been longing to hear ever since my screw up three months ago. Finally, to be back at the job that I love.

Janice grins, then hides her vape pen again, placing a reassuring hand on my uninjured leg over the covers. "Good work, Agent Slate."

I take a deep breath of the cold air as I step out of the car, a folder tucked under one arm. Behind me, a team of four FBI agents in from D.C. step out of similar, black cars. All of them arrived this morning on my request.

It feels good to be back.

I managed to slip out of my hospital room last night without causing too much of a ruckus. They wanted to keep me overnight for observation, but I wasn't having it. Instead, I met up with Liam and we went over our strategy for today. He's already in the station, arguing his case with Burke, trying to get the man to at least complete the paperwork saying he fired Liam with probable cause, which, of course, he doesn't have.

In my other hand is something known as a *handi-cane*, which is embarrassing as hell, but if I don't, it will take me twice as long to heal. The doctors said I only have to use it for two to three weeks, until my leg has regained some of its strength. But really, it's the aikido classes I'll miss that are making me more anxious than anything.

I motion to the agents, and we make our way up the steps to the station. Inside, Trisha sits with her book in her hand behind the plexiglass. She looks up with wide eyes when we enter. I have to imagine it's a fairly intimidating visual for her. I motion to the door and she nods, never blinking.

As it buzzes, I push my way through and lead the agents down the hallway, the click-clack of our shoes on the linoleum causing everyone to look up at once.

Burke's door is closed as we approach. I don't even knock before opening it. Instead, I swing it open, revealing Burke, his face red as he argues with Liam. He looks up at the five of us and all the color drains from his face.

"Chief William Burke," I say. "I am placing you under arrest for Obstruction of Justice, Evidence Tampering and

Conspiracy." I open the file folder and pull out the arrest warrant, showing it to him.

"You can't do this," he sputters, still trying to assert his power. But it's not going to work this time. Two of the agents circle around the desk.

"Put your hands behind your back," one of them says. Burke just sits there, not even acknowledging them. Instead, he's staring daggers at me. For a brief moment, I think he's going to fight it. That he might actually try to shoot his way out of this situation. His eyes drop to the sidearm strapped to his side, even in the chair. But before he can make a move, Agent McCoy takes Burke's head and slams it on the desk, causing him to grunt. McCoy removes the weapon from Burke's belt and he and Pearson wrench Burke's hands behind his back securing them before hoisting him up to face me. His face is full of indignation and anger, though it's also beginning to swell.

"This isn't over," he growls at me.

"You want to bet on that?" I ask. "You're looking at thirty to fifty years, and based on your overall health, I don't think you have that long." McCoy and Pearson have to physically pull him out of the office and down the hallway, fighting him the whole way. About halfway down he finally gives up, his body going limp and the fight leaving him. Liam and I follow until they're outside where the local news has showed up and they get footage of Burke being pushed into the back of a black SUV. A moment later, the two SUVs drive off.

"That was supremely satisfying," Liam says.

"Tell me about it."

He turns to me. "Conspiracy? I thought you only had the two charges against him."

"We added that little nugget this morning. Zara called me first thing. You'll never believe what she found: a paper trail from Rex Fuller directly to William Burke. Fuller paid Burke off to shut down the investigation the first time because he didn't want anyone looking into his sexual assault claims. That was why Burke was so intent on keeping the case under wraps. He was continuing to receive payments from Fuller in exchange for his silence."

Liam lets out a loud guffaw. I think it's the only time I've heard him belly laugh like that. "Oh man, everyone was screwing over Fuller! Who wasn't blackmailing that guy?"

"Right?" Thankfully the evidence Zara found will also help put Fuller away for years. He's looking at a similar slew of charges.

Liam wipes his eyes, still chuckling, then looks over to the news crew. It's the same one that had been at the motel the other night, with the same reporter. I can't imagine they have many in a town of this size. "How did the news know to be here?"

I shrug. "Who knows? Maybe someone tipped them off." I give him a wink for good measure.

"I better watch out for you." He laughs. "You're not playing around."

I watch as the SUVs disappear into the distance. "I think we can probably get you your job back now. I'd even be willing to bet thanks to your help on the case, the mayor might consider you for new interim chief until the next election."

Liam holds out his hands. "Oh, no. Not me. I'm done with the local cop stuff. I mean, I was happy to help with this, but I've got my sights set for something bigger."

"Yeah?" I ask.

"Well, I can't let you have all the fun, now can I?"

I take his words in for a moment. "Wait, does this mean you're applying to the Bureau?"

He nods. "I think it's time I finally get out of this town. Start to do something that really matters, you know?"

"I do," I say, beaming with pride. "I'll be happy to write you a recommendation."

"Oh, I've already got one," he says, smirking.

I furrow my brow, then it hits me. "Zara?"

He laughs again. "She was more than willing."

"Truth be told," I say. "I think she's got a crush on you."

"She doesn't know anything about me," he replies.

I give him my most skeptical look. "Trust me. If she knows your name, she knows *everything* about you by now. She doesn't work in Data Resourcing for nothing."

"Seems kinda unfair," he says. His gaze lingers on mine a moment and I feel that primal pull deep within me. Finally his eyes drop. "But maybe it's for the best."

"Yeah, maybe," I say. I'm thankful he's not trying to force this…thing…between us. Because if he did, I'm not sure how long my willpower could hold. And right now, I need to focus. He clearly heard what Wright said the other night about my husband, but he hasn't broached the subject and neither have I. I need to figure out what Wright knows first. *Then* I can make a game plan. I still have no idea if he was lying or not.

I check my phone for the time. "I need to get back to the motel to check out. Then I want a crack at Wright before he lawyers up. If it's not already too late."

"Understandable." He holds out his hand. "I'll guess I'll see you in D.C."

I take it, giving it a firm shake. "Looking forward to it."

Epilogue

"So, are you all packed?" Zara asks.

I glance at the phone on the motel's nightstand and roll my eyes even though she can't see me. "I only brought one bag. There's not much to pack."

"There's all the case notes," she says.

"Already in the car," I reply. I stretch my arms over my head, feeling a twinge of pain in my leg as I do it. It's been three days since I was "discharged" from the hospital. I'm supposed to go back in for a follow up which I would normally ignore, except for the fact I want to get some face time with Wright. He made it through both of his surgeries and it looks like he'll make a full recovery, though he's still got a few more days in the hospital. I made sure to confirm with the Stillwater police that he was handcuffed to his bed. They've assured me he's not getting away, though he's become something of a local sensation around here. That news organization is a double-edged sword.

"And we're going to lunch as soon as you get back," Zara says.

I sigh. "If I must," though there is a smile on my lips as I say it. "You know, I never could have done this without your help."

"I know," she replies. "And so does Janice. She's recommending me for field duty training."

"Really?" I ask. "That's great!"

"Yeah, I'm nervous about it. But fortunately, I already know someone who's been through all the ropes, so she can tell me exactly how to pass," she says with exaggerated confidence.

"That's not how it works," I say. "It's not just a test that you know the answers to. They'll test you on your skills in real time."

"Then maybe we need to set up a couple of sessions where you walk me through some examples. You know, just to get me ready."

I finish pushing my clothes into my bag, cramming them down into the sides so I can get it closed. "I guess I owe you that much."

"I mean, I did watch your dog while you were away, who I am considering adopting myself."

"You will not," I chuckle. "He loves me too much. I just want to come home and relax on the couch with him asleep on my feet."

"Uh-uh," she says. "I'm not about to let you stay a shut-in. You might be able to fool everyone else, but I know all your secrets."

I chuckle. "Okay, I'm headed off to my checkup and to chat with our friend Wright before he's transferred back to D.C."

"Be careful driving!" she says. "And we'll see you when you get back."

I nod and end the call, tucking the phone into my coat as I grab my bag and look around the room one last time. It wasn't the nicest place, but it allowed me to get the job done, and that was all I really needed. I guess Janice really had known what she was doing assigning me to this case.

As I drive back down to Stillwater Medical, I can't help but reflect on how lucky we were to break the case. Now with Wright going to prison for the rest of his life, his kids have a chance at a new life, though it won't be easy. They'll both be traumatized from what they had to endure at the hands of the person they trusted most in this world, and it's going to take a lot of love, patience, and time, but they'll be okay in the end. I spoke with Social Services who are committed to finding them a home together and one that recognizes their unique circumstances. Unfortunately, they don't have any other living family, given that both Victoria and Gerald—nee, Joe's—parents are dead.

I also gave Sheriff Park all the information on the case, informing him we'd found Laura Allen's killer. He's already told me both her parents and sisters are going to be coming to D.C. for the trial. I can't say I blame them.

I have to wonder how many other victims are out there we don't know about. It's one of the primary reasons I was able to convince Janice to allow me some time with Wright before he's taken into official custody. But the real reason I need to see him is I need to know how he knows about Matt and if his information is any good. Is this nothing more than an attempt to manipulate me into helping him? Or does he have some genuine information?

I can't believe he'd actually have something of value. I mean, it isn't like he knew who I was before I came to Stillwater, so how would he even know about Matt? My theory is once he realized we were looking closely into him, he used some of his power and influence to dig up details on my life, just for this eventuality. All he needs is the appearance of a bargaining chip, but the fact of the matter is I already know it's bullshit. No one killed my husband; he died of a simple heart attack, despite his young age. It's rare, but it happens. And trust me, I did plenty of research on the phenomenon after he passed.

For a while there, you could say I was obsessed.

I pull into the hospital parking lot, taking careful notice of the crowd of people gathered near the front. Many of them holding signs protesting Wright's presence inside. The general reaction from the public has been very negative; the people of Stillwater want him out as soon as possible, and they aren't afraid to let their views known. Outside also sits the same news van that was there the night we stopped him, as well as the day Chief Burke was arrested.

As I make my way toward the crowd the reporter happens to spot me. It would be hard not to as I'm the only twenty-something using a cane to get around. Her eyes light up and she makes her way over to me, her cameraman close behind.

"Agent Slate," she says. "Glad to see you here. How are you feeling?"

I glance up at the camera and see the little red light is on. "No comment," I say, moving past them.

"How about a few quick questions," she asks. "What was it like when you finally realized Gerald Wright was the man you'd been searching for?"

I ignore her and keep walking.

"Do you have any regrets about not finding him sooner? I understand you visited him twice before you came to the conclusion he was your suspect. If I may ask, what took so long?"

I feel the heat rising in my cheeks. But I have to keep my cool. I just turned everything with the Bureau around. I can't jeopardize that now with a sloppy interview.

"I'm just here to have my injury checked," I say, trying to pick up the pace. But with the cane, I'm limited as to how fast I walk. I'll never take speed walking for granted again.

"Are you confident you've found all of his victims?" she adds as I reach the doors. I want to spin around and knock that camera out of her associate's hands with my cane. Especially after I left them the tip about Burke. That was a big story for them. But it's never enough; they are always chasing after the next big thing. The media is insatiable.

I turn on my good heel, looking straight into the woman's eyes. "Have a nice day," I say, using all my strength to make sure it doesn't come out sounding anything but saccharine. She sets her lips in a line, narrowing her eyes at me as I walk into the hospital's main entrance. I know for a brief second there she thought she was actually going to get something from me.

Now, I just have to hope Wright isn't as stubborn as I am.

I pass the desk and make my way to the elevator. My appointment is on the second floor, but I know Wright is on the fourth. I'm not supposed to meet with him until after I see Dr. Naraki, but my curiosity is getting the better of me. I've thought of nothing else since that night. And even though I know this man is a trained liar, I need to look him in the face and question him. I need to know what he knows.

And given that he seems anxious for my help as well, I'm hopeful I'll be successful. But at the same time, I'll be in the same room as someone who has no compunction about killing to get what they want. The absolute worst of the worst.

My hand hovers over the "2" button, but then I push "4" instead. Leaning on the cane, I take a deep breath. Naraki can wait. And if he can't, I don't really need the checkup anyway. My leg already feels stronger and I'm pretty sure I'll be able to stop using the cane in a few days.

The doors open on the fourth floor and I find myself standing face to face with a young blonde woman, not much older than me, in a black trench coat. She gives me a sweet smile as she allows me to step off the elevator before she gets on. She looked at me as if she knew me, but I didn't recognize her face.

I shake it off and head down the hallway toward Wright's room. But before I can take five steps, a blue light begins flashing above my head and a code alarm goes off in the hall-way. Suddenly there is a flurry of activity around me as nurses rush past, some grabbing a crash cart and head down the hall.

As I'm watching the nurses scramble, something in my stomach bottoms out and I begin rushing down the hall myself. I almost stumble and the cane nearly goes flying, but I manage to grab onto one of the rails along the wall and steady myself. I watch in horror as all the nurses rush into room four-twenty-five, the room Wright had been assigned. Outside sits an empty chair where a Stillwater police officer was supposed to be on guard. I glance around, and see an officer come rushing up the hallway from the opposite direction.

"Where were you?" I yell at him as I make my way for the door.

"I had to use the bathroom," he says. "The nurse was just here, I saw her walk in!"

I make my way into the room to see Wright on his bed, his eyes completely glassy as a group of eight people work on him. The monitor to the side of the bed tells me what I already know: he's gone. The nurses are strangely organized as they work, and I catch everything they say as they work to bring Wright back. But as the seconds tick away, I can tell it's going to be hopeless; nothing they're doing is having any effect.

"He's gone into cardiac arrest," one of the nurses says and instantly I'm transported back to the moment three months ago as I was standing off to the side, tears streaming down my face as a flurry of people worked on my husband, doing every-thing in their power to bring him back.

It plays just the same.

The furtive looks on their faces, knowing it's hopeless but doing everything they can anyway.

The limp body of Wright, already beginning to decay even as the doctors and nurses send shock after shock of electricity through him, trying to restart his system.

It won't work. He's gone. They'll close his eyes, note the time.

And then everyone will walk away, their jobs done.

And I'll be left alone, once again.

My mind flits back to the woman at the elevator. The one who looked like she knew me. And now that I think about it, she might have had scrubs peeking out from under that trench coat.

I scramble back to the hallway, to the cop who has uselessly taken up his post again. "The nurse you saw, blonde?" He nods. "She's in disguise, a black trench coat. Find her!" He takes off down the hallway, yelling into his radio.

I follow, but by the time I take the elevator back down to the main floor and find him at the entrance, there's no sign of the woman.

Wright wasn't just trying to manipulate me after all. He knew someone would be coming after him. Just like he knew my husband didn't die of natural causes.

What the hell have I just stumbled upon?

The End?

To be continued…

Want to Read more about Emily?

. . .

When a federal judge's daughter goes missing without a trace, it will be up to recently-reinstated FBI agent Emily Slate to find her. Only Emily doesn't realize what dangers lurk at the edges of this unique case.

Special Agent Emily Slate is a woman on the hunt. After returning from the town of Stillwater, she's more haunted than ever. Ghosts she thought she'd laid to rest have suddenly reared their heads, and the only person who can answer her questions has disappeared.

Meanwhile, a Federal Judge's daughter is reported missing and it's up to Emily to find her. As she dives into the case, she discovers a clever and twisted mind working against her and every minute that passes could mean it's too late for his victims.

Find out what happens in *The Collection Girls*, available now on Amazon. CLICK HERE to get your copy now!

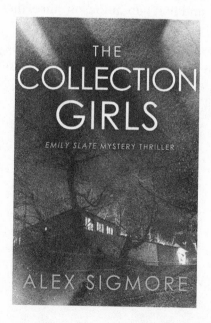

CLICK HERE or scan the code below with your phone to get
THE COLLECTION GIRLS!

FREE book offer!
Where did it all go wrong for Emily?

I hope you enjoyed *His Perfect Crime.* By now you're aware of the tragic circumstances surrounding her husband's death. If you'd like to learn about what happened to Emily in the days following, including what almost got her kicked out of the FBI, then you're in luck! *Her Last Shot* introduces Emily and tells the story of the case that almost ended her career. Interested? CLICK HERE to get your FREE Copy Now!

Not Available Anywhere Else!

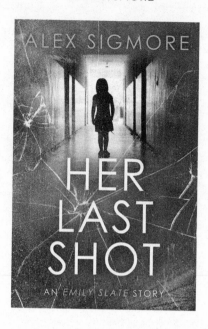

You'll also be the first to know when each book in the Emily Slate series is available!

Download for **FREE HERE** or scan the code below!

The Emily Slate FBI Mystery Series

Free Prequel - Her Last Shot (Emily Slate Bonus Story)

His Perfect Crime - (Emily Slate Series Book One)

The Collection Girls - (Emily Slate Series Book Two)

Smoke and Ashes - (Emily Slate Series Book Three)

Her Final Words - (Emily Slate Series Book Four)

Can't Miss Her - (Emily Slate Series Book Five)

The Lost Daughter - (Emily Slate Series Book Six)

The Secret Seven - (Emily Slate Series Book Seven)

A Liar's Grave - (Emily Slate Series Book Eight)

The Girl in the Wall - (Emily Slate Series Book Nine)

His Final Act - (Emily Slate Series Book Ten)

The Vanishing Eyes - (Emily Slate Series Book Eleven)

Coming Soon!

Edge of the Woods - (Emily Slate Series Book Twelve)

The Missing Bones - (Emily Slate Series Book Thirteen)

Standalone Psychological Thrillers

Forgotten

A Note from Alex

I hope you enjoyed *His Perfect Crime*. My wish is to give you an immersive story that is also satisfying when you reach the end.

But being a new writer in this business can be hard. Your support makes all the difference. After all, you are the reason I write!

Because I don't have a large budget or a huge following, I ask that you please take the time to leave a review or recommend it to fellow book lover. This will ensure I'll be able to write many more books in the *Emily Slate Series* in the future.

Thank you for being a loyal reader and giving me a chance,

Alex

Made in the USA
Middletown, DE
27 February 2024

50452119R00156